PENGUI

THE PATHS WE CHOOSE

Monica Rana grew up in Kathmandu and went to Harvard College before working in banking in London. At Harvard, she took multiple creative writing courses and won a few awards, including the Edward Eager grant and the Cyrilly Abels Short Story Prize.

ADVANCE PRAISE FOR THE BOOK

'Two sisters aged fourteen and seventeen caught in the teeth of an insurgency. The seventy-year-old reign of the Nepal monarchy setting, for certain. If the insurgency fails, what then? A heartfelt story of brave dreams, untold secrets, violence and intrigue which does not ever take its eyes off the young sisters braving their way along different paths'—**Kavery Nambisan, author of *Rising Sons***

'A moving story of friendship between two cousins set against a tumultuous time of civil war in Nepal. An honest portrait of a country in turmoil and the family ties that never break. I couldn't put it down'—**Firoozeh Dumas, author of *Funny in Farsi***

'A layered, well-told story and an impressive debut'—**Andaleeb Wajid, author of *The Henna Start-Up***

The Paths *We* Choose

a novel

MONICA RANA

PENGUIN BOOKS
An imprint of Penguin Random House

PENGUIN BOOKS

Penguin Books is an imprint of the Penguin Random House group of companies whose addresses can be found at global.penguinrandomhouse.com

Published by Penguin Random House India Pvt. Ltd
4th Floor, Capital Tower 1, MG Road,
Gurugram 122 002, Haryana, India

Penguin Random House India

First published in Penguin Books by Penguin Random House India 2025

10 9 8 7 6 5 4 3 2 1

ISBN 9780143471578

Typeset in Sabon LT Std by Manipal Technologies Limited, Manipal
Printed at Replika Press Pvt. Ltd, India

www.penguin.co.in

To Jes. Near and far, she brings them all. Small and large, of varied hue and character, they come. Each carried by her steady currents, lifted by her gentle streams. And here she rests, upon these boundless pebbled shores, facing the sun, her memory alight with grace.

May these stories live on

1

Mango Forests

(*Grishma Ritu*, Early Summer, 2001)

It had been Sumnima's idea to steal the mangoes. Everything of any real consequence always seemed to be Sumnima's idea. And now here she was, racing ahead, charging through the trees, leaving Rita trailing behind, and all Rita wanted to do was to cry out. But her breath came in squeezing, muted gasps. Her ankles repeatedly twisted and buckled, the uncertain *slap slap slap* of her feet thundering at the centre of her ribcage. A hard outline of something sharp pierced through the worn sole of her rubber slipper.

Then, an untimely thought: this Dashain, the biggest festival season of the year, when gifts were given and blessings received and the smell of charcoal-hot meat laced the air, she would ask Aama, her mother, for a new pair of slippers. Ones with thick soles, made with fresh white rubber and bright blue straps that stuck out like ears. Ones that made you feel like you were permanently walking upon lightly packed soil that was just turned. Sumnima would, of course, laugh at the thought if she ever got to know. After all, it could never happen; Aama certainly didn't have an extra rupee to spare. And now she could feel Dhire dai closing in on her with the angry swish of his stick that picked off skin from bare legs, leaving them as ripe and exposed as these mangoes she gripped, one in each hand.

That morning, Rita and Sumnima had awoken as usual in the quiet hours before dawn, hauled the *gagris* of water from the village tap a full twenty minutes away in the crisp air, fed the goats, cows and buffalo and picked the eggs. Then they cooked the first meal of the day: rice with watered daal, a boiled egg each and brinjal. She hated brinjal, the way it stayed slimy even after it was spiced and cooked, like eating the slugs that stuck to the bottom of rocks in the rainy season. Brinjal and gourd. That's all they ever seemed to eat in Rato Mato village. If it was not brinjal season, then it was gourd season. Gourds round as bottles, the pointy kind, the bitter kind, the spongy kind and then the twisting long ones that could be mistaken for snakes from a distance. Even Dalle the buffalo was kept fat on a diet of brinjal and gourd.

While they sat outside sipping hot tea and watching the sun light up the hills, Sumnima suddenly stood up and said, 'Let's go!'

'Go where?'

'Dhire hill. The mangoes will be ripening now.'

'What? Dhire hill? If Dhire dai finds us, he will kill us!'

'Have you seen that Dhire dai lately? He's *old* now. You think that old *budha* can outrun us? Stop being such a *darcherua*. Scared of your own shadow. Let's go!'

Rita opened her mouth to protest. After all, weren't they, too, old to be still climbing trees? But Sumnima had already turned her back, fitting her feet into her slippers.

Sumnima had a point. Dhire dai was rarely seen in the village these days, and the last time Rita had seen him, months ago at a festival, his hair had completely greyed. He looked even thinner than before, his knees sticking out beneath his lungi like thick knobs, covered in layers of loose folded skin. There was no way Dhire dai could outrun them. But as Rita picked herself up, dusting off her own skirt, she tried to ignore the list of things she had known all her life: to circumvent the swollen rivers in the monsoon, to watch out for snakes in the paddy fields, to avoid singular trees in a storm and, most of all, to stay clear of the fruiting forests high up on Dhire hill.

Sumnima lifted herself up the tree, clambering catlike from branch to branch with the same air of assuredness she had in everything that she did.

'Come on,' Sumnima called down, 'what are you waiting for?'

Rita looked up and took measure of the tree. Unseen in the canopies, parrots teased and catcalled as if daring her to try.

'I . . .' she hesitated, 'I don't think I can . . . reach.'

'Stop thinking and just do it!'

She moved closer and peered up into the thickness. *Yes*, Rita tried to convince herself. She could climb as surely as Sumnima had just done, harnessing every branch, bending them to her will. And in fact, she would go even higher up just to prove that she could. She grabbed a branch and hoisted herself up.

But two branches up, her fear was back. A familiar sensation, one that she had carried ever since she was a child. The distances between the branches seemed to grow wider and now as she stood on one branch, she could see that the only way she could get on to the next one was if she swung herself up with her legs. Slowly, she balanced herself, careful not to look at how far up she really was, one hand sliding along the trunk as the other reached for the next branch overhead.

Above, Sumnima had disappeared into the leaves. Rita was on the very tips of her toes, her hands so wet with sweat as if she had plunged them right down the river. Her fingers tightened around the bark and just as she was about to reposition them, the branch jerked forward. Her feet kicked air, and she managed to readjust one hand just as the branch jerked again.

'Stop shaking the tree!' she shrieked at Sumnima, hidden from view.

'Shh!' came the answer, then another sharp jerk.

Rita was flailing in the air now, her toes unable to find the branch she had just been standing on. The bark seemed to melt between her fingers.

'Stop it, didi!' her voice rose in panic, 'Stop it!'

'Shh! You want someone to hear you?'

Another sharp jerk sent one hand slipping off the branch and swinging wildly before finding the branch again. Just as she suddenly pictured herself lying face up and motionless on the ground, her toes finally touched rough bark.

She managed to hold on to the trunk when she heard the *thud thud thud* of ripening mangoes cascading on to the forest floor. And just as she dared to look down, realizing with an embarrassing surprise that she had not been so high after all—there, just beyond the green fruits, burst open and spilling their yellow insides—she saw a pair of feet.

Rita held still. Above, the tree was also still. The pair of feet stood there, motionless, then took two steps into the sunlight and stopped again. The last boy who had ventured amongst these trees, years ago now, still had the scars to show for it and no one had tried since. But then, Dhire dai moved, one foot turning followed by the other, disappearing back into the foliage.

It was a few long minutes before she felt the tree vibrate as Sumnima scrambled back down its length.

'You see!' she whispered sharply, punching Rita across the arm as she swung herself towards the lower branches, 'I told you to keep quiet!'

By the time Rita herself dropped from the lowest branch, feeling the infinite steadiness of the ground beneath, she was painfully stiff. She took a deep breath, pressed down her skirt, picked the two mangoes nearest to her that Sumnima had not already gotten, and put her slippers back on. That's when it occurred to her; even if Dhire dai hadn't seen them up in the branches, he must have seen their slippers, neatly arranged side by side at the base of the trunk! Rita opened her mouth to call out to Sumnima when, suddenly, the foliage behind her burst open—a strangled gargle followed by a deep-throated shout that sent a cacophony of bright green birds into shrieking flight and sent her slamming her slippers downhill, a mango squeezed in each hand.

'*Bhag*! *Bhag*!' the sounds followed her in hollowed abrasive shouts, 'Run away you thieves! You rotten, good-for-nothing thieves!'

She could almost feel Dhire dai's hand upon her. The sudden jerk at her collar that would send her toppling backwards, tripping over her own feet. The taste of the forest floor in her mouth. The swish of a stick that sliced mercilessly through the air and brought with it instant tears.

Rita felt her feet start to give way, melting beneath her. If Dhire dai didn't get her, she was sure her heart would burst open before she reached where the forest ended and the fields began.

Finally, at the bottom, she stopped. The trees behind her were quiet, the forest still. Just the echoes of her own heavy breathing, the aching of her ribs. She spun where she stood, searching, panting. And there, only a short distance away, with her back resting against a broad tree and her feet crossed before her was Sumnima looking at her and grinning haughtily, her skirt still full of mangoes.

'You see!' the words came out undefeated, 'I told you he was too old to get us!'

And then she laughed brightly and held out a mango. Small and green, beaded with plump drops of syrup around the stem. 'The first of the season!'

Sumnima bit a circular opening into the narrow edge of a mango and sucked the flesh right out, the juice dripping down to her elbow. She twisted her face at the sudden sourness and Rita laughed in relief, her limbs loosening.

'Here,' Sumnima pointed. 'Right here. We will build it right here.'

'Here?' Rita looked at her, 'But how will we get people to come?'

'Simple. They will walk up from there,' Sumnima pointed to the faint semblance of a trodden pathway that led up Dhire hill from the lower and more cultivated hill of Rato Mato far below them, 'and then we will build a new path that connects from there to here. And then all around the Dhire, to the back. From there, they will continue up to the mountains,' Sumnima pointed to the Himals, the revered destination of every tourist who ever visited these parts.

The idea of the guest house had first come to Sumnima on a trip to Pemba Monastery one year ago. Neelam didi, Rita's mother's friend and an aunt-figure for them both, had been with them, a huffing chaperone who had cajoled Aama into allowing them to come with her and then regretted every minute of it. The ascent up to the monastery was supposed to take four hours, the descent only three. Rita remembered relishing the climb; the air still held the chill of winter, the wind sweeping back leaves on trees, her face flushed with the freshness. But the higher the climb, the thinner the trees got, until towards the top, there were no trees at all. As if someone had swooped down with a giant sickle and felled them all down, leaving not a leaf behind with the memory of height. The sun seemed closer from up here, and one could smell it, beating down from a faultless sky. In front, loomed the enormity of the Himals, their spines running white, their bulk reflecting the light.

Rita remembered every bit of that day. How they had entered Pemba Monastery, their eyes adjusting to the darkness, smelling the thickness of a thousand butter lamps, the low reverberating hum of prayer horns. The outlines of a statue against the shadowed back wall—a golden Buddha, as high as the room, as broad as ten men, his arms folded in peace, his gaze a benevolence. The inside of the building was spotlessly clean, and it caught Rita by surprise. The Hindu temples she had visited were littered with bird droppings, runaway chickens, mangy dogs. Here the tiled floor was rubbed to a polish. All the people milling about dropped their voices to whispers and formed a silent line. Rita spotted two hairless monks, draped in orange robes, whisking up and down and gently manoeuvring anyone who did not remain in line. They did not speak a word.

Even Sumnima, straight-backed and tall in front of Rita, stood quiet as she shuffled from one foot to the other. Rita knew that Sumnima would dismiss anything that the monk told them. '*Nonsense*,' she would say, throwing her shoulders back. When it was their turn, Rita felt herself shoved forward, pushed down to her knees. All three of them knelt in front of a thin monk older than the rest. He was entirely hairless, and his leathered face seemed to hold an eternal calmness except for his black blazing eyes. He spoke so softly that Neelam didi had to lean heavily forward and another monk, standing in between, translated the words back in an audible pitch. Neelam didi rattled off her questions like the village matchmaker she was. These two, when will they marry? Will they marry well? How many children will they have? The older one is headstrong—how will her husband manage her? The younger one follows the older one, will she be able to manage her own household one day?

Rita could see Sumnima roll her eyes as the questions flew off Neelam didi's tongue. In response, the monk was silent, a small smile teasing the corner of his lips. Then he looked behind them, off to the left, behind Rita's shoulder and nodded. Rita remembered turning to look at who the monk was nodding to. But there was no one, just the polished expanse of floor. The monk kept looking off to the left for a long minute. Then he spoke.

'First,' he said, 'these daughters must find out their purpose. Why are they here?'

Rita wasn't sure if the monk was talking about this visit in particular, or life in general. Sumnima always said they were meant for more. More than their village, the daily routine of chores, the beaten stone paths that ran up and down these hills. Then the monk continued,

'But they must each fulfil their own destiny. And then the day will come when . . .'

Before the monk could go on, there was a shuffle behind them, and someone was prodding Rita to stand. The translator had silently stepped back, and they were being manoeuvred along now, other people from the queue moving forward to fill their place. Even Neelam didi decided against any resistance and merely grumbled on the way out.

Back in the sunlight, Rita remembered feeling a strange chill thinking of those words. *They will each fulfil their own destiny* . . . it was the singular intonation in the phrase that left her wanting. Sumnima, meanwhile, skipped out into the blue brightness and burst into loud dismissive laughter. Then she slapped Rita on the back and said, 'See! Didn't I tell you? I will marry a northern Bhote and have ten dull children and you will marry a southern Madhesi and wear a nose ring bigger than Dalle's!' Dalle's nose ring was as broad as Rita's hand. But Neelam didi let out a high ululation at the insinuation of either of them marrying out of their Brahmin caste, either to the north or to the south. Nothing was more important than the purity of the Brahmin caste, maintained through careful marriage and a multitude of children, of which male heirs were particularly cherished, to carry on the family line.

On the way back down, the three of them stopped at a tea shop by the side of the road. Neelam didi ushered them inside, deep into a pair of long benches that sat on either side of a thick greasy table littered with steel cups and plates. Around them, a bustle of people, some northerners from tribes who came from up in the Himals, some Nepalis but clearly not from these parts and a scatter of white people—tourists.

A northern woman in a long home-spun woolen *bakhu* skirt, with roped black hair down to her waist, came to take their orders.

'Three cups of tea and sel roti,' Neelam didi quickly said and then continued, 'How busy this tea shop is! You have so many people here every day?'

'We are not a tea shop,' the woman replied, her accent thick, her hands deftly clearing away dirty plates and cups, 'we are a guest house.'

'What?'

'Yes. We have rooms upstairs. Those tourists—they are staying with us.'

'Oh? They sleep upstairs and eat downstairs?'

'Yes. Every day is like this. There is always someone staying with us.'

Neelam didi leaned forward, her tone conspiratorial, 'Tell me, who owns this place?'

The woman looked up.

'I do.'

Neelam didi blinked, '*You*?'

'Yes. Now, just give me five minutes and I will be back with your order.'

Everyone knew that the northerners were different. Their social rules and mores were looser. Sometimes, Rita had heard it whispered, a northern woman would even keep two or more husbands. And, she saw now, they could own and operate a guest house. But it was Sumnima who was turning towards her, her eyes wide and in them, the brightness of an idea forming, taking distinct shape and before she opened her mouth, Rita knew exactly what she would say. *One day, we will open a guest house, just like this one.*

Now, by the mango forests, Rita considered Sumnima's plan. The stretch of land between where the forest stopped and the fields began was relatively flat and broad. Rita estimated it could accommodate a building with three large rooms on the ground floor and four smaller ones on the top floor. The current path the tourists took on their climb up to the Himals was two entire hills away, through the Nagapani valley. There were plenty of tourist guest houses out there, of course. But around here, there were none, the closest being the one they had passed on the route to Pemba Monastery. But if there were tourists who wanted to go off track and come to see the monastery with its humming mound of earth and prayer flags, then perhaps, Sumnima said, they would want to come see Rato Mato. After all, it was an idyllic Nepali village, one of the largest around, unchanged for generations. And an hour's climb up from Rato Mato on to Dhire hill were the mango forests—the only ones of their kind. Tourists could then circle around the Dhire and continue their climb up to the barren lands beyond. The whole detour would only add a day or two more to the standard trekking route.

'We should have five bedrooms,' Rita ventured, revising the dimensions in her head, 'four upstairs and one downstairs. I will do the cooking.' Although she didn't particularly like it, Rita wasn't a bad cook. Tomato achar, fried liver, curried river fish, dumplings. She had a few dishes in her repertoire. Because Aama and Kaaki, Sumnima's mother, worked the fields the whole day and she was the youngest member of the household, the task of cooking was often left to her. And Rita had deftly grown into what was expected of her.

'You can cook,' Sumnima agreed, 'I will serve the guests and do the cleaning. And of course,' she added, 'given you are the smart one, you will write the leaflet telling the world about our guest house.'

Suddenly, a flap of wings ruffled the air, and a parrot landed on a branch a few feet away from where they were sitting. It was bright green, as long as Rita's forearm, with a black collar and a flash of red beak. It cocked its head and watched them finish off the last of their mangoes. Rita looked down again at the faint path, beaten into the hill by habitual wear, and felt a sudden apprehension.

'But are you sure the tourists will want to come this way?' she asked. From this vantage point, the path from Rato Mato up to the Dhire looked far and steep, buttressed in between by rocky outcrops and wanton growths of earth.

'Of course, they will. They will want to come to our guest house because they will hear about it all the way in Kathmandu. You will know exactly what to write.' Sumnima laid down, stretching back on her elbows, the sun in her face. When they were younger, Rita recalled, Aama and Neelam didi would talk about Kathmandu, the capital city, calling it 'Nepal'. As if the whole of the country were encapsulated in the capital and everywhere else did not matter. The capital city, Kathmandu, was the beating heart of the country. To Rita, it felt like the centre of the whole universe.

Rita laid back on her elbows too. Their guest house would make enough money so that Aama and Kaaki would not have to work so hard in the fields. They could eat better—chicken every week, mutton maybe once every two. They could buy new clothes during Dashain. And the first item she would buy would be a new pair of white rubber slippers with bright blue straps that stuck out like ears. The parrot let out a chirrup and hopped closer.

'*Eh suga*! Oh parrot!' Sumnima laughed out loud, 'Have you come to spy on our plans?' She tried to shoo the bird away, but it would not budge.

'You better not come so close when we build our guest house,' she teased, 'otherwise someone might catch you and put in a cage!'

The bird cocked its head, studying them with one eye, then with a loud squawk, hopped away. It flew on to a low branch and sat there, still watching them. Rita felt bloated with indulgence—a warm luxuriant lull—and closed her eyes. After a while, Sumnima slowly lifted herself up, dusting her skirt. Rita followed, her feet finding her scraggy slippers. It was time to go home.

2

Rato Mato

Aama grabbed Sumnima first, pulling her by an ear and shoving her through the narrow door into the house. Aama did this when they were children but now it almost looked comical—what with Sumnima a full head taller than Aama. When Aama came for her own ear, Rita squealed in pain as she found herself shoved into the sunless innards of the house.

Aama stooped by the door, blinking sourly as her eyes adjusted to the dark.

'One of marriageable age, the other almost there, and behaving still like kids? Seventeen and fourteen years old! Do you think you are still children?' she bore down on them, the smell of stale sweat emanating from the fabric of her *cholo*, 'Don't bother lying to me! Anyone can smell those mangoes from ten feet away! You know what I was doing at your age?' she directed her gaze at Sumnima now, 'At your age, I had a newborn baby in my arms! That's what I was doing! Keeping another human alive! And you, what are you doing?'

Rita knew what Sumnima would say to her later. That when Aama was angry, her face puffed up and darkened, and she looked just like Dalle the buffalo. Rita felt a giggle rise and had to look across the room to suppress the urge to burst out laughing.

In the corner, squatting on a *churpi* seat by the wood fired stove, Kaaki was looking at them half-amused. But Rita knew that Kaaki hadn't grasped all the intricacies of the afternoon—the fact that Dhire dai's mangoes had been stolen by them, the two Brahmin daughters of a once priestly pujari house, and by doing so threatened to make the house known around the village as a retreat for thieves. Kaaki was a sensitive soul. She could be concerned by any number of things—Aama's anger, the visible redness of Sumnima's ear, the repeated mention of marriage, the monsoon threatening to be late again for a third year in a row, or even none of these things. No one was sure if Kaaki was capable of forming complex thoughts for she was unable to voice them, be it to ask questions or give answers.

Beside her, Rita felt Sumnima shuffle a foot.

'Where do you think you are going?' Aama was not done with them yet. 'You two are going nowhere! You are staying right here for the rest of the day. Do we not have enough work to get done? What will that Neelam say, the next time she comes around here? Do we not have to listen to enough from her as it is?'

Rita could hold it no longer and the giggle burst out of her, surprising the room in the dark. Aama, stuck in the doorway with the brightness of midmorning haloed behind her, blinked.

Aama and Neelam, or Neelam didi as the girls called her out of respect, went a long way back. Before Neelam didi married Dhire dai, the erstwhile guardian of the mango forests, and before Aama married Rita's father, the two had been neighbours. Aama would say that if she stepped out of her house and aimed a stone, she could send it within an inch accuracy of the same spot upon Neelam didi's tinned roof. When they reached marriageable age, they were brought together, a full day and night's walk up and down two hills, from their village to Rato Mato. There was one trumpet and one *madal* drum band, one pujari and one open fire, one common feast thrown for the village. It saved on costs to hold a two-in-one wedding. At least there were two husbands, they joked. There were plenty of times when that wasn't the case. But while Aama was married to the oldest son of an established Brahmin priestly family, Neelam didi was married to the dour loner who lived with his fruiting trees up on Dhire hill. There was no doubt which was the better catch.

It was the crimson soil that gave Rato Mato, or 'Red Earth,' the hill and the village alike, its name. Smooth and silky, the fertile soil gifted itself to paddy fields, fruit trees, corn, mustard and a myriad of vegetables of which brinjal and gourd remained the most popular. Aama would send Rita and Sumnima down to the nearest flowing water once every two weeks and the slippery dollops of fresh soil would leave their hair particularly shiny and smooth.

Dhire hill, meanwhile, had no obvious reason for its name and Dhire dai had not been born with that name. Everyone started calling him Dhire after the craggy hill and now no one seemed to recall what his real birth name was. Dhire dai represented the single house that constituted the Dhire hill inhabitation, the striding slopes of the hill itself and the forests of mango that ran across its southern face. The trees did not belong to him nor did the land upon which they grew. Yet being the caretaker of the mango forests was an honour, a unique role that Neelam didi tirelessly reminded everybody about every opportunity she got.

Her voice from outside, as if on cue: '*Eh launa,* is anybody in the house? *Aia, aia, aia*!' Neelam didi cursed as she lowered herself on to the steps of the courtyard outside. Her bad hip acted up whenever the air grew dense and made her lean heavily on to one side. Based on the condition of Neelam didi's hip, the villagers predicted that the rains should be coming soon.

'Water!' she called out, 'water, get me a jug of water!'

Aama's face hardened. She set her jaws and, throwing one last slant-eyed look at Rita and Sumnima, turned around and ducked through the doorway into the courtyard outside. Beside Rita, sitting cross legged on the floor, Sumnima yawned.

'You go!' she said.

'Why should I go? It was your idea! You go!'

'Just shut up and go. It was my idea, but you weren't complaining when you had that mango juice running down your chin, did you?'

'Ohho,' the call from outside again, more insistent now, 'Isn't there even a jug of water for a guest in this house? What sort of a house is this?'

Rita picked herself up reluctantly. She knew that one of them would have to respond soon before Neelam didi found one more allegation to level against their house. And Sumnima wouldn't respond to Neelam didi's request—she thought herself above such acts of mundane civility.

Rita aimed the jug and let the cold water run straight down Neelam didi's throat. As members of the Brahmin priestly caste, impurity was of special concern. The jug could be passed around from one person to another but none of them would touch their lips to the container. That way, the water inside always remained pure.

By now, Neelam didi would have heard. Dhire dai would have told her exactly who the thieves caught red-handed amidst his mangoes were.

Aama folded herself into a squatting position on the edge of the earthen porch. She was looking out, into the fields, a cigarette cupped in her fist. The length of white waistband around her midriff had come loose, curling in rough disarray.

'So,' Neelam didi cleared her throat, wiping her mouth with the back of a hand, 'whose idea was it?'

Rita looked down at the mud floor. Even though her cheeks burned, she felt tempted to claim their feat. They had outrun Dhire dai and eaten the first mangoes of the season and no one had been able to accomplish something like this for years.

'Chee-chee!' Neelam didi clicked her tongue, then nestled one knee beneath her wide behind and made herself more comfortable on the earthen porch, 'By now, Rita, you should know your own mind. How much do you listen to Sumnima? How much do you run after her? You are not a child any more. If Sumnima tells you to jump into the river, will you follow?'

Rita felt the hot flash of sudden indignation. Everybody always assumed everything was Sumnima's idea. *It doesn't matter,* she told herself. All that mattered was that one day, she and Sumnima would prove to the entire village that they were meant for more.

Sumnima ducked out of the house and flounced down on to the edge of the porch. In her hands, a cup of steaming hot tea.

'Go!' Aama stubbed out her cigarette. 'Go get us all some tea.' She had not addressed anyone in particular.

'You go!' Sumnima elbowed Rita.

'No!' Rita couldn't help herself and the response came out cutting, 'You go!' and she dug an elbow deep into Sumnima's side, hoping Neelam didi would notice.

Sumnima smacked her across the arm. 'You must go because I am older. The youngest always serves those older than them.'

'Rita!' it was Aama now, her voice hoarser after the cigarette, 'Sumnima is right. Stop arguing. Go get us all some tea.'

Rita clenched her teeth. It seemed to Rita that Sumnima always got preferential treatment around the house because she was older.

'Rita!' Aama's warning voice loud now, gruff.

Rita stormed inside. When it came to the two of them, Aama treated Sumnima as if she were her own daughter. Sumnima was Rita's first cousin, the daughter of Rita's uncle who was her father's sole brother. Why couldn't she, Rita asked herself, as Aama's own daughter and only child, ever enjoy even a momentary, fleeting sense of favouritism? Suddenly her annoyance at Neelam didi and Sumnima transferred on to her mother. But then Rita remembered again the story Aama had told her, the story that no one else knew. Many years ago, in a small, thatched lean-to, on a biting December night, Aama had bartered with the gods. Hidden in shadow, she had entered Kaaki's birthing hut, built away from the main house as per tradition, what with all that dirt and blood, only to find Kaaki flushed with fever, the newborn limp at her breast, the wood fire cold. Aama had lit the fire, smuggled in blankets, undid her cholo and brought the baby to warm at her own breast. She had broken the rules of gods and men alike by associating with the impure, for everything associated with the female cycle was considered impure, including birth. In doing so, she had secured Sumnima's life.

Rita balanced the small glasses of tea on to a steel tray as she walked back on to the porch. The afternoon was warm. At the edge of the courtyard, a white cat rested with her litter, the wriggling bundle arranged, at Aama's suggestion, in a wicker basket. The house where Aama and Rita lived was one of the larger ones that jutted on to an open square surrounded by a thin mud-swept porch, decorated with a string of dried chillies and nodes of yellow pumpkin left out to dry. Kaaki and Sumnima's house was connected to theirs but had a separate entrance. The other houses, belonging to other Brahmin and Chettri families, were situated either above or below theirs, separated by vegetation and terraces of cultivation that cascaded in symmetrical arches out of the side of the hill.

'It is time,' Rita caught Neelam didi mid-sentence, her back resting against the wooden post and her leg dangling stoutly just short of the ground, 'How much longer do we wait? And what are we waiting for? For you to grow into an old spinster? To still climb trees and steal mangoes when you are old and toothless? People will talk if we wait another year. They have started to talk already.'

Neelam didi had brought up the issue of Sumnima's marriage a year ago already. She spoke with authority on the topic, as she did on all topics, and Aama had not intervened. Sumnima, although three years older than Rita, had not been sent to school until Rita was old enough to join her and they could make the daily trek down the hill to the district headquarters together. As a result, Sumnima had started school late. After she had failed, falling a year behind, Rita and Sumnima had ended up together, both now in Class 7. Neelam didi thought that was more than enough. It was, after all, more education than any woman in the village had ever achieved. Any more would be a detriment—no woman should be more educated than her future husband.

'I've told you already,' Sumnima was leaning with both her feet dangling from the edge of the porch, her heels now exaggeratedly kicking against the sides, 'You can say what you like. I am not getting married any time soon. Why should I leave my own house and go call someone else's house 'home'? Why should I become a *nokkar*, a servant to a total stranger?'

Sumnima, Rita knew, was baiting Neelam didi. It would be a long and entertaining afternoon.

'Because that is the way of our lives. That is the right way. Everyone gets married, Sumnima. And those who don't, live to suffer for it.'

'What has marriage brought you? Any of you?'

'Never mind what it has brought us,' Neelam didi snapped, 'The question is what will it bring you? And the answer is simple. Respect. What is a woman without a husband? Nobody. Nothing. As an unmarried woman, even the village dog will not turn its nose in your direction.'

'Hmm!' Sumnima grunted in disdain, 'Should I give up my life for the village dog? All day, people just sit and talk. They say this and they say that. But later, will those people be there for me?'

'What about children?' Neelam didi switched tactics, 'Don't you want children? Who will take care of you when you're old?'

'You don't have children,' Sumnima shot back, 'and you seem to be taking care of yourself just fine.'

Rita and Sumnima knew Neelam didi had given birth multiple times but each time the infants had emerged either half-formed or lived for a few weeks or months, then passed on before their personalities could be formed. In the beginning, Aama had said, Neelam didi would sit on the earthen porch of her house at the top of Dhire hill and weep. Once she had even tried to end it all, climbing one of Dhire dai's fruiting trees armed with a rope.

'But what happened?' Rita had asked Aama.

'What else?' Aama had grunted, 'The branch broke.'

Neelam didi had escaped the branch episode with no more than a broken hip and since then, had transformed into the woman she was today. As a Brahmin herself, Neelam didi knew all the Brahmin families that lived in the cluster of houses surrounding Rita and Sumnima's family, but she also knew the families of the other castes. The Chettris, Rais and Magars. She would lower her voice in passing and, with pursed lips, comment, 'Those Bhotes,' referring to the northerners, 'they have horns like buffalo. Make them angry and run for your life!' One day, one of the dark-skinned Madhesi seamstresses who had moved to Rato Mato from the hot plains of the Terai a generation ago missed a stitch in Neelam didi's cholo. '*Mori*!' Neelam didi swore the moment they were out of earshot, 'Those rat-eaters can never do a simple task.'

'Rat eaters?' Rita had asked and Neelam didi had explained that down in the hot Terai plains, the Madhesi had found the perfect solution to do away with the fat rats that came to steal their grain. Rita had shuddered and felt she understood why the Madhesi were deemed impure, why the Brahmins and Chettris refused even a drop of water from their houses.

Behind them, there was a short shuffle of cloth as Kaaki ducked out on to the porch. In her hands, she carried a small circular brightly coloured package. Neelam didi sucked in her breath, her mouth still poised over her cup of tea.

'Ohho, *lati,* what do you have there?'

When Neelam didi addressed Kaaki as 'lati', dumb girl, she did so with a familiarity and fondness that made it acceptable, but still, Rita watched a shadow pass over Sumnima's face. It was not as if Sumnima was particularly protective of her own mother. Sometimes, it seemed to Rita that Sumnima detested the use of the word not in defence of her mother, but in distaste of the implied association.

Kaaki smiled, unwrapping the paper covering with care. Inside were biscuits—sweet glucose ones usually spared for special occasions.

Rita bit into her biscuit carefully, first neatly nibbling the circular rim before moving to the sweet middle. The biscuit tasted even better dunked in tea, but eating it dry kept it going for longer.

She watched as, on the other side of the courtyard, the cat jumped out of her wicker basket, stretched, and leaving her mewling litter to their own devices, approached the party.

Kaaki walked to the edge of the porch closest to the cat and squatted in a square of sun. She reached into the peels of wrapping, a smile stretched out on her lips.

'Look at my hip,' Neelam didi continued, her mouth hovering over the edge of the glass, 'Look how it acts up. Some days I can barely walk! What do you think will happen five years from now? Ten years from now? Who do you think will look after an old childless woman with a bad hip then?'

Now she threw her head in the direction of Aama, 'This is exactly what happens when there is no proper man in the house. Look at Sumnima! Look at how she talks back! No one to keep her in check!'

Aama did not respond. Rita's father, the head of the household, had left them years ago for better employment across the border in India. Then his visits had grown more and more seldom as had the money he sent home, until both stopped. A rumour went around the village that he had found another woman, one who had given him sons.

Rita barely remembered him. She only remembered his shoes. Polished, shiny black. No one in the entire village owned a pair of shoes like that. The shoes were made of leather, which only came from cows, the animal associated with the Goddess Laxmi, the Goddess of fortune. How could a priest wear the skin of a cow on his feet? For Rita, he would always be the unholy man for whom she had not been enough.

'And who,' Sumnima was not about to let it go, 'is going to pay for my dowry? Which man will want to marry a woman who has nothing to bring with her?'

'You don't worry about that,' Neelam didi dipped her biscuit in tea, 'we will make arrangements.' All the items brought in Kaaki's dowry, Rita knew, were already long gone, sold off piece by piece by her uncle.

The sound came so suddenly that Rita jumped. The biscuit dropped out of her fingers and plopped into her tea. The cat scattered in a flash of white. Aama stood up quickly and turned around.

The man was standing in the middle of the courtyard.

Rita remembered how her uncle used to be different. She remembered his bright laugh, the same one Sumnima had, that caught you by surprise and didn't let go. How, when they were young, he would swing each of them between his legs and then up, up, up into the air. He was nothing, she told herself, like her own father.

The same man stood in front of them now, swaying. His body thin, his face swollen raw, his eyes with no hint of recognition. The brown pants he wore every single day were rolled up to his knees.

Her uncle spent most of his days at the tea shop at the bottom of Rato Mato hill, playing carrom board and drinking *raksi* out of tea glasses. When he returned, late into the night, the smell of fermented rice strong about him, he usually demanded his food and went straight to sleep. Sometimes he scolded Kaaki for the food being too cold or too hot, and sometimes he pushed her out of his way. And then there were times he did not return home at all and the next morning, Kaaki would go searching, finding him curled up somewhere at the bottom of the hill, wet with dew.

Slowly, day by day, Rita's uncle dropped out of their lives. She tried to understand it. She had always been taught the importance of men: as heads of the household, as owners of all the village lands, as indispensable farm labourers, as conduit to the afterlife. Everything of any importance seemed to default to a man. And yet, most of her life, there was hardly a worthwhile man around. Neelam didi said that men like her uncle were those left behind. 'How much can a man dig a field?' she had spat. But sometimes, Rita thought that Neelam didi was wrong. It was not the men like her uncle who were left behind. It was the women.

Over time, Sumnima spoke less and less of her father and Rita became careful not to bring him up. They both were given more tasks around the house while Aama and Kaaki worked harder in the fields, making up for a lost pair of hands. Rita could see the defiance in Sumnima's tightly pressed lips, her upturned chin. The harder things got around the house, the bolder Sumnima seemed to grow.

Now in front of them, Sumnima's father opened his mouth, and then closed it again. Then he lurched forward.

In a sudden burst of confused movement, she felt Aama brush past her, reaching towards Sumnima. Then Aama was pulling them both away, past Neelam didi, who was now standing up. As she was dragged away, the strength of Aama surprising her, Rita turned around to look. Her uncle had grabbed hold of Kaaki—still sitting, still smiling.

'Eh dai, what are you doing?' Neelam didi's words were measured but her voice was loud enough to carry through the village and Rita could hear the rising panic in it, 'Ohho, what are you doing, dai?'

For a moment, Aama hesitated, stopping and turning half-way. Rita saw the craziness in her uncle's eyes, his body girded and throbbing with anger and alcohol. And then Aama decidedly yanked them both away, round the side of the building, and as she turned the corner, Rita saw that her uncle had now caught Kaaki by the hair. He dragged her off the porch and into the courtyard. 'Whore!' he was spitting thick swollen words, 'stupid lati whore!' and swinging his leg back with vicious strength to find Kaaki's exposed back, the soft space between where her dhoti skirt ended and her cholo began. Pushing her to the ground, he kicked her again and again, his feet gaining accuracy with the familiarity of fixed movement, the sickening dull thuds spilling into the fields.

Aama plunged straight into the growth of bitter gourd and it occurred to Rita that they were destroying the season's crop. There, in a hollow spot surrounded by scattered vines, Aama fell to her knees and pulled them beside her. They stayed like that, the three of them, hiding in the vegetation until the shouting in the courtyard died down.

In the silence that followed, her entire body pounding, Rita felt small, nondescript. The rough fabric of Aama's cholo, unwashed and blackened at the collar and sleeves, pressed into her.

'Chup! Chup!' Aama was cooing now, like she would do when they were children. And then 'Don't cry,' she was saying, 'Chup, chup, shh, don't show him your tears.'

And Rita, pressed against Aama's shoulder, realized that it was not she who Aama was addressing. Sumnima, a full head taller now than Aama, stronger, faster, bolder than them all, was crying hidden in a patch of vegetables. Sumnima, builder of dreams larger than the hills themselves, was crying in fear and shame.

When they finally emerged from the vegetable patch, they found Neelam didi doubled over in the centre of the courtyard. Rita's uncle was nowhere in sight. At Neelam didi's feet, Kaaki was lying on the mud-swept ground—her sari had come off down to the waist, her cholo was half ripped and revealed one loose breast. One eye was bruised purple, her jaw swollen and bloodied. Her hair was a matted halo, speckled with dust. *Pasu*, Rita kept thinking. Animal. He had turned her into an animal.

Aama rushed to help Neelam didi lift Kaaki back up. 'Ram, Ram,' Neelam didi kept keening, 'Ram, Ram,' calling upon the gods. Sumnima lingered at a distance, watching. She didn't speak—her face robbed of colour. Aama and Neelam didi called for hot water and a cloth to wipe Kaaki clean and Rita ran back into the house. Other villagers started arriving, asking what had happened. But when Rita returned, searching for Sumnima, she was already gone. That night, Sumnima did not come back home until late in the evening, after Kaaki had been fed broth with a spoon and laid to rest.

3

The Turning

In the school assembly line, they stood in order of height. Rita at the front, Sumnima behind Tsering Lama towards the back. The school principal stood straight as a ruler and regarded the students, his spectacles reflecting the white of the morning sun, his fisted hands stiff along his sides. Beside him, a small group of teachers stood to attention. The morning smelled of pungent earth and the crisp cold air that travelled down from the mountains. All of them were there singing the national anthem in unison—for God to protect the king of Nepal, for his reign to spread far and wide, for all his citizens to sing of his glory.

Rita felt a flutter in the furthest reaches of her belly. It was as if her entire being was connected to the ground beneath her feet, to the king in Kathmandu who was the reincarnation of Lord Vishnu himself, to the Himals the whole world came to see. As if all of them—the gathered students, the teachers, the principal, the fatly curved clouds above—rose with the fullness of that moment, a crescendo of voices lifted high. Rita felt larger than herself, heroic and whole.

The line moved forward across the yard in single file, each student raising their arms out to the shoulders of the student in front of them. Rita had just reached the front of the school building, the girls in front of her already disappearing inside into a growing din of voices, when behind her, she heard Tsering, the distinct lilt of his thick northern accent, the underlying viciousness of the words 'lati' and 'deserved it'. Rita stopped in her tracks and whipped around. Sumnima's hands had fallen off Tsering's shoulders. She was standing stock-still, staring as the boy brought his hand to his mouth to stifle laughter.

Rita hesitated, glancing at the turned back of the principal, then broke line and started walking back towards Sumnima. But before she could get to her, Sumnima abruptly reached up and grabbed Tsering's collar, letting her own knees give way, collapsing on to the ground and bringing him down with her. Then Sumnima was upon him, pummelling him with her fists, a string of expletives flying off her tongue.

Rita heard her own voice screaming for Sumnima to stop. She tried to fling herself forward, but a crowd had formed and someone was grabbing on to her collar and in the pell-mell that followed, Rita felt herself roughly pushed and pulled back to the outside of the circle. She stood up on her tiptoes to see but her hands shook and she could not find the courage to wade back in.

'*Nwaughty* girl! *Nwaughty* boy!' Principal sir spat out the words in English as he pushed through the crowd. No one else in all the surrounding villages had better mastery of the English language than him and he presided over every English class throughout the whole school. It made him one of the most important and respected men in Rato Mato and the surrounding villages.

'You monkey!' Principal sir's judgement came crashing down, 'You donkey!'

His ruler came swishing down next, moving so swiftly and fluidly that the crowd inhaled and took a step back. Rita winced as the ruler slapped indiscriminately against Sumnima's bare calves, her exposed arms. Rita watched welts rise on Sumnima's skin, her plaits undone, her oiled hair slithering loose down her back. Sumnima, despite the pain, looked straight back at Principal sir, her eyes black and unblinking.

'It's her fault, sir!' Tsering was trying to shout out in his own defence.

'Tsering Lama!' Principal sir mixed English with more familiar Nepali words, 'You shameless boy! Go to your classroom right this minute!'

'And you?' Principal sir looked at Sumnima from over the rim of his spectacles, 'Get up, you disrespectful girl! Is this any way for a young woman from a Bahun house to behave? Being a girl, how can you hit someone?' Principal sir spat out his final reprimand 'You *donkeyni*!'

Rita watched Sumnima's lip, bleeding now, slightly turn up at the corners.

Inside the classroom, an unusual silence had fallen over the rows of seated students. Particles of dust danced in the stream of light spilling in through the open doorway. Outside, the day was bright—a brilliant, teasing white.

'Today,' Principal sir announced, his voice solemn, his familiar composure well recovered now, 'we will be turning to the questions and answers for Chapter 2.'

Rita sat towards the front of the class and Sumnima with the older students sat at the back. They all had the Class 7 Mahendra Malla books open in front of them, dog-eared and dirty, passed down from class to class, one shared by every two or three students.

'Our Villages,' Principal Sir recited out the title. 'Question number one, why are people in the villages healthier than people in the cities?'

Rita knew the answer prompted by the text. People in the villages were healthier because they ate freshly grown food and exercised by working in the fields. The black and white picture in the book before her showed a village just like Rato Mato, nestled on a hill face, trees she recognized as banana, kaphal, orange. But the book did not speak of people like Aama, who carried loads so heavy that she groaned in her sleep. Or Kaaki, whose face still held purple bruises—her arm bent at the joint so that she could not stretch it out straight. Or Sumnima's father, drunken and spent on the wooden bench outside the tea shop down the hill.

A boy raised his hand and gave the rote textbook answer. Niraj Rai, the smartest in the class. Rita twisted around to look at Sumnima, who remained head down, staring at the book. Her lower lip was swollen thick.

Principal sir droned on, his voice a high nasal whine. Then he got to question number five, 'Discuss the development initiatives that our government has started in the villages.'

Niraj Rai raised his hand again. 'His Majesty's government,' he spoke softly, 'has developed multiple successful initiatives like building roads, irrigation channels and cottage industries to aid the development of our villages.' Rita always thought Niraj tried too hard.

'Well done!' Principal sir, Rita knew, prided himself on his Brahmin caste, his well-versed English and his love for king and country.

There was a momentary silence until Manju Thapa cleared her throat. Manju was one of the older students in the class and she never failed to show it. Rita did not like her and neither, she knew, did Sumnima.

'Sir!' Manju's voice was saccharine and a large blue ribbon held together a plait at the crown of her head, 'But if the government's programs were successful, then why have the rebels gained so much ground?'

Principal sir's face flashed shades of red.

'Who said they have gained any ground? Where have they gained ground?' Principal sir's voice rose.

'One of my father's friends said that they have taken complete control of the far west.' Manju's voice sounded perfectly innocent, the blue ribbon on her head nodding in agreement.

'These rebels you talk of,' Principal sir sniffed, 'are nothing but thugs and thieves. If they want to gain any real ground, they should act like any other party in our multiparty democratic system and fight to gain the people's vote!'

'But sir, then why do so many people support the rebels?'

From the back of the classroom came a giggle.

Principal sir's face stiffened. 'Nobody around here supports the rebels,' he declared. His hands gripped the Mahendra Mala, his knuckles shot white, 'The people here support His Majesty's government and the modern principals of multiparty democracy. That is the real people's choice. Now Manju, enough of your silly questions!'

Rita stole a glance behind Principal sir's shoulder. Hung up on the wall was a large coloured photograph of the royal family. She had seen the king once, on the black and white television in the tea shop down the hill. He had walked not on the ground but upon thick carpets, and Neelam didi said that in real life, the carpets would have been crimson red.

The school gong suddenly clanged, indicating break time, and Rita pushed through the crowd of students, searching for Sumnima.

In the bare yard, the only sign of the morning's fight was how the dust lay unsettled. Rita spotted Sumnima at the far end of the dirt yard, at the edge of a group of older students.

Manju was there with her sidekicks—three of them from class 8, one from class 9. The previous year, the one student who had graduated from class 9 had moved to stay with some relatives in Kathmandu to complete class 10 and take his school leaving exams. He had passed in the third division. It was the best academic accomplishment Rato Mato had ever seen. Rita squatted in the dirt next to Sumnima. She noticed how Sumnima shifted slightly to make room but did not acknowledge her.

'They have built a gigantic gate and on top, they have put a banner in red – "The Land of the Free",' Manju spoke, her eyes bright, the bow on her head dipping like a bird that had just landed, 'They are now controlling the entire district. The government, politicians and police—no one even dares to enter.'

'Even the police?' someone asked.

'*Nobody* dares to enter,' Manju's eyes flashed, 'And it's the people who have power. Rich, poor. Man or woman, it does not matter. Everybody is equal!'

'They have won the hearts of the people,' responded Niraj and his voice now had more conviction than Rita had ever heard in the classroom. Tall and thin, his shoulders were as narrow as his hips and he carried a dirty old cloth bag slung against his shoulder wherever he went. Niraj's parents, Neelam didi had informed Rita, worked as indentured farmhands for someone who lived in Kathmandu. 'Chained to the earth!' Neelam didi had declared.

'They have,' he continued, 'cleaned up the villages. They have banned carrom and all forms of gambling. They have banned alcohol. And,' here Rita noticed how his eyes seemed to shift hesitantly in Sumnima's direction, 'and they have started to take abusive men to account. All cases are decided by village committees. By the people themselves.'

Beside her, Sumnima made a small, almost involuntary movement.

'But Kathmandu does not say anything?' someone asked.

'Kathmandu does not care,' Niraj snapped back and Rita was surprised by the sudden aggression, 'Kathmandu has never cared about villages like ours. Not the government, not the politicians, not the king!'

'They are all too scared,' Manju raised her voice, quickly taking back control of the conversation, her eyes large and expressive. 'They are too scared to confront the rebels. And this is only the beginning . . .' Rita did not trust Manju's words, but still, a slow shiver crept up her arms.

'Shh!' someone whispered. One of the teachers was heading their way. The crowd dispersed.

That Saturday, Rita and Sumnima had finished all their early morning chores when they heard voices coming up the beaten stairs carved out of the side of the hill.

'Eh Sumnima!' Manju hopped up and skipped her way to the centre of the courtyard. Behind her, Niraj followed, slim as a shadow, his matted hair parted on to one side, his eyes narrow, nose shallow—features distinctly different to a sharp Brahmin face or a defined Chettri one like Manju's. The Rai people had a flat look, somewhat similar to the northerners, and they, too, were positioned at a rung towards the bottom end of the caste hierarchy.

Rita stopped grinding grain and Sumnima sat back on her haunches.

'What are you doing? It's Saturday. Come with us.' Manju's voice was a sing-song drawl.

The question was directed at Sumnima alone. Neelam didi said that the Chettri caste were political tacticians. That's why they had ruled the country for so long. They were eloquent and deceptive—they could charm you with their tongues and slice you with their knives.

'Where are you going?' Sumnima, squatting with her hands folded in between her knees, asked.

'Up, into the forests. We have other friends waiting for us. Come! You can't be spending all your time with *bhaibahini haru*, come spend some time with us.'

Rita started at the word bhaibahini, meaning younger brothers and sisters. A hot flash of anger shot through her.

'Why?' Rita spoke quickly, 'What is so special in the forests?'

Manju turned now to face her, her brows knitted together, a sharpness in her look. But it was Niraj who answered.

'We and some friends are having some conversations,' he said. 'Well, more like debates. We are debating things.'

'What things? Why can't you debate here?'

'Because,' and now Manju and Niraj exchanged looks, 'because there are many people around us who don't understand.'

'Don't understand what? Federalism, Nationalism, Maoism, Marxism—which one of those big ideas will you be debating? That the rest of us can't understand?' Rita relished how the words rolled off her tongue. She didn't grasp the full meaning of any of them, but she wouldn't let on.

Beside her, Sumnima shifted and lifted an arm to shade her eyes.

'Ohho!' Manju suddenly clapped a hand in surprise across her mouth, 'The bahini knows more than I had thought!' and when she released the hand, her mouth was laughing but her eyes were not. 'Maybe next time,' she said, 'we will take you along with us. But this time only, let your didi come with us, Ok? Look,' she swept an open hand in front of her, 'you have almost finished all your household tasks. And also, what will your mother and aunty say if they return and both of you are not here?'

Sumnima stood up. She brushed small flakes of husk off her tunic and slipped her feet into her slippers. Was Sumnima seriously going with these two? The situation was starting to slip away.

'Where are you going, didi?' Rita tried to keep her voice even. Sumnima stepped down on to the courtyard. She was much taller than Manju and as tall as Niraj. Her back straight, her forehead high, her hair falling in a neatly oiled plait, her eyes large and expressive, her features proud. She looked nothing like Rita with her slight frame and less defined, ordinary features. Sumnima was someone everyone wanted to have on their team. And here she was, being pulled away by these two outsiders.

'It's only for a short while,' Sumnima shrugged her shoulders, 'I will be back soon.' She made no effort to include Rita.

For the next few weeks, every Saturday, Manju Thapa and Niraj Rai climbed the steps towards their house to get Sumnima. Then one day, the visits stopped because, Rita knew, they were no longer required to convince Sumnima. 'Ok, I'm going,' she would say when Aama and Kaaki had left for the fields, and then she would disappear up the stone stairs.

Sumnima stopped talking about the guest house. She no longer argued with Neelam didi whenever she came around with a fresh string of gossip or piece of advice. She took on a serious, aloof, expression. All her—and their—old habits and interests seemed to swiftly slip away, as if they had been mere fleeting whims, easily replaceable. In the playground, when the boys chased after each other in the dust and the girls sat in small circles, fishing out wai wai noodles and roti from squares of cloth, Rita would find Sumnima in a corner with Manju, Niraj and a few others in a closed clique. She would look across the yard and Sumnima would be hunched in her new circle, her body close to the others, blocking out any slice of space in between.

Early summer winds came to the hills and pummelled trees, bending branches until they snapped, sending leaves sizzling through the air. Aama and Neelam didi busied themselves reinforcing the chicken coops and goat pen, the thatch that held Dalle, the rods that held the vegetable vines in place. Then they doubled up for lost time in the corn fields.

Every Saturday afternoon, Rita found herself alone, her day a long spell of restless silence. She lost herself in daydreams. They could build a brick ledge around the guest house and plant marigolds that would grow into bushes of bright orange and yellow flowers by autumn.

They could buy a kerosene stove with multiple burners even bigger than the one in the tea shop down the hill so that an entire meal could be cooked in one go. Rice, daal with ghee, chili potatoes, sautéed lamb. The tourists would hear about the guest house all the way in Kathmandu. Somehow Sumnima's dream had become hers alone.

One Saturday afternoon, Rita was crouched atop a wide pan made of twisted jute, separating grains of rice from small stones when Neelam didi came by.

'Ohho,' Neelam didi exhaled as she made her way across the courtyard and sank heavily on to the porch.

'Water!' she made a dramatic gesture in Rita's direction, 'Water! Some water!'

Rita stood up reluctantly and brought out the customary gagri.

'Aha!' she smacked her lips as the last drop of water fell, 'I'm too early, I know, they are not back yet from the fields. But,' and here she looked round the courtyard, 'but where is Sumnima? I came all this way to try and talk some sense into that girl and bring her some news, and now she's not here!'

The last thing Rita wanted to deal with was Neelam didi's nosy questioning, her pointed self-righteous words.

'What news?' Rita asked, trying to stall the inevitable.

'Ahh,' Neelam didi sighed in satisfaction and puffed out her chest. 'Wouldn't you like to know! But that is for me to tell Sumnima. Where is she?'

'She has taken the goats to graze.'

'But why are you not with her?'

'She's gone with . . . others.'

'Who others?'

'Some friends from school.'

Rita stared at the grains of rice in the pan before her.

'Eh Rita!' Neelam didi almost sang out now, 'Which friends? What, are you not talking or what?'

'Friends from school, I told you.'

'Do these friends have names?'

'Manju Thapa and Niraj Rai,' Rita snapped, the names bitter on her tongue.

'Ohho!' Neelam didi drew in her breath.

'Manju Thapa!' Neelam didi nodded knowingly, 'She's got quite the cheek, that girl. And of course, that father of hers. That man is a *total* bullshitter. He calls himself a businessman? *Eesh* business. You know what he does? Uses big tractors with big teeth to break and sell rocks by the river. Without government permission. Mark my words, that man is selling our very hills from under our feet. And if a thief like that is a self-made businessman, then I am the queen of Nepal! And Niraj Rai?' Neelam didi raised her eyebrows, as if in afterthought, 'That family, barely a shirt on their backs. What is Sumnima doing with Manju Thapa and that rat-poor Rai boy?'

'I told you—they have gone to graze the goats.'

'Niraj Rai is grazing goats with the two girls?'

Rita did not respond.

'He is quite a reader, I hear. Maybe that boy will be the next one from this village to finish Class 10 and take the SLC exams. They say he reads all the time. How he manages to study in that one room with all his siblings crawling over him is beyond me! But maybe he will study his way out of this village one day.'

Neelam didi only ever commented on the academic achievements of boys. Last year, when Rita had returned home with a 2nd division report card, Neelam didi had wrinkled her nose, her face full of suspicion. Later she whispered to Aama, 'Too much education can spoil a girl.'

When Rita looked up, she saw that Neelam didi was wholly focused on her, her head cocked to one side, her eyes knowing.

'And they did not take you with them?'

Rita made a small movement, imperceptibly shaking her head.

'Never say,' Neelam didi continued 'never say I did not warn you of this. Everyone grows up, Rita. Even our Sumnima. Why, she should already have been married off a year ago! In our day, girls her age were already with a baby or two in their laps!'

'She has not gone off to get married,' Rita retorted, 'She has gone to graze the goats.'

But even as she lied on Sumnima's behalf, Rita felt a tangy sharpness at the thought of Sumnima, Manju and Niraj debating words that sounded important but meant nothing in the context of their village lives. Federalism, Marxism, Republic—words that were whispered around the school building, but were as formless and empty as the clouds that passed by, none of them carrying any rain.

'Yes, yes,' Neelam didi slapped her thigh. Then she lowered her voice conspiratorially, 'Don't tell Sumnima, yet, but I have started making inquiries. And my efforts have brought up not one, but two leads. Both solid. Good families, both SLC graduates. Mark my words, our Sumnima is going to be married before the year is out!'

4

Ghosts

It grew hotter by the day, the air stifling and expectant. Rita spent every Saturday by herself now. As she sat in the courtyard, she recalled all the things Neelam didi had threatened Sumnima with and became convinced that they would happen to her alone: she would become a bitter old maid, without any respect, even the village dog would not sniff her in passing. Then sometimes, in her loneliness, she felt *not* alone. As if there were others nearby—unseen, unknown. Watching and waiting. *It is only the wind*, she kept telling herself. But she was not the only one.

The villagers of Rato Mato started claiming that they were seeing things, up in the forests. Indescribable creatures, sometimes at dusk, sometimes at dawn, half-hidden by leaf and bark. Some said they heard voices. Barely audible whispers, caught on a passing gust. '*Bhoot ayo*,' they said. Ghosts had come to settle in their hills.

In the west, the rebels captured a hilltop police post, killed all twenty-one policemen and confiscated their weapons. It was the largest attack in a previously non-rebel-held area and it occurred in broad daylight. The news spread from hill to hill. Meanwhile, a few hills away to the east, forest fires were raging, feeding off the dry wind. In the late afternoons, when the wind ran its hardest, Rita thought she could smell a hint of smoke out in the courtyard.

One evening, Rita and Sumnima squatted on their haunches behind the house, in front the sprawl of vegetables that ran up then dropped into terraced fields. Bit by bit, the fields were starting to get cleared for the planting season. Freshly turned earth reflected rusty hues of the last light. Beyond, closer to the horizon, the darkening forms of hills loomed, silhouetted against a speckled sky and birds chattered and called all around, settling into trees. Sumnima concentrated on the pot before her, her hands scrubbing it with rough bark smothered in ash. The concoction worked even on days old rice stuck stubbornly to the steel bottom.

Rita blurted out, 'Where do you go?'

She wasn't sure what made her want to shatter the silence that sat heavily between them. But she missed the times when it was just the two of them. When life felt less uncertain and ordinary, and she less uncertain and ordinary in it.

Sumnima remained silent.

'With Manju and Niraj, what do you do?' Rita insisted.

'We go up into the forests,' Sumnima shifted on her feet, the leggings under her tunic rolled up, her bare calves bronze against the last light. Rita felt a rush of relief that here they were, talking again. 'And we just . . . discuss things.'

Rita looked at her sideways. Sumnima's face was illuminated a light brown, her brow high, her cheeks chiselled. Her eyes were large and gently curved at the edges. In a bride's veil with kohl around them, she would be considered beautiful. A desirable woman.

'If you are just discussing things, why can't I come with you?' Rita ventured, emboldened by the moment.

Sumnima did not reply immediately. Then said, 'Because you are too young,' but the words dropped out flat and shapeless.

'Too young for what? This winter I will be fifteen. We are in the same class. I can read better than you.'

'That classroom is not the real world.'

'But we are taught by Principal sir and he has the best English in these hills, they say he even has the ear of Kathmandu!'

'Ha!' Sumnima's lip curled at the end, 'So what if he speaks English? That man has nobody's ear. Have you seen that jacket he keeps wearing? A hole under the armpit large enough to fit a fist through.'

Rita found herself grappling for words. Here was Sumnima, forgetting all the things they had built together. All the things they had yet to build. Here was Sumnima, dismissing her wholly.

'Neelam didi and Aama are going to marry you off before the year is out,' Rita suddenly spat out, feeling the dark satisfaction of her words, 'Neelam didi has already found a match. Not one, but *two*.'

Sumnima readjusted her tunic. 'You seem in a rush for me to leave this village.'

'You seem to be in a rush to leave it yourself.'

'This village . . . it can swallow one whole.'

'Is that why you are planning to join the rebels?' Rita felt her own face twist, her mouth screwed in distaste, 'You will escape this village by running away with them instead. What are they teaching you up in the forests? How to fire a gun?'

Suddenly, Sumnima whipped around and grabbed Rita by the wrist. Her nails dug deep into Rita's flesh.

'Promise me,' Sumnima's voice lashed out in a fierce whisper, her black eyes flashing, 'you will never ever say that out loud again!'

Rita winced, her wrist shooting pain.

'Never speak of the rebels again, do you hear me?' she tugged hard at Rita's arm.

Rita gulped and nodded.

'Promise me! Never repeat what you have just said. Promise!' Sumnima bore down on her.

'Promise,' Rita's voice came out in a squeak.

Sumnima stood up, brushing past Rita back into the house.

Rita sat outside a long while. Sumnima's ferocity left her breathless. A feeling, cold and sweaty, crept down the tunic along her back. Somehow, she had lost Sumnima completely.

From that day on, Rita kept her distance from Sumnima. They passed by each other almost like strangers, in the courtyard, by the small clay stove inside, out by Dalle's shed and the chicken coup. With the rains yet to come, there was so little water left that every morning Rita started going down to the village tap and standing there for hours just to collect two gagris of water. She would carry the water up to the house, one gagri balanced in a *doko* basket down her back, the other on her hip.

Usually by this time of the year, the sky would start to turn, groaning and rumbling. Then, before long, the monsoon would gush down, water running from terraced field to terraced field, collecting in shallow pools. But this year, like the previous two, the skies remained silent and the irrigation channels dry. The villagers diverted some of the spring water, flowing down from the Himals, and fed them into the fields, but the flow was only a trickle.

As a child, paddy planting season had always been one of Rita's favourite times. Ploughing the terraces was a messy process. It involved the boys and men of the village running thick wooden ploughs behind oxen and buffalo knee-deep in slush. It was one of the few activities even the carrom-playing men showed up for. Later, when the soil was broken, all the women would gather in the fields. They would wear their brightest colours and bend for hours, their hands deftly inserting bright green saplings. By the afternoon, someone would end up sloshing mud on someone else and the planting session would turn into a full-fledged fight, fresh patties of mud whizzing about, bodies and clothes lathered in rusty red. The terraces would echo with shrieks and hoots of laughter, faces made unrecognizable with dripping mud except for the whites of eyes and teeth.

This year, Sumnima refused to go until Aama insisted that it would be Rita carrying and handing over the food and water. They could not let Rita face her uncle alone, not after what had happened.

For the last three days they had been making the same journey, Sumnima walking ahead, Rita behind. They had found Rita's uncle on the first terrace each time, cursing and heaving the heavy wooden plough behind the pair of borrowed oxen. Red dust covered his exposed legs and arms, his eyes striking amid the dirt that layered his face. Despite his efforts, there seemed to be barely a dent in the earth. Half a dozen other terraces trailed behind, still left unploughed.

Each time, Rita handed over the food tentatively as Sumnima watched from afar, not a word spoken. She felt her pulse race every time she approached him, and when he reached out to take the container from her hands, she could not help flinching. She wondered if her uncle felt any remorse. But as she walked away, she knew that what he had done to Kaaki was not uncommon and there would be no consequences. Her uncle would remain the man they all had to defer to, the man who came home one night out of two, demanding his food, his tongue thick and rolling in his mouth. The man on whose name these lands now rested, the fields, the house. This, she knew, was the way of their village, and all the villages around. Without him, there would be no plantation, no food to eat, no surplus to sell.

Approaching closer, Rita could see that the first terrace lay empty, and she felt something lift inside her—her uncle must have finally moved on to the next terrace. Sumnima must have noted this too because she stopped momentarily in front of Rita. Then, from beyond the rim of the first terrace, they saw the broad backs of the oxen, their tails moving in unison, swishing at flies. Where was her uncle?

In front of her, Sumnima quickened her pace. By the time Rita reached the rim of the first terrace, Sumnima had already leapt off the walkway on to the terrace below.

Not far from them, lying prostrate, his face swollen in the sun, his pants stained wet down to the knees, her uncle snored with his arms folded over his exposed belly. The plough wasn't even harnessed to the oxen.

Sumnima remained still, staring, her face unreadable. Then she picked up a handful of dried earth and let loose, hitting the inebriated figure of her father. He did not move. Rita watched as Sumnima slipped first one foot, then another, out of her worn slippers. She walked right up to the snoring body and prodded him with a foot. It was deeply disrespectful, to touch an elder with your feet, let alone your father. And then, abruptly before her, Sumnima started kicking him.

Rita dropped the still warm roti and water jolted out of the jug she carried.

'Didi!' Rita heard her own voice come out in a harsh begging whisper, 'Didi! Stop it! Stop it! What are you doing?'

But Sumnima did not stop. She continued, a choking sound emerged from her throat but her eyes were dry. This, Rita knew, was the thing she had seen deep within Sumnima—the shift in the air, a turning over that was now revealing another person, someone she had never seen before. Neelam didi was right. Sumnima was too much, a thing uncontained. But then other, more practical thoughts raced through Rita's mind: what if the man before her, in a drunken stupor but now starting to groan and cough, woke up? Should she scream? But what if, through the cloud of alcohol that still held him thick, he recognized her voice?

She ran towards Sumnima, grabbing her by the hand. She pulled but Sumnima was too strong and simply batted her away.

'I will shout!' Rita threatened, 'I will go tell Aama!'

'Go!' Sumnima lashed out, her breaths now coming in gasps, 'Go tell!'

'Didi stop it!' Rita reached for her again. 'Stop it otherwise I will tell, I promise!'

Sumnima turned around sharply, 'Go tell, you darcherua! You coward!' She grabbed Rita's shoulder with one hand and shoved her away.

Rita looked desperately around. There, lying an arm's reach away on the ground, was a flat rock the size of her palm. Rita snatched the rock and aimed it straight at Sumnima.

The rock found its mark and rolled off Sumnima's hip with a dull thud.

'Why are you doing this?' Rita's voice climbed.

Sumnima looked back, blinking, then marched straight towards her.

'Because he deserves it! And we deserve justice!' there was a cruelty in her words as she approached, 'Go tell, you darcherua, go tell the whole village!'

Sumnima pushed her hard and Rita fell backwards on to the packed earth.

Never before had Rita seen a woman hit a man, let alone a daughter kick her own father. What if people saw? She turned around. But there was no one on this side of the hill. Only empty fields, readying for the rain. What if her uncle decided that he had had enough of them all? What if he became one more man to leave the village, what if he sold the lands, the house, and turned them all out? What if he awoke and attacked Sumnima back? She remembered Kaaki. How, in that moment, sitting listless upon the courtyard dirt, unable to stand up, unable to see, Kaaki had looked non-human. Pasu, the word came again to Rita's mind. Animal.

Rita ran back towards the house, momentarily losing her balance and falling off the walkway before picking herself up again. Sumnima was only half visible beyond the edge of the terrace, the heavy wood of the plough now balanced upon the strength of her shoulders. High in her hand, the swish of a stick. Rita heard the oxen protest as it came down hard upon their backs. It occurred to her—she had never seen a girl plough a field before. But then, another deeper realization dawned as her own stunted shadow chased alongside her. How could she ever tell on Sumnima? How could she ever betray her?

In the days that followed, forest fires raged uncontrolled and seemed, each day, to come closer across the hills. The stories of ghosts and unknown creatures multiplied. The villagers talked of the *kichkandi*, waiting to suck the life out of unsuspecting men. They spoke of lost spirits and the *banmanche*, half-beast and half-men. Down at the tea shop, Sumnima's father insisted, shaking over a cup of hot tea, that a creature had caught him by the legs, lifted him clean up in the air, flipped him upside down and shaken him till his bones almost came loose. He rolled up his pants and showed the swells and bruises, bright and multiple, to prove it. But the creature, he insisted, was not half-man. It was half-woman.

* * *

One morning, Neelam didi arrived just as Rita finished mopping all the floors with the mixture of antiseptic cow dung and mud. 'Ohho!' she spat out as she slowly lowered herself on to the shade of the porch. 'This heat is going to kill us. No rain in sight and yet my hip pains as if we were all going to drown. Eh Rita! Go, get me some water!'

Inside, Rita wavered. She did not want to face Neelam didi. In fact, she did not want to face anybody these days. She went from task to task in solitude. At school, she felt herself gaze out the window. An image kept playing itself over and over before her—Sumnima and the look of surprise in her eyes as the rock bounced off her hip. It was the first time Rita had ever turned against Sumnima and it made her feel as if she somehow had turned against herself.

Rita stepped out with a small gagri of carefully allocated water.

'Listen!' Neelam didi wheezed, 'Tell your mother, Kathmandu is sending NGO health workers and even doctors up to the hills. They are saying we are all going to starve if we don't plant the rice soon and they are blaming us for drinking the same water as our buffaloes. But if the spouts and streams are dry, what are we supposed to do? He Ram, He Ram! Oh God! Anyway, I hope Kathmandu won't be coming here empty-handed. They may even bring some supplies with them. Tell your mother. She must take Kaaki and get that arm straightened out. She must go down to the district headquarters and check—do you hear me? And where is Sumnima?'

'Grazing the goats.'

'Again? With Manju Thapa and that . . . Niraj Rai?'

Rita did not say anything.

'Hmph!' Neelam didi lifted herself painfully, 'As soon as the rains come, we will marry that girl off. I just got news that one of the boys' family has agreed. So, it has been decided. Mark my words, we are close. This Mangsir, the date has been set!'

As Rita watched Neelam didi descend back down the stairs, she felt a vague, thumping hollow right in the centre of her being. Sumnima's marriage had always felt somehow abstract, a faraway distant possibility like old age or death. But suddenly, it was here, only months away now.

A sudden inexplicable urgency took hold of Rita in that moment and she left the gagri lying on the floor, her feet moving towards the stone path Sumnima had taken up into the forests. She climbed up, step after step, and even the thought of ghosts wasn't enough to stop her. After a while, she left the Rato Mato hill behind and started up the northern face of the Dhire. The path faded into undergrowth and around her, the shrubs grew thick, straggly, their leaves brittle with thirst, their thorns unsheathed. The higher she climbeds the shorter the trees grew, stunted by earth that had turned sandy, shifty, the shade a paler, grimier red. Rita climbed a long while until she felt like she had broken through the circumference of the surrounding hills, into the brightness of unfettered air. Behind her, forest fires clawed red across the valley.

Then suddenly, Rita stopped, daring not to move. From higher up the thickly forested hillside, came the distinct echo of what sounded like clapping. She took careful steps towards the sound, her heart pounding in her throat. The sound came again, from still further up.

Then she heard other sounds—the beat of a madal, muffled voices, the soft flurry of more clapping. Rita crouched low, moving warily forward until she could see, amidst the shadowed play of leaves, colour and movement. She clambered over to a bush thick with thorns.

In front of her, between a ring of small trees, was a gathering of people. Most of them sat cross-legged on the floor. Rita saw a boy playing the madal and recognized him immediately. He was the boy from Class 9 picked to play the madal during cultural events at the school. Next to him, Rita recognized Manju, but she was not wearing her blue school uniform skirt or the blue ribbon bow. Around her forehead was a bright red bandana, a white star emblazoned on its front. She was dressed in dusty green and Rita realized that Manju was in fact wearing pants, just like the boys around her. She was so focused on the faces closest to Manju and the madal player that it was only after a few seconds that Rita turned her attention to the couple the crowd was cheering on. With their backs turned to her, was a slender boy and next to him, a tall girl, her hair in a tight bun, her legs also in forest green pants. They were gyrating, stepping in unison, their hands whirling in the air and with a sudden shock, Rita knew the movements. The broad shoulders, the elegant long fingers that reached up, the feet that moved with a certain discordant hesitancy. Sumnima had never been a good dancer. And yet, here she was, a red band donning her forehead, her legs in pants that did not belong to her and stopped short above her ankles. With a final high note of the madal, the dancing abruptly stopped. The crowd clapped and Rita ducked back behind the thorn bush. Someone spoke. An unfamiliar male voice, older, distinct and commanding.

'Let this song', the voice was saying, 'be an eternal reminder of the spirit of the revolution. This is only the beginning, comrades. Only the beginning. Long live the revolution!'

And then in unison, the crowd echoed, 'Long live the revolution!'

The gathered people were on their feet, their fists pumping into the air. Rita stayed hidden as she could hear a commotion now, of things being packed and gathered and banter about which paths would be taken to return to various villages. And suddenly, someone rustled through the branches above her as they approached. Rita watched as Sumnima disappeared behind a tree, then emerged clothed in the same clothes she had worn that morning before she left the house. Behind her, Rita could hear voices dissipate. The rest of the crowd was already starting to make their way down the hill. How would Rita get back to the house before Sumnima did? Then, Rita recognized Niraj. Here he was, walking right up to Sumnima, grabbing her by the wrist and pushing her back against the tree. His head was tilting as his face touched hers and his arms rose around her. Niraj made a small movement and then Rita saw it, the touch of lip upon lip, mouth upon mouth. The familiar curve of Sumnima's closed eyes, her carved cheek against bark, flush with the implication of pleasure.

Rita had a sudden overwhelming urge to get away as fast as possible. As she turned, she fell on all fours. Somehow, she moved, crawling, through brittle space. It felt like an eternity to reach the next bush, the next dwarf tree. She smelled smoke, fear and something else—more powerful but as yet unnamed—stretching towards her. Finally, her feet were slamming down the hill, the soil shifting, powdery.

The image of the back of Niraj's head, his fingers splayed and linked around Sumnima's against the tree kept flashing in her head. She saw Sumnima's closed eyes, her open mouth. The red star of the rebels brandished high upon her forehead. Not only was Sumnima doing the forbidden, she was doing it with the low-caste Rai boy. All these days and weeks, Sumnima had been building another life. One without her in it. By the time she reached the familiar bend above the village of Rato Mato, halfway down the hill, Rita was choking on her own tears. Sumnima and the rebels. Sumnima and Niraj. Sumnima, for whom she had not been enough.

Every day after that, Rita woke up to Sumnima's betrayal, to its thick insistent accompaniment. Her mouth felt parched, her feet hot and caked dry. She imagined the things Sumnima would have done with Niraj. She was sure that any day now, Sumnima would elope, leave this village, leave her. Rita felt her own mind tear itself apart with the images, the ones she had just seen, the ones she hadn't but was sure she would. And with each image she felt the bitterness grow. In school, Rita noticed how Sumnima would pass by Niraj in the dirt yard as if she did not know him. And yet, for days in a row, Sumnima did not show up in class and neither did he.

The Saturday when the men came, Rita was mopping the porch for the second time. Her hands were red, the smell of cow dung clinging to her, persistent and sharp.

She heard them before she saw them, striding purposefully up the side of the hill and on to the courtyard. Both tall and sturdy, dressed in bright blue jeans and clean shirts, their collars crisp, on their feet a pair of laced shoes. They were not men from these parts.

A few years ago, a man from the health services in Kathmandu had come for a similar visit. Both Sumnima and Aama were home at the time. Alongside the man from Kathmandu, dressed very much like these two men, was a white woman. The white woman had been from an NGO, a non-governmental organization based in Kathmandu. Rita remembered the woman's hair, how it lifted in the air, consumed with sunshine, her eyes the colour of the sky. She wore a vibrant tunic, not too dissimilar to Rita's own. As if by dressing like them and bending into a deep namaste, the white woman could somehow become less of an anomaly, could become more like them. She had been overly friendly, greeting them multiple times before sitting them all down in a line on the porch. Then, from the backpack at her feet, she took out papers, medicine, big colourful pictures. The Kathmandu man had translated. The woman spoke quickly, spending a full half hour telling them about the virtues of washing their hands, boiling the tap water before drinking it, consuming small, neat packets of *Jeevan jaal* when taken by a bout of diarrhoea. And then, she had eyed Sumnima and Rita before pulling out a picture of a balloon from her bag.

'This,' the health worker had translated, 'is a condom.'

Aama had immediately brought her hand to her mouth and stood up.

'Tell this white woman,' she had said loudly, 'there are no men here. What is she teaching our children?' The white woman, embarrassed by the interruption, had gone blazing red and Sumnima and Rita had fallen atop each other in laughter. Rita wondered now if Sumnima and Niraj used a condom when they did what she was sure they were doing, up in the forests.

The two men were calling out greetings to her and she noticed how one of them was holding a pen and notepad.

'*Eh nani*,' one of them called out, 'is there no one else at home? We've been going from house to house taking this survey. Here, look,' he held out his notepad of lined paper, 'it's the National Census. Can we sit down for a few minutes and ask you some questions?'

Rita was conscious that she was all by herself. Aama and Kaaki would not be coming back for another half hour at least and who knew when Sumnima would show up. But Rita had heard all about these new arrivals from Kathmandu and she felt a certain curiosity. What did these two men hope to achieve with this census? Kathmandu, she thought, would not be here without a reason.

She brought out two cups of sweetened tea. When the men started asking her questions, the answers were easy enough. How many females in the house, how many males? What were their ages, approximately? How many years had Rita been in school for? Then the questions started going deeper. What had happened to all the men? What did Aama and Kaaki do for a living? Did the people of the household vote in the last election? Who did they vote for? What did Rita think of her classes at school? What did she learn about the government and the king?

The men asked about Sumnima. Who did she associate with, what did she think of the classes at school, what did she think of Principal sir, a self-declared royalist? It was the first time anyone had asked Rita such questions. And what was more, they seemed genuinely interested in what she had to say. And as Rita answered question after question, the big words of Federalism, Nationalism, Republic teeming in her mind, she remembered what she had promised Sumnima. That she would never speak about the rebels. Not to anyone. But what was her promise now worth if all of Sumnima's own promises, had been forgotten and fallen swiftly away?

Bit by bit, Rita told the two men everything. She gave them names. She told them about her uncle, why he was not working. About Aama and Kaaki, how they worked all the time. About Principal sir, who was oblivious to all the changes afoot in his own village. About Sumnima, who would be going away soon. They could count her in their survey if they liked, or not. It did not matter. Overhead, clouds gathered, thick and shiftless. As she answered question after question, Rita felt, at times, like she could reach out and touch them, closing in all around her. At times, like she could fall right into them, be swallowed whole.

5

Dhire Hill

(*Barkha Ritu*, Summer Monsoon, 2001)

Two weeks after the men from Kathmandu came calling with their survey, a small boy went running through Rato Mato village, banging on every door.

'They are coming! They are coming!'

Neelam didi came hobbling up to the house as fast as she could, her face so heavy with emotion and strain that it looked swollen.

'Fifty!' she panted, her lips dry, her cheeks flushed a dark tremulous red, 'There are fifty of them! All armed and moving fast!'

'Who?' Rita sprung up from the porch.

'Soldiers,' Neelam didi gasped for air, 'rebels.'

'Who saw them?' asked Aama, her brow furrowed.

'Hari's boy.'

'How do we know he isn't lying? That Hari's boy is always making up stories.'

'This is no story,' Neelam didi wheezed, 'such a story, not even Hari's boy could make up.'

'But where did he see them?' Sumnima was watching Neelam didi, motionless.

'He saw them across the pass. Walking single file. With guns slung across their shoulders.'

'And where was the boy?'

'On the southern hill face. He looked up while grazing the cows and there they were, marching. They must have been heading for the bridge. They will be here by sundown.'

'And did he stop and count?'

'He swears by fifty. Maybe he only saw twenty. But what if there are more to join? Seventy? A hundred? How do we know? But we know one thing at least. They are planning an attack. They are going to attack the district headquarters!'

Before Rita could process the news, she noticed Sumnima make a movement, then stop, as if changing her mind. What did Sumnima know?

Aama stood up and studied the sky. Then she turned to face them all.

'Sumnima, Rita,' she ordered. 'Go hide the rice and corn. Behind Dalle's shed. Leave only one or two sacks behind. Hide everything else.'

'But why?' Rita found herself asking. In the corner, Kaaki squatted unmoving, her eyes fixed on Aama.

'Because a marching army is not going to pass by this village hungry. And if they finish our stores, and the rain doesn't come, we will have nothing left to eat. Go, go quickly!'

Rita ran for the cattle shed. Behind her, Sumnima was stalling. Dalle the buffalo watched them approach with one roving eye.

In the closed space inside the shed, Rita heaved up sacks half her size. She watched as Sumnima, usually so swift, moved as if she were shuffling ankle-deep through running water.

'So,' she said as Sumnima readied herself to haul a sack up by its ears, 'aren't you and your new friends going to join the rebel army?'

Sumnima let go of the sack and looked up, blinking in the half-light. It had been weeks since any words had been shared between them.

'Why would I join them?' she asked in surprise, but her voice sounded unconvincing.

'They are coming, aren't they?' Rita was pleased by how pointed her words were, 'Isn't this your chance?'

'How would I know? What did Hari's boy really see? Neelam didi, she makes a drama out of everything, multiplies everything.'

Sumnima reached for the jute, grunted and lifted the sack up, her arms strong. But Rita felt herself weighed down by confusion. The rebels were marching to Rato Mato. Why was Sumnima here instead, with her?

Aama straightened up as Rita and Sumnima returned to the house. She motioned for them to come.

'You two,' her voice was rough. 'It has been decided. You two are to go up with Neelam to the Dhire. Stay there until the rebels leave.'

'But why the Dhire?' Sumnima asked.

'Because,' Neelam didi jumped in, 'because those revolutionaries are nothing but thieves. First, they will come steal our food. And then, they will steal our children. What if they take you with them when they leave? What if they do other things?'

Rita had heard stories. How in other hills further down west, the rebels had started recruiting children into their armies. How they would pass by schools and fields, taking them away, either through persuasion or by pointing the gun.

'The Dhire . . .' Sumnima opened her mouth, but Aama cut her off immediately.

'Right now. Nobody will find you up on the Dhire. The decision has been made. Go with Neelam didi, right away.'

Sumnima did not continue but Rita could see things were left unsaid in her face. Kaaki had walked around and was now standing next to Sumnima. Rita could see the similarities in the curve of cheek, the angle of chin. But that is where the similarities ended. Where Kaaki was thin and frail, Sumnima was tall, strong, her shoulders straight. Kaaki reached for Sumnima's sleeve. A smile hovered around her mouth but Rita could see the tears in her eyes. Kaaki's heart understood, even if her mind did not, and in that moment, Rita felt as if Kaaki's heart understood something beyond them all.

Aama and Kaaki stood in the courtyard, watching them leave. The wind picked up and played with the edges of the two women's dhotis, wisps of hair about their faces. Just as they turned a corner, Aama reached out to Kaaki, steadying her by the elbow.

Following Sumnima and Neelam didi up the stone path, Rita's mind was full of questions. Why was Sumnima coming with them? Where were Manju and Niraj?

Midway up the Dhire, the wind picked up and started blowing in gusts.

'*Aia*, *aia*, let me rest for two minutes,' Neelam didi stopped and sat on the side of a wide rock by the path. Rita wondered how she managed all these steps, twice a day every day, with her painful hip and pronounced limp. But these steps, she knew, were all Neelam didi had. Carved and flattened with stone, they linked the singular house up on Dhire hill to the life below.

Sumnima looked at the thick clouds over the valley and cleared her throat, her face a shapeshifting canvas. 'Let's keep moving,' she said, her voice strained, 'otherwise we are going to get caught in this storm.'

For the second half of the climb, Neelam didi spoke endlessly, her voice rasping above the growing sound of the wind, interrupted only by heavy panting. She told them about a new calf born to the Madhesi cluster of houses, the celebrations that followed given it was the first calf birthed since the cluster had moved to these hills. She told them about the new Magar bride—only a child—brought from another village a few hills away. She told them about the Chettri girl who had eloped, running all the way across the border to India. 'How can she not be scared,' Neelam didi was incredulous, 'after all the stories one hears about women being tricked into prostitution in India, how can she be sure that boy would not sell her?'

They were midway up the Dhire. The clouds had overtaken them, consuming everything in a thick moving fog of white. In the distance, they could hear thunder gathering. It leapt over them now, a deafening sound breaking the sky.

'Ram! Ram!' Neelam didi shouted out, 'Ram! Ram! Let's hurry, hurry!'

Rain fell in sudden sheets, lashing at them, churning the earth to gushing mud. Rita couldn't recall the last time she had experienced rain this hard. Around her, the world was flooding quickly, consumed in darkness. Neelam didi unfurled her wool shawl, revealing a small torchlight hidden in its depths.

The rain came down harder and Rita could feel her toes slip into the flow of mud. In front, Neelam didi was shouting something but she couldn't hear her above the sounds of the wind and rain. Veering from the edge of the cliff, Rita recognized where they were—an outcrop of bamboo that grew in a thicket at the sloping bend of the hill. It was still a long walk from here to the house at the very top.

'Let's wait here, the rain is too heavy,' Neelam didi crouched down, squatting right in the centre of the leafy enclave. She cleared her throat, then flapped her shawl like a large bird resettling its wings.

'Sumnima,' Neelam didi spoke, her voice lifting above the sounds about them. There was something about her tone that made Rita look up sharply.

'I have come by the house now several times. But every time I come by, you are never there. I hear that you have made new friends. That Manju girl and . . . and Tilak Rai's son.'

Sumnima looked up, her eyes unreadable, painted in oblique shadow.

'The village is starting to talk. Did it never occur to you that someone would find out? Did you think that chatterbox Manju would keep your secret?'

Rita felt her heart stop. What did Neelam didi know?

'Did you ever stop to think about your own mother, about Aama, about Rita?' Neelam didi's mouth turned up in a sneer, contorted by wavering light, 'Has your family not suffered enough as it is? Did you not stop to think,' her voice was as unrelenting as the rain, 'what would people say about a Brahmin girl with a Rai boy?'

Rita started. Of course, Neelam didi knew. She made it her business to know everything that happened in the village.

'That insignificant village, all the useless people in it,' Sumnima burst out, 'They have nothing better to do than concern themselves with things that don't matter. What about the fact that most of those people don't even own the land they were born on, the land that they till their whole lives? What about all those women, sold off like cattle before they even bleed. What about the injustice and poverty? Does anybody talk about that?!' Sumnima was angry. 'They are nothing but fools. And you, you are a fool to listen to them.'

'Shut your mouth!' Neelam didi roared, 'People are not fools. They only talk because they see. You are the only person here with your eyes closed. A Brahmin girl with a boy of a lower caste. Think about your family. Haven't they suffered enough? Your drunkard father, not enough money in the house and now you.'

'And what, he is not a human being? Just because Niraj is of a lower caste, his life does not count?'

'Stop your nonsense. You think you will live an easy life marrying a Rai? No land and not a penny to his name. Will you eat stones?'

Neelam didi's acknowledgement made it suddenly more real. Sumnima was going to run away with Niraj Rai. In a flash, Rita saw the worst of all her imaginations coming true. But just as she turned to face Sumnima, she heard a sound. A sound that didn't belong to the storm.

Neelam didi heard it too.

'Shh! Shh!' she batted at Sumnima and rose slowly from the rock, the torchlight pointed in one hand. She listened for a few breathless seconds, took two steps into the dark. Nothing. And then, there it was again.

And suddenly, Rita saw them. First one, then two, then three. Outlines of figures, just visible in the distance, climbing over the edge of the cliff. Hauling themselves up in the bruised light, beyond the skirting of the bamboo grove.

Neelam didi switched off the torchlight. The three women breathed in darkness.

'Run!' Neelam didi whispered. 'They haven't seen us. We must hurry!' she moved deeper into bamboo, a shadow amongst shadows.

Rita felt a sudden weakness, a slackening in every part of her body, her heart and head both thundering on, leaving behind a shell of herself. The outlines of Neelam didi and Sumnima moved quickly forward and thinned into the trees. But Rita's feet wouldn't move.

'Didi wait!' Rita hardly heard the sound coming out of her own mouth, 'Didi wait for me!' She stumbled. All around, the whip lines of hollowed stems closed in on her, thrashing and battling each other. Then, she felt movement, close to her. She felt fingers grabbing at her wrist, pulling her with force, lifting her through the writhing mass of stems. Sumnima. Sumnima had come back for her.

By the time they scrambled up to the house at the top of Dhire hill, banging on the door until Dhire dai flung it open, Rita was disoriented by the darkness, the rain, the raw fear that threatened to choke her.

Neelam didi whispered in panicked urgency, 'Shut the lamps! Bolt the doors!' Dhire dai hadn't needed much explanation and did exactly as his wife said. They shuttered the windows, bolted the door, even moved a long wooden chest of drawers that had come as part of Neelam didi's wedding dowry in front of it.

'The rebels are here,' Neelam didi rasped, 'They are here.'

Sumnima had crawled to a west-facing window. She unbolted it now, opening a small crack. Balancing on her knees, she peered out.

'Look, there!' Sumnima pointed with a finger in the dark, but Rita could barely tell which direction she meant. The rebels were here, below them somewhere, on the skirting of the Dhire.

A wavering light in the distance. Coming and going, disappearing and reappearing again. Like someone moving in and out of the trees, torchlight in hand.

'There! There!' Neelam didi's voice lifted, her breath heavy in the enclosed space. But she was pointing in a different direction. And Rita, turning now towards the opposite side, could see a second light, this one a yawning distance away from the first one.

The first light flitted on the side, towards the northern flank of the Dhire. The second light came from where the base of the Dhire meandered slightly to the west, jutting out in a spindly elbow that opened into a wide vista of the valley below. In the middle, tucked in between the north and west, was a deep gorge.

The lights came and went, and then there were more. On either side of the gorge, a line of flickering lights, like columns of fireflies making their way through the night—men, moving through trees. Then, barely audible in the downpour, came what sounded like a high-pitched whistle. It was answered by another whistle from across the gaping darkness, this one nearer, breaking through the rain. Back and forth, like the synchronized calls of night birds across the depths of the gorge, the whistles rang.

'What are they doing?' Sumnima asked, every muscle tensed by the window.

'They are communicating,' Dhire dai's words sent an instant chill up Rita's spine. 'They are talking to each other.'

'What do we do?' Neelam didi asked, a high whine.

'Shh! Keep quiet. They are obviously planning something. Something big,' Dhire dai's voice hovered over the four of them crouched in the darkness, 'I think . . . they have climbed on to the base of the Dhire to attack the Rato Mato headquarters from above.'

'What will we do?'

'Nothing, we just stay here. They will not come this high up.'

'What about Aama and Kaaki?' Rita felt a sudden panic, 'What is going to happen to them?'

'Don't worry,' it was Sumnima who answered now, her breath fast and clipped, 'the revolutionaries will not hurt them. They are here to protect people like our mothers. There is nothing to fear.'

'Chup chup, shut up!' Neelam didi sharply elbowed Sumnima, 'Stop your nonsense. What do you know about the rebels?'

But before Sumnima could reply, there came a sudden, deafening blast. A roar that seemed to sweep through the night, up the hill, through the house, through their bodies. Sumnima gasped, pushed open the window further and stuck her head out. Beneath them, down the hill, where only a short while ago lights flickered on either side, the darkness had split open in a blaze of sharp light. Shouts, wails, and the metallic *rat tat tat* of what seemed like a hundred guns bursting into motion ripped through the night.

Rita fell to the floor. Beneath her, the earth moved, rocking slowly back and forth. Somewhere close to her, she heard moaning. A low endless sound. Sumnima. When Rita opened her eyes, Neelam didi's bulk was pressed against Sumnima, her thick arms clamped around Sumnima's body. Dhire dai was on the other side, restraining Sumnima's legs. Rita blinked, confused, until she realized that Neelam didi and Dhire dai were stopping Sumnima from running outside. Sumnima fought and thrashed for a long time, while outside, the heavy gunshots fell to occasional, distinct, cracks. Until finally, only silence reigned outside the open window. Sumnima stopped fighting. They lay there, the four of them, a spent heap upon the floor, while the rain stopped, the darkness thinned, and a distant glow broke forth over the Himals.

At the first break of daylight, they hesitantly emerged from the house and descended the peak. Sumnima stumbled ahead, her face bleached of all colour. Rita followed, her legs watery-weak. Behind her, Neelam didi and Dhire dai were wordless as they climbed down the hill. They were soon joined by others from the village.

At first, they found nothing. Only trails of blood seeping into red earth. Bullet casings, someone's shoe. It was only on the western flank that they started finding the first bodies. Stuck precariously between rocks down the steep slope, caught by the crags of trees and rain-swept thickets. Someone wept. Someone else started retching, bent on all fours on the ground soggy with last night's rain.

Sumnima ran from body to body, pushing aside others to look. There was more blood seeping into the red soil than what the bodies could account for. Someone said that the rebels must have taken most of the dead and wounded on their side with them. Rita felt like someone was squeezing her chest. Then the villagers found others, dressed in blue, some faces they recognized and some they didn't. Policemen from the district headquarters below Rato Mato. Policemen brought from nearby hilltops, posted by Kathmandu, in the district headquarters. Reinforcements. Kathmandu had already been expecting a rebel attack on Rato Mato.

By mid-morning, the whole village of Rato Mato seemed to have assembled around the base of the Dhire. Dressed in multihued tunics and dhotis of red, green and yellow, it almost looked like a wedding or a fair to Rita. The villagers gathered and whispered, huddled into small groups with a man or woman wiping an eye with the edge of a dhoti or a sleeve.

They heard it before they saw it. The first helicopter, its splayed wings furiously whipping air as it prepared to land upon the plateau. Jumping out now, a dozen armed policemen. Two more helicopters landed next with more police, grave-faced men barking at the villagers to step back. From the third helicopter emerged two men without uniforms, armed with a large contraption that one of them carried on his shoulder, trailing loops of wire. 'Video,' a hushed whisper went around, 'video camera.' One of the men now lifted a mike to his mouth and started to speak into it in clipped sentences.

It was afternoon by the time they lined up all the bodies they could find next to each other atop the plateau, the crest of a false rise. Sumnima stayed close, at one point catching

Rita by the elbow and pointing, her mouth open wide in shock. At the very edge of the line lay two bodies smaller than all the rest, their braids oiled and plaited, fastened with identical blue ribbons. Girls, dressed in green fatigues. *Manju!* The thought jetted through Rita's mind but no, these faces were unfamiliar, not from these parts. The girls were not much older than Sumnima and Manju. The sight knocked Rita sideways. She could imagine how they would have been, two village girls in green camouflage, their guns resting nearby, standing side by side and braiding their hair just as Sumnima and Rita braided theirs before heading to school every morning.

She saw it then—a lone tear running down Sumnima's cheek. These were the revolutionaries Sumnima so admired. This was their fight, the price they paid to bring about all the things they talked about. Which one of the big words had been worth this? What, Rita wondered with a sudden revulsion, would Manju have to say about all this? Or Niraj?

Aama found them in the crowd, her mouth set in a thin, tight line. Rita could see the fear in her eyes, rounded and black. 'Here you are!' she whispered in her rough smoker's voice and Rita could hear the hiss of release.

The men with the cameras walked by, half tripping over the lines of wire that trailed between them.

'Did you see that one?' one asked the other, 'How old do you think she is, sixteen, seventeen?'

'What will Kathmandu say?' the other asked before they moved through the crowd. They moved too quickly for Rita to pick up the response.

Kathmandu. Rita found herself thinking, Nepal. What will Nepal say?

Later that evening, gathered about their colour televisions in their big painted homes, the people of the capital would be seeing these same images she was seeing now. The rich businessmen, the politicians, the king himself. She wondered if they would feel fear in the same way, smell its acrid stench, laced with metal.

The policemen carried with them a multitude of large plastic bags. They were lifting the bodies now, one by one, and fastening them in plastic before placing them into the bellies of the helicopters. It was only when the two helicopters had already lifted off with their loads that the rumours started through the crowd.

Neelam didi whispered it to Aama. 'Some of the dead are from our village.'

Sumnima grew stiff. Rita reached out a hand, but Sumnima moved forward, making a first uncertain step. And then she was running, racing towards where the newly found bodies lay, bodies in rebel green, the dead left behind. By the time Rita caught up to her, Sumnima had dropped heavily to her knees. Laying just before her—with limbs twisted in angles that were not meant to be—was a man. Rita forced herself to look down, running her eyes above the narrow hips in dirtied forest green and then stopped at a bloodied gash. She recognized him instantly. Niraj Rai. Rita felt herself fall heavily beside Sumnima. Sumnima's mouth was twisted into a wide soundless O.

Before any sound came out, Neelam didi was upon Sumnima. She swooped her arms around Sumnima and was struggling to lift her back up on her feet. Aama was suddenly there too, reaching for Sumnima, and Rita felt a slow, emerging realization. Aama knew. All this time, Aama knew, but had said nothing at all. Aama laced her arms around Sumnima and heaved her up. Neelam didi had one palm wrapped around Sumnima's open mouth, and was saying, 'Take them back down, take them away from here.' Rita could see the fear in her eyes. The fear, it dawned upon her, of association.

Aama and Neelam didi were dragging Sumnima now, hoisting her on to Dhire dai's back. Dhire dai staggered to his feet, his bare legs thin as wires and tottered. Then he regained his balance, moving quickly down the hill, bearing Sumnima on his back. As if she were a bride, carried as per tradition, leaving her father's house for the last time. Sumnima's head rolled off his shoulder, lolled listlessly to one side.

They stayed awake the whole night with Sumnima thrashing around inconsolably on the mud-swept floor. It had taken all three of them—Kaaki, Aama and Neelam didi—to restrain her. It was only in the watery darkness of early dawn that she had fallen into an unsteady, whimpering sleep. Rita had laid down beside her, feeling faint and disembodied, her mind yet to fully comprehend what had come to pass. Outside, there were voices and the scuffle of feet, someone's low hoarse whisper, 'They will do a search. They will go house to house. They will not leave a single stone unturned.'

Dhire dai locked them all in and waited outside. When Rita awoke to the sounds of dawn, the rooster crowing obliviously in his coop, Dalle the buffalo calling for his morning meal, Sumnima was gone.

6

The White House

Out front in the courtyard, Dhire dai had kept watch all night. But the open window, just big enough for Sumnima to climb through, was at the back of the house.

Rita's first thought was to check the village. Before anyone could stop her, she flew down the hillside and ran through the village until she reached Manju's house. She rapped breathlessly on the door. Then, she called out. No answer.

'They left,' a neighbour poked her head out of a doorway, 'yesterday evening.'

'Left? To where?'

'Kathmandu,' the old woman coughed, 'they took everything with them.'

Was Manju with the rest of the family? The woman peering out at her couldn't be sure.

'They all left, took everything with them,' she repeated. Somewhere in the distance, a dog barked and was answered by another.

Rita ran to a side window and peered inside. Manju's house was empty, swept clean. It was as if the house had never been occupied.

By the time Rita ran back home, Aama and Neelam didi were hunched, sitting on the porch. Kaaki's head rested on Aama's lap, her eyes shut, her face swollen and dirtied with tears.

'You know we have to do it,' Neelam didi was saying as Rita approached, 'we have no choice. *You* have no other choice.'

Kaaki groaned and turned over.

'Chup chup, shh shh,' Aama softly keened, her thick calloused hand smoothening out Kaaki's hair, 'We will find her, we will find her.'

'They will be coming soon,' Neelam didi continued, her gaze levelled on Aama, 'asking questions. Looking for accomplices. She is now a liability. To herself and to all of us.'

Rita felt a moment of confusion, who were they talking about?

'We need to get her out!' Neelam didi raised her voice.

Aama looked away, out to the hills. 'But we don't know where Sumnima is, she could be anywhere,' she suddenly looked old, as if the years had been sucked right out of her.

'Where do you think she is?' Neelam didi almost spat out, 'She's gone to join the rebels, that's where she is. That girl has never had a sensible idea in her head.'

'Don't speak against her,' Aama raised her chin.

'She has brought this on herself. And now on all of us. She has put Rita at risk. If they come searching, there is nothing we will be able to do. *Nothing*.'

'But,' Rita heard her own voice, the tremor of dawning realization, 'But . . . you are talking about me, aren't you? But . . . where will I go?'

Neelam didi turned to her, her eyebrows raised, as if in surprise, as if she were seeing her for the very first time, 'Dhire dai will be here any minute now. He has a plan.'

'So, he will take her there?' Aama's voice sounded resigned.

Neelam didi hesitated. 'It is the only place he knows.'

Rita looked from one face to the other. Aama seemed to understand.

'How will she survive there?' Aama said, 'She knows nothing.'

'There is no other alternative.'

Rita felt a keening in her ears, 'Where will Dhire dai take me?'

Neelam didi's voice was softer, solemn, 'Kathmandu.'

'Kathmandu?' Rita repeated, her mind stunned.

'There are,' Neelam didi hesitated again, ' . . . there are people he knows there.'

'But how long will I go there for?'

Neelam didi turned her gaze down. She looked at Kaaki, her hair spread out around her in a stringy matted halo, and didn't respond.

'Aama?' Rita felt her heart thump faster, knocking at the back of her throat. 'Aama?' she whipped around, reaching for Aama's sleeve.

Aama let out a slow exhale.

'As long as it takes,' she said, her fingers warm and roughened, reaching up momentarily to pat Rita's hand before falling away. 'For as long as it takes.'

When Dhire dai arrived, a sack strung on his shoulders, their farewell was brief. Neelam didi held her, pushing her tight against her large bosom. Aama avoided her eyes. She walked into the house and emerged with a small jute bag. As she handed it to Rita, she rested a hand upon her shoulder, giving a brief squeeze before turning back towards the house. Rita wanted Aama to weep, to press her close, to call out to the gods. But she knew what Aama was doing. She had seen it before. Aama was building walls inside herself. Walls that would allow her to carry on, heaving a doko larger than herself, bending hour after hour in the fields, a mere witness as the gods played out this hand too, this karma.

During the whole trip, Dhire dai spoke little. He had never been one to talk and in the present circumstances, words seemed to fail him completely. They avoided the village paths and crossed through fields. They moved quickly downhill, dropping from terrace to terrace until finally they dropped down to the main road and Dhire dai flagged down a passing bus. The next two days and nights they spent at the back of the bus as it wound through the narrow road carved out of cliffs and hillsides. Rita fell in and out of sleep, her mind numb, unable to wrap itself around all that was happening, her body limp. When they stopped to refuel at dawn on the second day, Dhire dai stood up, said he would be back soon and returned with a large bag of unshelled peanuts.

'Here,' he said and laid them gently on Rita's lap.

Dhire dai mostly smelled of red earth and *khaini* tobacco, but somewhere, underlying the pungency, was the sweetness of mango. His thin sleepless face was grizzled and his hands roped with veins. His eyes watched the river outside. This unlikely man, Rita realized, was the closest thing to a father she would ever know.

Outside, it started to rain. The rain came and went and then came again, pummelling the ground in the darkness and then petering out in the dawn, a light tap-tapping against the bus window.

As the bus entered the valley of Kathmandu, the roads widened, making way for more buses, trucks, cars and bicycles splashing over potholes and tooting their horns. There were people and dogs, children and cows. Shops selling bright cloth and freshly strung meat. A dark man in a loincloth passed by, carrying a basket full of sweets upon his head. Madhesi, Rita imagined. The bus inched past a massive advertisement with the face of a woman as big as a house. *Colgate Toothpaste*—the giant letters read in dazzling red, and the woman smiled with over-sized sparkling white teeth. After a while, Rita noticed the wooden poles everywhere and the thick electric wires that zipped across them—bulging and crisscrossing, a tumble of sparrows flitting in between.

At some point, Rita fell asleep again. It was the bustle of people that woke her, a cacophony of voices—men and women squeezing hurriedly past each other in the tight innards of the bus, picking up bags, clothes, tiffin boxes. By the time they got off the bus with their sparse belongings, the sky had turned dark again.

Rita stepped on to the muddy ground of a bus parking lot, her body stiff, and looked up. Beyond the empty stretch of the bus park, rose the outlines of buildings. Even in the gloom, she could make out their colours. A sunnily disposed blue, rose pink, sand yellow and a bright green that looked like something she could reach out and taste. They came in all sizes and shapes, some wide and ridden with antennas, others that stretched up five–six–seven floors high, adorned with clusters of balconies. The same electric wires she had seen on the road ran here too, from one building to the other, balcony to balcony, a net of black wire that stretched through the city. There were open windows and large billboards and clothes hung out to dry, and flowerpots that sprung precariously from ledges. Beside her, Dhire dai cleared his throat.

'Kathmandu,' he said and pointed with his chin. 'We have to take a tuk-tuk from here,' he added.

They walked out on to the street. A woman hurried past, her red sari hitched up in one hand, the other laden with plastic bags. Then, a bicycle came hurtling, jumping on to the pavement and swerving next to Rita before clattering back down on to the street. Buses and cars honked at each other—the vehicles strung in a long unmoving line. She felt Dhire dai reach for her, steadying her by the arm, 'We are almost there,' he said. She noticed something brush against her leg and looked down to see that they were being followed by a thin three-legged dog.

'*Pakh, pakh*, wait here,' Dhire dai lowered her on to the pavement and made her sit, with Aama's jute bag and the bag of peanuts arranged by her side. He crossed the street hesitantly, looking back and forth on either side, putting a foot forward before withdrawing it again. Rita noticed that the other men and even some girls on the street were wearing pants and shirts. Dhire dai was wearing a traditional *daura suruwal*, a *bhoto* vest, cloth shoes and a topi. She looked down at herself—her bare feet in too-thin slippers, her worn leggings beneath a faded tunic, dirtied at the sleeves, her bare brown hands, the single metal bracelet that adorned her wrist. She looked like a village girl. For the first time, she stopped thinking about where she had come from but thought instead about where she was going. Where was Dhire dai taking her?

On the opposite side of the street, Dhire dai approached a line of parked tuk-tuks, and dipped his head through the front door of one. An exchange of words was followed by furious headshakes from the driver until finally, Dhire dai turned back and crossed the street.

'Get up,' Dhire dai pulled her by an elbow, 'We have found a tuk-tuk.'

Rita had never been in a tuk-tuk before, with its three wheels and canvas-covered body that made it look like a bicycle with the aspirations of something bigger. The driver watched with bloodshot eyes as she entered the dark womb of the back seat, holding tightly on to the metal frame reaching like hungry ribs all around. At one point, the driver swerved and they pressed between two trucks hurtling ahead, one on either side, and Rita squeezed the metal frame until her fingers went numb.

The tuk-tuk laboured up an incline as the houses seemed to grow larger and further apart, bright brick compound walls broken only occasionally by metallic gates. They seemed to go on for a long time. Finally, the tuk-tuk stopped at a pair of large gates, wide and wrought in black iron, and Rita felt her strength drain away, her body dip forward. She had the vague notion that someone was reaching in and holding her by the shoulders, slowly easing her out of the suffocating canvas. She heard, as if from a great distance, the clanking of metal and the last thing she remembered was the smell of mangoes.

* * *

'Here, here,' a dark face hovered above her. From somewhere came a hiss, the clank and clatter of pots and utensils.

Rita slowly opened her eyes, the brightness glaring. Above her, a dark woman with a thick face was mouthing incomprehensible words. Rita slowly picked herself up and noticed that someone had wrapped a *khasto* shawl around her shoulders. Dhire dai was next to her now, his familiar face looking relieved, helping to lift her into a sitting position, her back against a wall.

In front of her, Rita registered an array of shelves, a tiled floor, the shape of a stranger. She heard again the tinkle of dishes but the sound was not metallic, like up in Rato Mato. She recognized the sounds from her visits to the tea shop at the bottom of the Rato Mato hill. This was the sound of porcelain.

'Here,' the dark woman was back in front of her now and handing her a cup of warm liquid, 'Drink this, you will feel better.'

Slowly, Rita lifted the cup to her lips. She recognized the sweetness of Horlicks. Up in Rato Mato, Horlicks was a luxury, bought very sparingly for pregnant women or the sick. She could feel the warmth of the malted liquid run right through her body.

Suddenly, a door at the other end of the bright room threw open, startling Rita. A young man walked in, straight shouldered and slender. His mouth was open wide, his teeth bright and in perfect alignment. It reminded her of the toothpaste advertisement she had seen from the bus.

'Ohho!' the young man's hand shot up to his mouth, 'She's awake!'

With a flourish, he pulled up a stool and sat close, leaning in, his face almost directly in front of Rita's. She could smell fresh soap and something else—a hint of fragrance. He studied her, his eyes running over the con tours of her face, his mouth spread into a grin.

'It was a long trip, Krishne,' Dhire dai spoke warily, his topi still crunched tightly in his hands. 'We have seen a lot these past few days.'

'Hmm, we know,' the young man, Krishne, nodded. Then he sat back and folded his arms. 'We saw everything in the news. But now, you are in Kathmandu. The Jarsap is having his lunch.' Krishne stopped short, as if that was all the explaining that was required. He was quiet for a moment, his eyes still on Rita's face and she did not know what to make of him. She carefully averted her gaze.

The Jarsap. Rita recalled Neelam didi's breathless stories about the once powerful general who owned the entire southern flank of the Dhire hill, the mango forests that she and Sumnima had stolen from and of which Dhire dai was the hereditary caretaker. The Jarsap was a member of the Rana family, a family that had ruled Nepal for over 104 years and still held substantial power in the capital. In her Mahendra Malla books were chapters about how the Ranas had ruled behind a puppet Shah king, the palaces they had built, the martyrs they had made. They were known to be ruthless rulers.

Krishne turned his attention to Dhire dai now, bantering about the late monsoon, and Rita took the opportunity to let her eyes move around the room. She was in the kitchen with its walls hung with cabinets, a large stove—much larger than the one in the tea shop at the bottom of the Rato Mato hill—multiple pots singing and sputtering simultaneously. Gas-run, she noticed. At the far end, a large tap and basin piled high with plates and bowls. She was right, all white polished porcelain.

She wondered who Krishne was and what his connection to the Jarsap was. Only after making a full sweep of the room did Rita realize that the woman who had given her a cup of Horlicks was gone.

Rita had just begun to feel as if she was finding her bearings in this tiled and stainless environment when the main entrance door flung open again and a tall older woman strode into the room. Her face was wrinkled and sour and a shock of white hair was wrapped into a tight bun at the crown of her head. She wore a crisp cotton sari in pale green, her full sleeved cholo a bright starched white.

'Namaste, Bajai!' Dhire dai called out instantly, standing up, his hands closed palm to palm in greeting and Rita quickly got to her feet, following suit. Bajai said nothing, just nodded briefly in acknowledgement and headed straight to the stove. She lifted the lids of various pots in a swift and clanging orchestra and a mix of thick aromas filled the room. Chilli and onion, ginger, egg. Rita heard her stomach rumble. She had barely eaten in two days.

Krishne suddenly stood up, frowning, cut his conversation with Dhire dai short and abruptly said, 'Come! While we wait for the Jarsap to finish his lunch, I will show you about the house. Are you able to walk?'

'Yes, yes, she's fine,' Dhire dai answered for her and Rita felt Dhire dai's hand tugging her up.

Outside, they stepped on to damp brick, cutting right across a large open courtyard. The building extended around them in an enclosed square, and at the very centre stood a wide rain-battered tree.

Krishne moved quickly to the tree and then stopped, turning around. Suddenly, his face was open again, bright in welcome. 'This,' he announced, his hand sweeping before him, 'is the Seto Bangala, the white house. This is the main quarters—the kitchen and dining rooms are over here and those are the living quarters and bedrooms.' He bounced on the balls of his feet, 'This is the Ranisab's quarters,' and then he twisted, pointing to the very back of the courtyard, 'And that is where the servants live.'

Rita looked up, wondering who the Ranisab was and who were these servants the young man referred to. The dark faced woman she first saw, she suspected, must have been one of them. The building surrounding them was three stories high, its façade broken by evenly spaced pillars lined with carvings and large windows that were intricately etched and brocaded. The walls, painted a luminous white, stretched to a sloping tiled roof, a row of pigeons cooing and lining its awning.

'Rita *mayya*,' Krishne was smiling at her again, 'have you ever been to a zoo?' Rita shook her head, a deep blush growing at the attention.

'I didn't think you had,' he chuckled. 'One day I will take you to the Kathmandu zoo. But until then, you will have to make do with this place which is, mind you, very much like a zoo. Come, let me take you to the garden. You will see what I mean.'

In between the white wings that held the kitchen and the servants' quarters, an arched passageway led to a vast open space populated with islands of green and punctured by pools of muddy rainwater. Meandering through were brick pathways, high enough to avoid the elevation of rainwater and hedged on either side were rows of bedraggled bushes that would have been, she saw, uniformly manicured before the rains. Despite the aftermath of the monsoon, the effect was one of a perfectly fluid continuum, curving and arching around the entire garden. They walked down a pathway now and Rita looked at the many trees and plants, most of which she didn't recognize.

'Harke!' Krishne called out, 'Eh Harke! Come here! Come meet our visitors.'

A small man appeared from behind a bulbous bush. He was the same height as Rita but his face was leathered. He wore an oversized, buttoned shirt and blue shorts that revealed legs bent out like bows.

'This is Harke Bahadur Tamang,' Krishne announced, 'Harke, as you can see, tends the Jarsap's gardens. Eh Harke, aren't you going to say namaste? Say namaste to Rita here!'

Harke stood and stared uncertainly at Rita. She felt like she was watching a child making up his mind. Abruptly, Harke brought palm to palm in a namaste, his mouth spreading open in a wide gummy grin, and Rita saw that he was missing half of his upper teeth.

'Harke is,' Krishne whispered, 'a gentle animal. Soft as a rabbit. Harke has been in this house his whole life. And we in turn are gentle with him, you understand?'

The young man continued up the pathway to the back of the garden, where a row of tall pine trees stood in a line. Beyond them, was a cemented clearing with a high running wall around it, broken only by a large black gate.

'Gurung ji!' Krishne now called as they approached a squat two-storied building along the far wall. Rita noticed that the top floor of the building had two small windows and the lower floor was fully open, door-less, like twin caves. The ground floor, she saw now, was in fact a parking space with two vehicles, one large blue jeep, and the other a smaller grey car. Above their heads, a window unlatched and a man's head stuck out.

'What is it, Krishne?' the man demanded.

'Namaste, Gurung ji!' Dhire dai called up jovially before Krishne could answer. Dhire dai, Rita noticed, reacted differently to every member of the household. He seemed to know which ones to pay extra deference to and which ones he could be more familiar with.

'Eh Dhire!' the man in the window gave a friendly salute, 'It has been a long time, my friend! I'll be down soon. See you back in the house!' He smiled once again at Dhire dai, gave Rita a cursory curious glance, then retreated from the window.

'That,' Krishne shuffled closer, his hand cupped to his mouth, 'is Gurung ji. Gurung ji is the Jarsap's driver. He used to be in the army, together with the Jarsap. Isn't he beautiful?' He chuckled, 'If anybody comes within two meters of the Jarsap's cars, Gurung ji will stick his well-oiled hair right in your face. Gurung ji is our very own resident peacock!' Krishne slapped his thigh at his own joke and then proceeded back into the garden.

After more walks up and down the gardens, Rita suddenly found herself at the front of the big house, facing the façade of the Seto Bangala. She felt as if she were looking at a picture torn right out of her Mahendra Malla textbook. In the 104 years that the Ranas ruled the country, they had built vast palaces and mansions across the country. And here, right in front of her, was one of them.

'Shh, come quietly.' Krishne had his finger to his lips and whispered as the wide wooden front door slowly creaked open. Rita was not sure why they had to be quiet, but she felt so small amidst the immensity around her that she dared not even breathe.

'Are you sure?' Dhire dai lingered hesitantly at the door, 'We should be using the back entrance.'

'It's ok,' Krishne's eyes gleamed with a mischievous confidence, 'no one will know.'

They stepped inside and the door clicked shut behind them. It took a few seconds for Rita to adjust her eyes and there, opening up before her, was a room with a sweeping marble floor and a high ceiling far overhead from which hung an enormous dripping apparatus of sculpted glass.

'This,' Krishne offered in explanation, 'is the entrance hallway. Take your shoes off!'

Shoe-less, they passed by painted vases reaching as high as Rita's waist, chairs embroidered in velvet and a metallic temple replica large enough to fit a village child. At the end of the hallway was an alcove, then a stairway carpeted in red that swooped upward towards the ceiling. Rita clutched her slippers to her chest, her eyes feeding off everything she saw. They passed through two more doors and corridors before finding themselves back where they had begun, in the *bhanchaghar*, the kitchen.

Bajai was still there, standing at the stove, but now another woman had joined her in the room. Short and plump, the woman was younger than Bajai, and the moment she saw Rita, she exclaimed, 'Ohho! Nani, you have arrived! You poor thing! Come come, let me see you!'

Rita found herself held by the shoulders as the woman clucked and Rita warmed to her immediately. 'We saw it on the evening news,' her voice was a high syrupy lilt, 'What is happening to this country, to our villages! After all you have been through, how tired you must be! You poor thing.'

The woman turned her large, flushed face towards Dhire dai, 'Tell me Dhire, was it as bad as what they showed on the news?'

Dhire dai dropped his eyes. But before he could answer, Krishne stepped forward, dragging two stools with him. 'Ohho, Thul didi! Why are you upsetting our guests?' He offered one stool to Rita and sat primly on the other. 'Come, let us welcome them instead!' As if on cue, the gauze back door swung open and filing in now were Harke Bahadur from the gardens, Gurung ji from the garage and the dark woman Rita had not seen since the morning.

'Please, everybody!' Krishne addressed the gathering, 'Please everybody, let us take our seats. Some of you have already met Rita but let me now introduce her to the rest of the house,' and then he turned to Rita and winked, 'Don't worry. Before you know it, you will feel as at home here as the rest of us!'

Rita could see that the young man was in his element, enjoying his own show, and yet she felt the slither of a cold sweat.

'This,' Krishne crossed the room in a fluid sweep, 'this, everybody, is Rita. Rita is going to be the newest and youngest member of our household. She has made a long and dangerous journey to get to us. So please, everybody, make her feel comfortable.'

Rita watched Krishne's exaggerated gestures and thought the young man looked like someone who belonged on the television.

'Gurung ji and our very own Harke Bahadur you have already met. And this here is Thul didi,' he positioned himself behind the friendly plump woman, resting his hands upon her shoulders. 'Thul didi is the caretaker of the Jarsap's granddaughter. But she is also everyone's caretaker. Isn't she soft and huggable? A pukka Kathmandu Newarni, look!' he clipped his tongue against the roof of his mouth, 'She can't pronounce her Ts!'

Thul didi let out a hearty laugh and made as if to chase him but Krishne leapt out of her reach. Rita had heard about the Newars, the original inhabitants of Kathmandu valley, but she had never seen a Newar before. Thul didi was fair, her features broad and flat.

At the front of the room, something let off a shrill whistle. Rita looked up to see Bajai ladling a large pot.

'As I told you, Rita mayya,' the young man dipped away, 'this house is very much like a zoo. This here, as I am sure you have surmised is Bajai!' He twirled around. 'Bajai is a Brahmin cook. Bajai is the only person allowed to cook the Jarsap and the Ranisab's meals, and in fact, is the person who cooks for us all. Even in this day and age, we still eat like we did 100 years ago!'

'Eh! What are you saying?' Bajai brandished her tea ladle high and faced Krishne. Her face was ageless, pulled tightly away into her hair knot, 'How much are you yapping?'

But before Bajai could make another move, Krishne slid his hand under the ladle and jumped back with a stolen slice of bread.

'Bajai, as you can see,' Krishne looked straight at Rita and winked again, 'is the biting kind.'

As she watched him, Rita felt her limbs loosen. Krishne, she concluded, was harmless.

Bajai started distributing cups of tea and plates of buttered bread to everyone, her face turned up in distaste as if the task were an unbecoming necessity.

'Now this person here, you have met already,' the young man folded a second piece of bread, dipped it into his tea and shoved half of it into his mouth, 'But you have yet to be officially introduced to her. This here is Kali.'

Rita turned to look at the dark woman standing at the edge of the room, the first face she had seen upon arrival. The woman was tall, broad and quiet. 'Everyone says she is named Kali, black, because of the colour of her skin. But I think otherwise!' Krishne cupped his mouth but made no effort to dim his voice, 'I think she was named after the Goddess Kali and mind you—she is just as fierce!'

Kali, Rita saw now, was a Madhesi. How had someone at the very bottom of the caste hierarchy, from far down in the south, come to be here, in this big house?

'And last but not least, me,' the young man stood in the very centre of the room, 'they call me by the name of Krishne. Just pukka like Lord Krishna himself. As good a dancer and certainly as good with the *gopini* girls,' Krishne broke into a wide smile now and Rita felt again the heat of a deep flush against her neck.

'Stop yapping, Krishne,' Bajai barked again, 'Take the girl to the Jarsap. How much more time are you going to waste?' It was the first time Bajai had acknowledged Rita's existence.

A momentary shadow passed across Krishne's face but he downed his tea and said theatrically, 'Come. Let us leave the bhanchaghar. And let me take you to the *baithak*, the living room.'

Up on the walls in the hallway, they passed by life-sized portraits of men and women, one after the other, dressed in capes and layers of cloth, their heads adorned in jewelled crowns. Rita felt Dhire dai reach for her shoulder. Then at the end of the hallway, Krishne opened a large creaking door and disappeared behind it. Dhire dai stopped, hastily turning Rita around to face him.

'Rita, listen,' he started and she could smell the earth on him, the damp crimson soil of Rato Mato, the sharp sting of khaini.

'Forgive me,' he said, 'forgive me because I have not told you everything. I have not told you about your new life. All I will say is, you will be safer here than in the village. Remember, this is a big house. And we are very small people. Do what they tell you. You must always be obedient and work hard.'

He held her by both shoulders and Rita looked into his eyes, searching. It surprised her, how Dhire dai's eyes seemed to momentarily moisten but when she searched again, they were dry and tired.

The large door creaked open. Dhire dai stood up to face it and placed his topi carefully back upon his head.

Inside, Rita's eyes adjusted to the darkness. Beyond the high walls, she heard a distant roar and realized that outside, it was raining again. And then suddenly, she saw them. A large tiger, teeth drawn in a vicious snarl, lunging up from the wall to her left. To her right, a bear, claws outstretched, bearing up on its hind legs. Next to it, the long swirling horns of deer, the tips as pointed and sharp as blades. A small yelp escaped her before she felt Dhire dai's hand fall back on her shoulder. 'Shh,' he whispered.

'Dhire is that you?' a drawling nasal voice came from across the room.

'*Hajur*, *Darshan*, *hajur*,' Dhire dai answered with salutations of the highest respect.

And before she knew it, Dhire dai was pulling her over thick layers of woven wool that was spread over the floor, her bare feet sinking deep into the weave. Dhire dai moved with more enthusiasm than she had ever seen him move before, his topi tilted high upon his brow.

Dhire dai stopped and dipped at the waist into a deep bow. She followed him, bending herself into a deep namaste and when she looked up—her gaze running over her own bare feet, the weave of thick carpet, the oblong shadows of lamplight—she saw a deep velvet cushioned seat and in it, a small man.

7

The Ranisab

The first thought Rita had, staring at the small man in the deep seat, was that he looked nothing like the pictures of his ancestors up on the walls. The Jarsap was thin-chested with a protruding belly and balanced a pair of glasses on the tip of his nose. His army days were long behind him.

He looked up from a newspaper spread across his knees. 'So, you have finally come!' his voice was larger than the space he occupied and a tinge of disapproval lined his words, as if he had been expecting Dhire dai weeks ago. She felt the Jarsap's gaze move towards her and Rita dropped her eyes immediately.

'I read about the incident in the newspapers, and I saw the broadcast on TV,' he declared, 'How are my trees?'

It struck Rita that the Jarsap asked first about the trees, rather than about the village or its people or the terrible state of things. As if everything that happened had already been analysed and explained, making Rita feel like an untrustworthy witness to her own account.

Dhire dai bowed profusely as he spoke and Rita noticed how he seemed to speak a lot but said little.

'About the girl,' the Jarsap nodded now towards her. Rita was not sure how, but Dhire dai had laid the path for her arrival already. 'You can leave her here. Krishne will arrange everything.'

The Jarsap's generosity sounded like a dismissal. Dhire dai bowed some more, his hands folded before him, words of praise flying off his tongue, but the Jarsap's attention was already back on his newspaper. They slowly backed away, past the terrifying hung pelts, to the door. Rita felt her panic rise with every step that grazed the carpet. How would she survive in this big, strange house by herself?

That evening, they ate in the bhanchaghar together with all the servants. Rice, black daal in ghee, curried egg and fried liver. Rita had never tasted food this good. Krishne, Thul didi and Gurung ji sat with them on the stools. Harke squatted and ate by a far shelf. And Kali, the Madhesi woman, ate just by the back door, apart from everyone else. It occurred to her that the bhanchaghar was, in some ways, like Rato Mato. Here too, caste and ethnicity outlined a strict definition of roles, the household integrated yet segregated at the same time.

Afterwards, Kali took her across the courtyard to a room with a bare electric bulb suspended from the ceiling and two beds at opposite ends. 'This is your bed,' she pointed, 'and that is mine. Keep your things to your side of the room.' Rita nodded, glad that on the first night in this vast house, she would not be sleeping alone. The cover pulled up to her chin was too thick for this time of the year and across the room, Kali snored softly in the dark. Rita's mind wandered to Rato Mato, to Aama and Kaaki left to manage the house on their own, to Sumnima on her way to someplace else. It felt strange—being apart from Sumnima for the first time in her life. As if she were missing a part of herself, an arm or a limb, a sliver of who she was. Just before drifting off to sleep, Rita thought about how up in Rato Mato, she never played with the Madhesi children in school. And here she was now, sharing a room with one.

The next morning, when she entered the bhanchaghar, Rita expected Dhire dai to be there but he was not. At the stove, Bajai was already banging about, her tea ladle deftly apportioning tea into cups and biscuits on to plates. Krishne, sprawled on a stool, looked up and smiled widely when he saw her hover by the back door.

'Ohho, Rita mayya, come in! Come in!' he reached for his cup of tea and slurped loudly, 'welcome to the first day of your new life. Dhire left a few hours ago. Did he or anyone else tell you about what all you are supposed to do here?' He cocked his head to one side and looked at her, bemused.

Rita felt her pulse quicken. Dhire dai had left without saying goodbye. 'No,' she replied, and her voice came out in a barely audible whisper.

'Ok, listen,' Krishne cleared his throat, 'Here, come and sit. Take your tea. I will tell you everything you need to know.'

'First of all,' Krishne continued, 'we all have our charges and our specified roles in this house. I am the Jarsap's key manservant. Gurung ji, who you met yesterday, is the Jarsap's driver. Thul didi takes care of the Jarsap's granddaughter. Bajai, as you know, is the cook. Harke tends the gardens. And Kali takes care of things that the others don't. Like washing the clothes and cleaning the house. And you,' Krishne looked at her and suddenly his expression was serious again, 'you will be a servant to the Ranisab, the Jarsap's mother.'

Rita found herself staring. Nokkar, servant, she suddenly heard Sumnima's voice in her head. Sumnima had spat the word out, repulsed.

'The Ranisab,' Krishne was now swinging one leg atop the other as he spoke, his hand reaching for the biscuits, 'is getting along in age. But don't worry, there is not much you need to do. Kali and Bajai take care of all the basics. What the Ranisab really needs is company. An arm to lean on, if you will. And also,' Krishne looked at her curiously now, 'I hear you are quite a good reader. That could be useful. There is nothing the Ranisab appreciates more than a good book.'

Rita felt a rising sense of dread. The Ranas, she knew, had ruled with absolute power. Anybody who stood in their way, they ruthlessly terminated. She had heard Neelam didi whisper stories of men bricked up and cemented whole, enemies lathered in honey and left to the bees, of unspeakable things done to female servants under staircases and at the ends of long corridors. *Their ghosts*, Neelam didi had rasped, *still wander about the big houses*.

'When dealing with the Ranisab and the house in general, there are a few basic rules you need to know. First, always say "hajur", the highest form of address, before you start a sentence and after you finish it. Second, never speak unless you are spoken to. Third, always receive and give things with your right hand only. After all,' and Krishne let out a snigger, 'everyone knows you villagers use your left hands to clean your behinds!' and Rita felt herself blush at the sudden intimacy, 'Fourth, when you leave a room, never turn your back to the family. And lastly, always keep your shoes off and always sit on the floor.'

'But what . . .' the words came out tentative, her voice unfamiliar to herself, 'what do I need to do for the Ranisab?'

'Oh, there is not much you need to do,' Krishne waved his hand dismissively, 'Just a few things really. Make sure the Ranisab takes her medicines on time, massage her legs, help her in the puja *khota*, the prayer room—that sort of thing. But, one thing,' and Krishne lowered his voice, 'one thing is that you need to be patient, give the Ranisab time. Give her time to get used to you. The Ranisab can be . . . difficult.' He sat back, appraising her.

'How do you mean?' Rita whispered.

Krishne laughed, his teeth flashing and when he spoke again his voice was self-contained. 'You see, to understand the Ranisab, you need to understand where she comes from. The Ranisab was once one of the richest Ranas around. They say she was still a child when they brought her to Kathmandu. She came of age in Singha Durbar, the great palace, and they married her to the man who was to become prime minister, the next-in-line. She was his youngest wife. You know what that meant?' Rita could see that Krishne was relishing his own words, 'That meant that when the old man died, all his remaining wealth went to her, and to her only son. They say,' and now Krishne lowered his voice again, 'the last Rana prime minister would do anything the Ranisab asked. She was, at one point, even more powerful than the queen of Nepal!'

Later, it was Kali who took her across the brick-laid courtyard to meet her new charge. Rita wanted to call out to the Madhesi woman, to ask her more about the Ranisab. But Kali did not stop and did not check to see that Rita was still following her.

Inside, they entered the same cool marbled hallways that ran through the main building. Rita looked up, her eyes moving over the high walls, stopping momentarily at another cascade of suspended glass and then rested at the base of the carpeted stairs, flanked on either side by two enormous curves of tusk-like bone.

Kali halted abruptly, 'Take off your shoes!'

Upstairs, the walls were lined with framed images of deities in bright colours. The Lord Brahman in eternal repose, the earth a painted dot upon his forehead. The Lord Rama and his brother, Lord Lakshmana, both dressed in the garb of beggars before they entered their jungle exile. The Goddess Laxmi, a river of gold coins flowing from her upturned palms. And Goddess Kali, her power raw even in the painting, her skin a deep dark blue, her eight hands armed with a variety of weapons and under her feet, the severed head of a demon. At the end of the rows of deities stood another door and from inside came the smell of incense, thick and sweet.

Rita stepped into a cavernous room. It had a large four-poster bed on one end with a mosquito net cascading down from the ceiling in a white sheen. Along the opposite wall stood a heavy chest of drawers, a pair of handsome wooden wardrobes and a large steel cabinet. Closest to Rita, lining the wall, were rows of open stacked shelves, heavy with books—more books than she had seen in her whole life. Rita felt her breath catch in her throat. Directly opposite to where Rita stood, were three large windows that stretched from floor to ceiling, and before them, velvet sofas and a high-backed armchair.

Kali stood at the entrance and cleared her throat. 'Ranisab, hajur,' she said and her voice sounded inordinately loud in the room, 'the new girl is here, hajur.'

Rita looked around the room, searching for who Kali was speaking to. But she saw no one.

Kali waited for a few breaths before raising her voice, 'Ranisab, hajur!'

The armchair creaked and swivelled towards them a few inches. Only then did Rita notice the stick, a sleek black one, that jutted out the side of the chair, anchoring it to the carpet. In the middle of the black leather armchair that was now turning to face her, Rita saw a bundle of khasto wraps and peeking out from within their soft folds, the face of an old woman.

'The girl,' Kali repeated, 'she is here.'

The old woman's eyes were shut and her face flowered with creases. She held the black walking stick in a tiny claw-like hand. 'Kali, bring me my tea.' The voice was both larger and stronger than the body.

'Yes, hajur.' Kali waited and then, slightly more insistent now, 'The girl the Jarsap mentioned. She is here, hajur.'

The Ranisab opened her eyes. They were small like the rest of her, but black and intensely alive. Rita felt their light bore right into her.

'Who is this?' the Ranisab snapped. A layer of khasto shawl dropped around her shoulders, revealing wiry grey hair arranged in a loose bundle.

Rita felt herself shrink. But Kali continued, her tone flat, her accent heavy, 'This is the girl the Jarsap has arranged for you, hajur. Her name is Rita.'

'I don't need a girl,' the Ranisab turned her face to the window. It was a simple statement, not a question or an argument. 'Bring me my tea.'

But Kali continued to hover at the door.

'Her name,' she pressed, 'is Rita. The Jarsap says she is to stay with you, hajur.'

'Hmph!' a grunt from the armchair and a shuffle of cloth. Suddenly, Rita noticed that the carved head of the walking stick resting against the leather chair was the head of a precisely sculpted bird. Its beak rounded, its beady eyes staring straight at her. The bird almost looked alive.

'The Jarsap said . . .' Kali started again but before Rita knew what had happened, a cushion went flying across the room and the black stick with the bird head was now thump thumping against the carpeted floor.

'I don't care what my son says!' the Ranisab was shouting, her voice shockingly strong, 'I don't need any girl! Now get out!'

Rita jumped and rushed out of the room, not waiting for Kali. Out in the corridor, her heart pounding, she pushed up against the wall like a small, trapped prey. Kali stepped out behind her and closed the door with a soft click.

'Let's go,' she said quietly and without further explanation, headed back down the stairs.

In the kitchen, Krishne was waiting, expectant, with Thul didi by his side. Kali did not have to say anything.

'Ohho, nani.' Thul didi's voice dripped with sympathy, '*kathai bari*, you poor thing.' Rita blinked back tears. It was the acknowledgment that made it worse, that seemed to strip her of her very essence.

Krishne pushed himself off the shelves, 'Let it go!' he waved a hand, 'Forget the *buddhi*, that old woman. Come, have a cup of tea. It will make you feel better in no time.' Rita was struck by Krishne's use of such a casual term in reference to the Ranisab. Such language was forbidden she was sure, and yet, his disrespect made her feel less small.

The tea made with cinnamon and clove warmed her insides. She had never wanted to be a nokkar in the first place, so why had this old woman upset her so?

* * *

'Ranisab, hajur!'

The next day, Kali stood at the door and addressed the Ranisab exactly as she had the day before, 'The girl is here.'

Rita peeked in but the old woman was not in the armchair. The room was shaded, the curtains still drawn against the harsh early monsoon light.

'Please, hajur, time to get up,' Kali used language of the highest respect. Rita lingered by the door and watched as Kali stood by the four-poster bed, propping the pillow, handing the Ranisab some pills from a drawer at her bedside and a glass of water from a jug, then bringing forth the Ranisab's slippers. Finally, Kali handed the Ranisab the black walking stick and Rita recognized the face at its head. The bird was, in fact, a parrot. Carved in polished white bone, its eyes on Rita's face.

'What is she doing here?' Rita was so focused on the bird that she had not noticed the Ranisab, now sitting at the edge of the bed and staring straight at her.

'This,' Kali explained patiently, 'is Rita, the girl that the Jarsap sent for you. She is to stay with you, hajur.'

'Didn't I tell you yesterday? I don't need any girl!'

'But the Jarsap said . . .'

The Ranisab snatched the parrot by its throat and was pointing the chiselled beak right at Rita, 'Get out! You! Get out of here!'

Rita felt her heart leap up to her mouth. But despite her best instincts to run out of the room, she held her feet firm. The Ranisab lifted her stick and brought it down, stabbing into the carpet.

'Is she deaf? Or is she stupid? Get out I say!'

Rita gritted her teeth. She would hold on, she told herself, but from behind the Ranisab, Kali was now motioning for her to exit. Outside in the corridor, Kali shook her head. 'This will be hard work,' she muttered, then proceeded back down the corridor.

The servants, led by Krishne, held a conference amongst themselves, and it was decided that Rita was not to be taken to the Ranisab for the next three days. A short break was deemed necessary before attempting to introduce her again. Rita slumped in a corner of the bhanchaghar and felt herself fold into tinier and tinier pieces. She had failed. She wasn't sure what she had failed most at—not gaining the Ranisab's approval, not slotting herself neatly into this big house, or not matching up to what was expected of her.

That evening, Rita hid herself in the room she shared with Kali. She pulled out the jute sack that Aama had given her. Inside were her few sparse possessions—a wool shawl, a brown toothed comb, a tunic, hand-me-down underwear, two pairs of knitted socks and her copy of Mahendra Malla. Rita fingered the leathery paper as fat tears fell on to the pages. She thought of Aama and Kaaki, alone in the house in Rato Mato. Who was mopping the floor or collecting the water? Who was feeding Dalle and the livestock? How would Aama and Kaaki manage the workload by themselves? Then she thought of Sumnima. These days, Sumnima seemed larger in her memory, fierce and indomitable. If she were here, she knew exactly what

Sumnima would say to her. *How can you let that old woman frighten you? Don't be such a darcherua!*

The next three days, Rita did nothing. She shuffled from the bhanchaghar to her room and back again. The servants gathered four times a day for meals. Breakfast and teatime were hurried but lunch and dinner were lengthy, informative events centred around heaped plates of food. Rita had never eaten food so good, and it reminded her of the guest house that she and Sumnima were supposed to build. She would learn how to cook some of Bajai's dishes and one day serve them to their guests.

Kali entered their shared bedroom with a pile of clean clothes in her arms. 'Here,' she motioned, 'these are for you. Make sure you change twice a week and wash your clothes out back. Here is soap.'

Rita could not tell if the clothes were new or hand-me-downs but it did not matter. The sleeves of the tunics were only slightly too long and the leggings that came with them had to be tucked and adjusted at the waist. Pink with embroidered white flowers, lime green print with gold seams, a bright blue—Rita had never seen, let alone owned, tunic sets of such intricate design. Everything around her seemed so vast and plentiful, unconstrained by the things that defined their daily lives up in the village.

On the fourth day, she woke up to the sound of Kali quietly leaving the room in darkness. The woman was always the first up, her various duties starting before sunlight. Rita waited for the sound of doors unlocking across the courtyard then slowly crept out. At the outhouse, she ran cold water over her face and held herself steady, repeating over and over again, *don't be a darcherua*. Then sidling along the building, she opened the door to the depths of marble and made her way, barefoot, up the carpeted stairs. Rita entered the Ranisab's room swiftly, then did exactly what Kali had done. She reached up, drew open the heavy curtains; then approached the bed, deftly pulling back the covers. The Ranisab was lying on her side, her frail back to Rita. Then quickly, before the Ranisab had a chance to turn around, Rita grabbed the black stick, avoiding the parrot's gaze, shoved it against the bed within easy reach and scurried across the room. She headed straight for the wall of shelves and without another thought, grabbed a book and plumped herself down upon the carpet. Then, she started to read out loud.

Rita did not understand a single word before her, but they came easily, the letters piecing together and flowing out of her in a fluid melody. In her mind, she heard Principal sir as she read—her voice tracing his intonation, his precise pronunciations, the way he built up a sentence before letting it go, catching it just before it fell. She had finished the entire page and moved over to the next one when she heard the door swing open next to her. Kali stood in the frame, blinking, her mouth gaping wide.

'What are you doing here?' she whispered in harsh astonishment.

'Shh, shh!' Across the room, the Ranisab was sitting, propped up in the bed. Her eyes amused. She put a finger on her lips and motioned for Kali to be quiet. 'Kali, go get me my tea.'

'Hajur?' Kali looked stunned, still standing in the door's frame.

'Get me my tea,' and then, as an afterthought, 'and get Rita here a cup too.'

A rule of the house, Rita knew, was that masters and servants were never to eat together. And yet, despite her surprise at the words, Rita did not stop reading. The next time she looked up, the Ranisab had dropped down from the bed, the stick clutched in her hand. Slowly and creakily, she sat herself down in the armchair.

'Look at me,' the Ranisab said after a while.

The Ranisab peered into her face and Rita held her breath, her legs folded at the knees, her hands folded over the book in her lap. Rita saw herself now the way the old woman must be seeing her. The new lime green tunic a smudge too large for her. Her bare, calloused feet. Her singular metal bracelet, plain and dark, coloured by the grime of her skin. And suddenly, Rita felt as though she could smell it, across the short expanse of the carpet, what this rich and powerful Ranisab must think of a village girl like her.

'How far have you travelled?' the Ranisab's voice was sharp, just like her eyes, two things as yet untouched by time.

Rita swallowed.

'Two days and one night,' she whispered. 'From Tanahu.' And then she remembered. 'Hajur,' she added quickly.

The Ranisab did not seem to have registered her error.

'By bus?' the Ranisab asked.

Rita nodded. She found herself wondering if the Ranisab ever left the sanctuary of this vast house. If she did, Rita was sure, it was to be driven in a private car, the ones standing in the open-mouthed garage outside.

'Did you cross the Marsyangdi river?'

Again, Rita nodded, surprised by the question. She found herself asking: *when the Ranisab looked out of her car window, what did she see?* Other cars and shops, bright with sweets and saris. A woman like the Ranisab would never look at the public buses, crammed with people, or up towards the hills.

'Hmm,' the Ranisab nodded as if she knew, 'the river must be just a foot below the road this time of year.' Rita blinked. The Marsyangdi did not flow into the Kathmandu valley—*when had the Ranisab seen it?* Kali was back, swiftly entering the room, placing a cup and saucer with a tinkle on a side table and handing Rita a steel glass of hot tea on her way out.

'Continue. Read!' the Ranisab commanded.

Rita turned the page of the book, feeling its texture between her fingers, and only then did the words start to make sense to her.

The Bagmati river, a body of holy water flowing through Kathmandu valley, is revered by thousands and yet has reached levels of hazardous degradation that would have been unimaginable only a generation ago. The decline in the river's ecological health not only is a detriment to the maintenance of biodiversity and the flora and fauna that depend upon her waters but threatens the entire cultural civilization that she has birthed upon her shores . . .

'Here,' the Ranisab interrupted, 'come sit here, closer.'

Rita felt suddenly self-conscious as she moved to a spot by the window.

'Start again, from the beginning.'

She returned to the top of the page.

'There!' the Ranisab exclaimed, '*Gi-ra-wat*, degradation. You must pronounce it properly. Try again!'

For a moment, Rita felt as if she were back up on Rato Mato, in Principal sir's classroom. The ruler in his hand, his spectacles catching the morning sun.

'*Gi-ra-wat*! Again!' the Ranisab picked up her stick now and thumped it upon the carpeted floor.

Rita felt her hands tremble and the book shook. She opened her mouth and inhaled, felt her lungs expand. Then she reread the line, slower this time, carefully going over the word. *Degradation*.

'Hmph! Good. Continue.'

Rita read until the end of the page and noticed that although the Ranisab had closed her eyes, her face was screwed into a tight scowl. The old woman exhaled—a deep dissatisfaction writ large on her face—and Rita felt her stomach quiver. She contemplated slapping the book shut and fleeing the room but then, the Ranisab opened her eyes.

'Degradation. It is not only a crime, it is a sin! What the people of this country have done to their own rivers and forests is a sin! When I was a girl, the Bagmati river was the giver of life! There used to be cranes that came in the summer, all the way from Siberia, and they would land right here, upon the Bagmati. Thousands of them—so many that you could hear them from miles away and they shadowed the whole lands as they passed overhead. Thoo!' the old woman spat out, 'this city is full of temples and yet its people are totally godless!'

Rita blinked, she did not know where or what Siberia was.

'Hajur,' she whispered and was not sure if the word came out as agreement or interruption, 'shall I continue?'

The Ranisab seized the parrot's gullet and sat back in the armchair. She twisted its head round and round and every time it faced her, Rita could feel its beady gaze, 'Continue.'

By the end of the morning, after reading two dozen pages, Rita was given permission to leave. Kali was waiting for her outside in the corridor.

'Aabii!' she exclaimed, her eyes round and startled in her thick face, 'I don't know how you did that. But it has . . . worked. Aabii!' It felt to Rita that Kali was looking at her differently now, as if Rita had just become something more than another task.

The next day, the Ranisab was already waiting.

'Here,' she handed over a book. The book, Rita could tell, was old. It had a hard rust coloured cover and no title, or at least, the title had completely faded. 'Start reading. Don't forget to make every word count.'

Rita sat on the floor by the windows and opened the first page. A book of poems, the first by Lekhnath Paudyal, one of the most famous poets in the country. The poem was titled 'Pijarako Suga', the Caged Parrot. Rita opened her mouth and steadied her voice.

The poem was a monologue in rhyme, spoken by the parrot itself. It lamented being locked in a cage, of how its parents were far away in a corner of the forest. With whom could it share its despair? It spoke of weeping at times, at times sitting still as a corpse, at other times jumping relentlessly in a crazed frenzy. It remembered the forest. The abundance of fruits and freedom. And while enunciating every word, her voice rising and falling, cresting through the emotions, Rita saw Dhire hill in her mind. The swathes of mango blanketing its southern flank. The flocks of green birds that fed on their ripe yellow insides. The plot of land, at the line of the fields, where she and Sumnima would build their guest house one day. When the poem ended, there was a stillness in the room.

'It must have been difficult,' the Ranisab spoke, her voice startling Rita, 'to leave your village.' Again, the Ranisab spoke as if she knew. 'But you know, you are lucky.' She rearranged herself in the armchair, kicking up a thin hidden leg beneath a large khasto blanket.

Rita waited for the Ranisab to continue, but the old woman sat, staring out the window, her black eyes stealing light, transported, her attention withdrawn.

Finally, after swallowing a couple of times, Rita whispered, 'Hajur?'

'You are lucky,' the Ranisab blinked, and her eyes were back in the room, 'You had a bus. In my days, there were no buses. I was brought to Kathmandu by bullock cart. It took us two weeks to get to Kathmandu. That's how I came here first. By bullock cart.'

Rita opened her mouth and closed it, unable to find a response.

'I was much younger than you when I was brought here,' the Ranisab continued, 'Back then they married us so young. Just a child. It was my father's ambition, "You will become the youngest wife of the next maharajah!" he had said. In those days, who would protest against a father's decision?'

The Ranisab suddenly stretched, unfolding another thin leg from under the khasto blanket. A socked foot fell on to the carpet and Rita was shocked by how small it was.

'When my day came, how I held on to my mother and wept. I didn't want to get into the bullock cart. I remember, it was driven by an old man with a long stick. When we started off, the cart creaked forward, the man hitting the oxen with his stick. I could have travelled faster on my own two feet!' the Ranisab smiled, 'The dogs ran alongside us. Chased me right out of my own village.'

The Ranisab was quiet again. She looked down at her hands. Small, just like her feet. Rita wondered: *Had the Ranisab ever told this story to anyone else?*

'Where was your village, hajur?' Rita could not tell what, but something gave her the courage to utter the question. Another rule of the house, Rita knew, was not to speak unless spoken to. But here, in the stillness of the room, in the quiet rainy light, the rules were being bent and twisted out of shape.

'A village close to Biratnagar,' the Ranisab responded, 'in the east. My father was a big landholder there.'

'We travelled half a day before I noticed him. Isn't that strange?' she continued, 'He must have been sleeping. Or maybe he was just shy of me. But I hadn't paid any attention to the piece of cloth at the very front of the covered cart. I had been sitting like this, with my heads in my knees,' the Ranisab motioned, 'when suddenly, I heard someone say "Don't cry!"'

The Ranisab looked out the window now, the memory bright in her eyes, 'I remember I was so scared, I forgot to scream! I thought I had imagined it. And then, he cursed.' The Ranisab smiled again, close-mouthed.

'"What are you waiting for? Hurry! Hurry!" he shouted.'

Rita wanted to ask, *who?* But she didn't dare interrupt the telling.

At that moment, Kali walked into the room, a tray balanced in her arms. She briskly pulled up the side table, placed the cup of tea and saucer and a large array of biscuits arranged in circular order around the plate. Square and round, some striped with lines of sugary pink, others with buttons of rich brown. She also shoved a small steel glass into Rita's hands. She had not forgotten.

Rita waited until Kali retreated, closing the door. The Ranisab took a few lengthy sips before Rita brought her own glass hesitantly to her mouth.

'It took me a lot of courage,' the Ranisab spoke again. 'A lot of courage to look under that piece of cloth. But when I did, you should have seen my surprise! You know what was under that cloth?'

Rita shook her head.

'A parrot! Bright green and as long as my arm,' the Ranisab motioned, 'and once he started, that bird would not stop talking!' The Ranisab reached for a biscuit. Rita eyed the stripes of pink, as bright as cloth dye. And suddenly, the Ranisab reached out with her other hand, picked up another biscuit and handed it to Rita. She hesitated, but the Ranisab motioned again. Rita took a small bite and held the sweet piece in her mouth, too afraid to make loud crunching sounds.

'Ram, Ram, what stories he told me! He told me about the Ramayana and the Mahabharata, intricate details I would never have known if not for him. And you know, the funny thing is, he wasn't just a parrot that repeated things he had heard. After three days in that bullock cart, he wasn't just answering me, echoing back my own voice and words. I would say something, and he would respond, as if he understood. The parrot, you see, was actually speaking and carrying out entire conversations!'

The Ranisab turned away, facing the garden and Rita took the opportunity to swallow the piece of biscuit.

'You will not believe me,' she spoke from the shadow, 'but what I say is true. And one day, you will know that it is true for yourself.'

There was a stretch of silence and Rita ventured, eager to continue the conversation.

'Hajur, did the parrot also come to Kathmandu?'

The Ranisab spun back into the room. Then she placed her cup with a distinct rattle back on the table. 'Yes,' a small smile grew at the corners of her lips, 'I insisted. When we reached Kathmandu and the palace guards came to meet us, I threw up a wail and said I would refuse to marry anyone unless the parrot came with me. The guards must have paid off the bullock cart driver handsomely. We were taken from the cart and put into a horse-drawn carriage and when the carriage passed through the great iron gates of Singha Durbar, we stepped foot on to the palace grounds together. The parrot and me. Soon, I was carrying him on my shoulder, wherever I went. You see, when a bird has been caged for too long, it forgets how to fly.'

For the first time, Rita glanced out the window. The garden was sodden and a guava tree rose from its centre, boughs out-stretched, fruit scattered before it like an offering.

'You should have seen the Singha Durbar back then,' the Ranisab continued, her voice gaining a lilting cadence, 'over 300 rooms the palace had. All divided between the old maharajah's family—his sons, nephews, hundreds of servants and bureaucrats. When I finally came of age and was married to the maharajah's younger brother, the next-in-line, I had an apartment of my own. He already had other wives, then. But I didn't mind. I had my parrot. He was the one thing, in that whole palace, that was my own. I had made swings for him, pools of water and cushioned seats. How he entertained everyone. Even my husband, to this day, I believe it was not me he came for, but my parrot. He loved me to the end, my husband did.'

Rita had only ever read about Singha Durbar in the Mahendra Malla, a black and white photo of the palace stuck at the very beginning of the chapter. Built by the Ranas for their own personal use, it later became a seat for the Nepal government when the Rana regime was overthrown. She remembered the book saying that the vast palace now stood as a proud symbol of Nepal's democracy.

'Then once, in the middle of the night, a gong sounded through the whole palace. "Fire!" they all shouted, "Fire!" Everyone was in a panic. Servants screaming, people running, children and women crying. Somehow, I found myself in a crowd of people rushing down a corridor. And then, I remembered. I had left him in his cage. I ran back, pushing against the wave of people, running back inside just as everyone was running out.

'When I got to my chamber, there was so much smoke—stinging my eyes, clawing at my skin—I could barely breathe. I stumbled to his cage. It was empty. Maybe one of the servants had remembered to let him out before running. Outside, I searched everywhere. I asked everyone I saw. I knew he couldn't have made it out on his own, someone must have taken him. They even took some of the palace guards away from fighting the fire to search for him. How I prayed to hear him call me. How I waited and cried and waited. It was on the third day when my husband came to me. He swore to me, his eyes red raw, that on the day of the fire, both he and his manservant remembered seeing a strange scene. They remembered seeing bright green wings flap out of a billow of smoke and soar right over those flames into the night sky.'

The Ranisab was quiet.

'You know,' she turned now to Rita, 'sometimes, even a bird as small as a parrot can change who we are, how we see the world, who we become. The poet you just read, Lekhnath Paudyal, he knew that. That one poem changed the fate of this country. One poem about a caged bird that had forgotten how to fly contributed, in its own way, to ending 104 years of Rana rule. The poem, you see, spoke about the desire for freedom. The same desire the entire country shared. It spoke of the desire to fly, to unleash oneself from the yoke of a hereditary dictatorship. Not too long after, events started to overtake themselves and finally, the Rana regime ended.'

Rita remembered the fragments of history she had learned in school. The Rana rule crumbled with infighting and brother pitted against brother. In the end, the puppet Shah king slipped away right under the noses of the ruling Ranas and ran away to India. When he came back, he came bearing democracy. As power changed hands, the Ranas lost many of their great palaces and lands. Today, the Ranas remained rich and well-connected as aristocrats of the land, but they were no longer in government, they had no real say anymore and what they owned was a sparse reminder of what once was.

'But you see, now . . .' the Ranisab continued, 'Again, they hear him. The parrot. Out there, in the hills, the people of this country hear his call. They feel his need to fly. Again and again, he comes back. He keeps coming back.'

The Ranisab turned again to the window. 'Sometimes . . . I think the parrot comes to each of us. Even now, I still dream of him. And if you listen carefully, in silence, you can hear him. He calls, inside of you.'

When Rita left the room, crossing the long corridors, her footfall silenced by layers of thick carpet, she felt somehow changed. As if deep inside her, an unfamiliar, undiscovered pathway had opened. She thought of Dhire hill, Sumnima climbing step after step before her, the buck and whirl of events that followed. And she felt as if she were on the threshold of a revelation, something subtle yet profound that she had never understood before.

8

The King

Rita was quick to learn the concoctions of daily medicines and various massage oils, the precise schedule that started first with the puja khota adjoining the bedroom and then moved on to the bookshelves, the serving of meals, the slow meandering walks around the garden. She felt a sudden urgency to absorb everything, to swallow every sliver of new information whole. As if with each new lesson in this big house, she was discovering everything that had come to pass and by extension, her own self—more layered than she had ever known—piece by piece.

After lunch, the Jarsap, the Ranisab and the older servants all took their afternoon naps. Krishne retreated to his room and Harke Bahadur deserted the gardens. Gurung ji lived on the floor above the garage during the week but on weekends, he went to his wife and children at the outskirts of the city. Sometimes Rita slipped a new book out of the shelves and took it to her own room, other times she used the quiet afternoons to wander the house. She stole through the stretch of reception rooms in the main house, the baithak, the adjoining dining room and the library. She hovered over intricate pieces of art and decoration, scrutinizing framed photos. But inside of her, there was a turmoil made of things pushed down and hovering just out of view—all the unanswered questions, the visceral memory of fear, the recognition of loss, Sumnima. *Where was she now?*

One day, she carefully lifted a photo of the Jarsap with another man and realized with a startle that she was staring into the face of the king of Nepal. It was a hunting photo—the Jarsap and the king shoulder to shoulder, guns slung down their backs. The king looked surprisingly human, his skin mottled like any ordinary man.

She studied the picture of the Jarsap's son, his daughter-in-law and granddaughter, staged at a photo studio. Krishne had told her that the Jarsap's son was a major in the royal army and was posted down south in Birgunj, and that his wife had accompanied him there. The man in the photo wore a uniform, his shoulders broad, his head held high. The woman by his side was diminutive, her hair arranged into a rounded coif. Their daughter, only a baby in this photo, had been left behind at the white house, in the care of Thul didi. But the picture was one of a perfect family.

Some days, Rita found herself drawn away from the main house to the wing that held the Ranisab's apartments. On the ground floor were rooms that were no longer entered into, except by Kali with her dustpan and broom. The largest of the rooms carried a large map stretched against the back wall that revealed the topography of Nepal. Dotted lines dissected the country into zones and districts while blue markings traced the rivers. The Marsyangdi was traced out towards the west, white caps signified the Himals to the north, green shades denoted the Terai forests in the south and a white star marked Kathmandu city in the centre. The

Ranisab had once used these rooms for entertaining guests but now they lay silent, caught in a perpetual stillness. Sometimes, Rita felt a sudden chill across her skin that caught her unawares and she would hurry out of the room. It would take her days to gain the courage to come back.

After several weeks, just like that, the rains stopped. Outside, the sun shone sharply, as if to make up for lost time. At the far tip of the building, Rita discovered an unused stairwell that led to a locked attic and a square terrace above it. She hoisted herself up and sat on the concrete ledge, looking out at the stretch of Harke Bahadur's lawn that ate into rows of fruiting trees and ran up the compound wall in a blanket of moss. Beyond the wall were other houses—all of them at an elevation lower than the Seto Bangala—stretching downhill to the distant, crowded centre of Kathmandu city.

Sitting on that ledge, it occurred to Rita that the white house was like a microscopic reflection of the dusty wall map in the Ranisab's empty rooms. From east to west, it contained a Tamang, a Madhesi, a Kathmandu Newarni, a Gurung and herself, a western Brahmin. It almost felt to her as if all the contents of the house—things and people alike—were curated. Then she looked up at the distant hills. She thought of how they held people in the unlikeliest of places—at the lonesome peaks, at the base of groaning cliffs, by fast moving tributaries that could decide to flow down a different way for no good reason on a moonless night. She thought of Rato Mato and the Dhire. How they stood side by side—one shorter, the other steep and craggy. But from here, she could not tell which was which. Inside, she felt the emptiness again, like a wide gaping mouth. Out loud she muttered, 'Sumnima, where are you?'

'Krishne!'

The bellow whizzed around the compound, resounding off the walls.

'Eh Krishne!'

Rita—suddenly afraid of getting caught in her new hideout—flew down the stairs and burst out into the courtyard from the Ranisab's quarters just as the Jarsap appeared at the kitchen back door at the opposite end. The Jarsap had only ever entered the kitchen once since Rita had been at the white house.

'Krishne!'

Krishne was sitting on a stool in the courtyard, splashed with sun, dressed only in a thin undervest with the handheld radio raised up and blaring into his ear.

'Hajur, Jarsap!'

He leapt up, his hand shooting up to slap his forehead in a sharp salute.

'I have been looking for you all over the house. Where have you been?'

'Hajur, Jarsap!' Krishne repeated, smacking his forehead for a second time. Rita wondered where he had learned to salute like that and kept as still as she could, not wanting to bring any attention to herself.

'The palace just telephoned!' the Jarsap's voice rose. 'Dinner! Next week on Saturday! Start the preparations!'

'Hajur!'

The gauze kitchen door whined and slapped as the Jarsap retreated in a rustle of silk back into the bhanchaghar. Rita scurried over to Krishne.

'Did he say the palace? The king's palace?'

'What other palace is there? *Damn it*!' Krishne swore, 'A damned royal dinner party, Bahuni. You know what this means?'

'Is the king coming here?'

'It means a lot of work for us. That's what it means. *Damn it*, Bahuni!'

Krishne had stopped calling Rita 'mayya' about a week into her stay and started calling her 'Bahuni' instead. Partly, Rita knew, it was to tease her. But the bigger reason, she suspected, was to tease Bajai. With Rita's arrival, there were now two high caste Brahmins in the servants' quarters and Krishne would not allow Bajai to forget it.

'Ehh,' Krishne sank back down on the stool, 'how I pity him.'

'Pity who?'

'Who else? The Jarsap, of course. One telephone call from the palace and the whole house is turned upside down. You will see. But after? In five minutes, he will be forgotten.'

'Forgotten by whom?'

Krishne had his eyes and ears everywhere. Whenever she was with him, Rita had the nagging feeling that she was missing half the plot in everything that she saw.

'The king, of course. His Majesty only remembers the Jarsap when he wants to be entertained. They grew up together, you know. But later, His Majesty was quick to side-line the Jarsap and surround himself only with men who mattered. Advisers, politicians, men who grease with their tongues. In today's Nepal, you see, the Ranas are powerless.'

Rita looked up at the expansive white building, washed clean, surrounding her on all sides. It seemed impossible that all this did not signify some semblance of power still. But before she could think of another question to ask, Krishne had pulled himself to his feet. 'Come on, Bahuni! We have work to do.'

Over the next few days, the house exploded into activity. Forgotten cupboards in the baithak were opened and intricately painted plates and porcelain bowls extracted under Krishne's close supervision. Carpets were unrolled and hitched to posts outdoors and beaten with sticks of bamboo. Silver was lined up on stretches of white muslin in the courtyard, Kali bending meticulously over them with cloth and polish. Even the pelts were dragged out and sunned; tiger, bear and leopard leaping out upon great plastic sheets laid on the grass of the white house. In the middle of it all were unfamiliar people coming and going, tradesmen and borrowed help—some stopping to stare at the tableware shining in sunlight, others hurrying past the open jaws full of sharp teeth. Outside, the shrill bell at the gates of the Seto Bangala kept ringing and Harke Bahadur was permanently stationed in the parking lot.

In the bhanchaghar, Krishne kept them abreast of the latest. The Jarsap's son and daughter-in-law would be coming from Birgunj the day before the party, making it just in time. Also, there would be catering. Sweetmeats and black forest cake from a five-star hotel in the city centre. Rita did not know what a black forest cake was and it only added to her excitement. 'You will see,' Krishne assured her, 'they make the best food in all of Kathmandu!' He threw a long sideways glance at Bajai at the other end of the bhanchaghar and Rita felt a giggle rise.

But in her chambers, the Ranisab was taken over by a sour mood. 'He just can't stop himself. Again, another party! How many parties does he need to throw? Does it look like I have nothing better to do at my age than to pay homage to every juvenile Rana and Shah in this land?' Rita nodded solemnly, but for the first time in weeks, her whole body was abuzz, distinctly alive. She could hardly believe it—the king of Nepal himself would be here, in this house.

When it came to the Ranisab, Rita scurried about in preparation. She worried over saris and petticoats, experimented with the rose water and powder puff, backcombed the Ranisab's hair until it stood up like a great ball of cotton fluff, until the Ranisab caught her own reflection in the mirror and scowled.

'Eh Rita, are you trying to impress the king or turn this old woman into a clown?'

'Hajur, do you think I could see him?'

'Who? The king?'

'Hajur yes, I thought . . . I have always wanted to see him. They say he is a god.'

The Ranisab guffawed, 'Who said he is a god?' It seemed strange to Rita, coming from someone who started every morning in the prayer room, whose divinities included the Lord Vishnu. The king of Nepal would be no ordinary human, she was sure.

'Let me think about it,' the Ranisab said. Quickly, Rita slipped down to the linen room, so that, just in case, her new tunic—the one with the pink embroidered flowers—was pressed and ready.

The day of the big party, Rita awoke at dawn to high-pitched voices. Bajai had employed both Thul didi and Kali in the kitchens, Thul didi as the purer Newarni inside to mind the rice, and Kali as the impure Madhesi woman outside, squatting in the courtyard with an old knife and a bucket of potatoes. Bajai had already been cooking for the full week and at the moment, the usual instructions of caste seemed to contain exceptions. Krishne reported that there was no more space in the fridge and the Jarsap hollered before telephoning somebody to borrow an extra one. She could hear him now as she crossed the courtyard, his voice amplified in the marbled hallways, 'Krishne! Eh Krishne!'

Rita slipped into the bhanchaghar, pouring herself a cup of tea. Then she took her stool outside, out of the way, watching Kali work.

'What are the potatoes for?'

Kali's hands moved deftly. She reached over and chucked the pieces into a large blue plastic bucket.

'Fried potatoes,' she said, 'they are the queen's favourite.'

'The queen's favourite is the common potato?' Rita's eyes rounded in surprise.

'They are not just any potatoes,' Kali threw a glance over her shoulder, 'the old Brahmin witch fries them using a combination of spices that apparently no other house knows how to replicate, a recipe she learned in the great palace itself.'

Rita contemplated Kali for a while. Then she said, 'Kali didi, how did you come here, to the Seto Bangala?'

She had done it purposefully, addressing Kali as didi. Up in Rato Mato, a Bahuni would never have addressed a Madhesi as didi or 'big sister'. And here too, Rita knew she sat higher in the hierarchical order than Kali. But the woman squatting in front of her had been a strong presence ever since she got to the white house and this rule, too, she thought, could have an exception.

Kali took a while to respond and Rita was not sure if the variance in address had registered with her.

'I was brought here when I was a bit older than you.'

'From where? Who brought you?'

'From Biratnagar. The Ranisab brought me.'

Biratnagar. Rita remembered the Ranisab saying that is where she had grown up, in the far east.

'But how did the Ranisab find you?'

Kali said nothing. She collected the cut chunks of potato in large handfuls. Rita could see that the Madhesi woman never remained in a room or in a conversation for longer than was necessary. She would have to find another way.

'But how did the Ranisab know you? There must be . . . a story there. I would love to hear it, didi.'

Kali hesitated. She opened her mouth then closed it without a word.

'The Ranisab did not know me. But she had heard of me.'

'Oh?'

'She had heard of the *kamlari* girl working for a family close to the house where she had been born.'

Rita took a sharp intake of breath. Kamlari was worse than being chained to the earth. It was being chained to a person. It was what happened to the poorest, those born at the very bottom of the caste hierarchy. It was, Neelam didi had carefully explained, slavery.

'Did she,' and Rita felt a sweep of denial even as she asked the question 'did the Ranisab buy you?' Once, Aama had put a price tag on Dalle the buffalo and advertised it at the village headquarters. But the price had been too high and no buyer had come forward. Aama had refused to lower it. 'He is worth every penny and more,' she had said.

'Yes,' Kali wiped her forehead with the back of her hand, 'She paid off my master.'

'She bought you and brought you here.'

But Kali shook her head.

'No. The Ranisab paid off my master and set me free. But I had nowhere to go. I had no one. So, I followed her and came here, to this house, of my own free will.'

She threw a last handful of potatoes that rang out loudly in the bucket then stood up, wiping her hands against her tunic. Rita sat outside for a while longer, thinking about the Ranisab. About the carved parrot's head, the great fire, this story here of Kali and felt like they were all expressions of the same aspect—the Ranisab was someone who stood apart.

By noon, the sun rose to a peak, pulsing down thick steamy heat. The household skipped their afternoon nap and nerves started to run raw. At the front gates, the bell rang repeatedly. A van brought the second borrowed refrigerator. Then another van brought the sweetmeats and black forest cake hidden in a large paper box. In the bhanchaghar, Rita peeped in and saw a crate filled with bottles of expensive looking alcohol. Then one more bell brought Harke Bahadur rolling a drum of gasoline across the grass to the white house. At any moment now, the Jarsap's son and his wife would be arriving from Birgunj.

Rita was in the Ranisab's chambers when another peel of the bell was followed by a hum that seemed to rise through the house. The Ranisab turned expectantly to the door, 'Go see!'

By the time Rita raced down the corridors, the household's servants had already gathered and lined up at the entrance. She saw him just as she slipped in next to Gurung ji. A tall man, his chest wide, his face a clean square. The man from the photo, his features unlike the Jarsap's. Large eyes, a straight nose, a high forehead.

Krishne said the Jarsap's son looked just like his mother. He strode up the steps and through the front door.

In Rato Mato, Rita had witnessed different versions of this scene—households welcoming their sons during Dashain, visiting from various cities or over the border in India. The sons, unrecognizable from the boys they had once been, would be fed eggs and mutton and in return, they would press notes into the hands of those left behind. Later, Rita and Sumnima would spy on them from rocks above the crest of the district headquarters, watching as they boarded the bus back to someplace else. And Rita would feel giddy, just imagining herself in their shoes.

The Sano Raja, or 'little king' as the servants called him, swept into the hallway, briefly ruffling his daughter's hair as she half-hid in Thul didi's sari, then proceeded down the length of polished marble, towards the baithak. A timid woman, his wife, followed after him. Rita could hear an exchange of words with the Jarsap but almost immediately the Sano Raja reemerged and headed towards the Ranisab's quarters. He flung open the Ranisab's door as Rita scurried behind him and fell on one knee in front of his grandmother, the old woman swallowed into a large embrace.

'Bled right in front of the doctors,' Krishne had recounted the story of Sano Raja's birth, 'the doctors could do nothing. In the end, all they could do was watch.' The Jarsap came back from the hospital without his wife and a small baby wrapped in a nurse's arms in the backseat. The Ranisab had fixed everything. Kept the nurse on for three months, arranged a nursemaid, found a nanny. Set up the newborn and the nurse in her own sprawling wing, far away from the howls that rose and fell in the main house every night. It was years before the Jarsap held the boy in his arms. The blame, Krishne said, needed time to take its leave. Through it all, the one constant the boy had was his grandmother. Rita could see it now in the ferocity of their embrace.

By mid-afternoon, just before the king's party, the white house was steeped in a golden sheen that caught in the trees and reflected off the windows. With the arrival of Sano Raja, the house took on a new energy. The Jarsap barked orders, Krishne whinnied responses, and Bajai shrieked over the clamour of her pots and pans. From somewhere in the big house, Rita heard the sounds of laughter, the giggles of a child. And beneath it all was the low drawl of the Jarsap's son—commanding, cajoling, his presence large with life.

The Ranisab sat on the edge of her bed, humming a forgotten tune. When the time came to dress her for the evening, Kali came to guide Rita and the Ranisab handed her a set of keys from her bedside drawer. Carefully, Kali unlocked the fortified steel cabinet in the corner and brought out thin boxes which she set out on the bed—velvet-lined red, blue and green.

Rita gasped and stepped forward to see. Inside, nestled in satin within the first box, were gemstones, large and green. Earrings, rings, the largest drop-shaped stone set in the centre of a swooping necklace. *Snap, snap*. Kali fiddled at the brass clasps and opened box after box. Strings of tightly-knit pearls. Diamonds, catching the last of the sunlight—a sudden spark that danced in a square of brilliance about the room. The Ranisab's Rana-era jewellery. Everything they said up in Rato Mato, everything Neelam didi used to tell them in animated whispers—it was all true. Jewels larger than ripe fruit, large enough for crows to spot from up in the sky. 'Stolen,' Sumnima had promptly replied then, 'stolen from the people.'

Rita had never imagined this is what they would look like, all laid out in in front of her.

With a flick of a wrist, the Ranisab dismissed them all. More boxes were brought out. Heavy dark gold, a bright unearthly purple. And then, just as Kali reached to open yet another box, her hands looking inordinately large and rough against the velvet, a tumble of sky blue dropped off the bed and spun on to the floor. A ring rolled right down the carpet before circling and sitting just in front of Rita.

'Here,' the Ranisab motioned, 'what is that one?'

Rita knelt clumsily to pick the ring up, the bright blue burning into her palm.

'Aah,' the Ranisab peered, 'that is sapphire. An unlucky stone. At least, unlucky for my horoscope. Ha!' she chuckled, 'I don't even remember where that one came from. Here, Kali, take it away.' And almost instantly, Kali had the bright blue stones back in the box and in the steel safe.

When the Ranisab was dressed, Kali turned to Rita, 'The Ranisab wants you to accompany her. Dress quickly and come. And remember, do not make a sound. Do exactly as I say.'

Downstairs, they moved through the brilliantly lit house with Rita on one side of the Ranisab and Kali on the other.

They entered the baithak and Rita was startled to find the room full of people. Saris milled about in bright colours—verdant green, sun yellow, poppy red. Bangles tinkled, voices lilted. Someone guffawed before a hushed silence fell upon the room. Those seated stood up, each bending deeply at the waist and bowing to the Ranisab in deference. Rita tried not to look at the many faces, focusing her gaze on the carpeted floor, imagining what the wealthy guests must think about a simple village girl like her.

They had just reached the arrangement of sofas at the far end of the room when an urgency of whispers volleyed about the room.

'Ranisab hajur,' Rita heard Kali's thickly accented voice, 'here is your seat. Rita will wait behind you.' Rita felt herself grabbed by an arm and shoved behind the sofa, into the thickness of curtains. Then Kali was gone. In front of her, the room was still, every face turned the other way, towards the door. And then, there he was. Across the length of carpet, directly in front of Rita.

She squinted, taking in his pale skin, the thin line of moustache above his lip, his face framed with a pair of spectacles. He looked soft and kind, and he moved like an ordinary man. The king joined palm to palm in a namaste, greeting the bowed people around the room. Behind him, Rita saw the queen and jogging behind them both was the Jarsap. She noticed the Jarsap's smart Nepali topi and traditional suit, an array of medals crowding his chest. He had a sense of urgency about him, as if everything whittled down to this one moment—the approval of the king.

The king and queen walked right up to the sofas and after receiving a feeble standing greeting from the Ranisab, took their seats. The king signalled, and the entire room followed suit with a collective sigh of cushions and seats. Suddenly, the queen turned towards the Ranisab, leaning in.

'My mother-in-law, the queen mother,' she said, her voice ringing clear, 'has been asking about you.'

The Ranisab nodded, 'Please, Your Majesty, send my old friend my regards as well. Old age, it may constrict our movements, but the heart does not forget.'

Then the queen turned back, whispering something to the king. Rita felt breathless, careful not to appear like she was staring at the back of the king's head. Around her, glasses tinkled, and various concoctions were poured into cut crystal. A man, with a white cloth strapped across one arm and a tray balanced in the other, whisked around and with a startle, Rita recognized Krishne. Suited and polished, he wore a topi that matched the Jarsap's. Krishne, as graceful as a dancer, stepping and whirling.

At the far end of the baithak, someone turned on music and Rita could hear the distinct beat of a madal. The song was one that she had heard many times as a child up in Rato Mato and she felt it now, the same proud rise in her belly that she had felt in the school assembly. She imagined telling the whole village about this day, the look on Neelam didi's face.

'Hajur, if I may?'

To her left, a small distance away, the Sano Raja approached the set of sofas. He bent deeply at the waist and waited. Rita watched as the back of the king's head nodded. Then the Sano Raja approached, pulling forth a free chair, bringing it closer to the sofas but not too close. He sat down, perched at the edge, his hands still joined together at the palms.

'Hajur, Your Majesty,' he repeated, 'Your Majesty had asked for me?'

Rita stood stock-still as the king spoke. But his voice was soft, his face turned the other way, and she did not catch his words. Facing the king, the Sano Raja balanced at the edge of his seat, listening intently, his brows knitted in concentration.

'Your Majesty,' Sano Raja nodded, 'Yes, Your Majesty,' repeating the address with every acknowledgement.

Rita strained her ears and was reminded of the time she had watched the king on the black and white TV at the tea shop in Rato Mato.

Then Sano Raja's voice rose in response to the king: 'Your Majesty, we will crush the enemy! We will get them wherever they are hiding. Just release us, release the army and we will fight!' Rita's eyes darted to Sano Raja's face. His eyes were black and large, his lips curled into a snarl. Suddenly, he looked different, a stranger to the man she had seen embrace his grandmother.

The king, half turned, looked out the side window beyond a gap in the curtains into the darkness outside. Rita could clearly see his profile. And then he spoke, a shift in the air.

'But how can I allow one Nepali to kill another Nepali? How can I watch my own people turn against each other?'

'Your Majesty, but they are no longer your people. The rebels have turned against you. They have turned against this country. Allow me to speak plainly, Your Majesty. Amongst your people, there are ways of distinguishing who is the enemy and who is not. By *infiltration*. By using the enemy's own strategies against them. That is exactly what the armed police did in the Rato Mato Hill case. That is exactly why it was so successful.'

Rita felt her heart stop, her chest flood cold.

'The men were sent there weeks before. They were placed everywhere. In the district headquarters, in the health posts, in the villages themselves. Your Majesty, please! The villagers themselves gave all the information that was needed!'

The king's gaze was still locked on to the darkness outside. And then he shut his eyes, drawing out a long exhalation.

'But once I let the army out . . . the situation will spiral.'

'Your Majesty!' Sano Raja leaned in further, 'We can keep tight control of the situation. Using modern methods of intelligence gathering, the armed police were *waiting* for the attack. They knew exactly where, when, who. The counter-attack came before the rebel attack on the district headquarters even started! The timing was set to perfection, just as the rebels gathered in formation.'

The king was now nodding, the topi high upon his brow standing up and bowing down. Rita suddenly found herself start to shiver as the cold spread down to her toes, seeping right into the floor and taking everything with it.

She remembered the two men from the health post. She had given them names. Manju Thapa. Niraj Rai. Others. The gathering she had seen up in the forests. Communism, Federalism, Republic. Big words with no beginning or end that filled her mouth like unchewable sinews. All the while, she had felt anger. Anger at what Sumnima had done with Niraj. Anger at the rebels for taking Sumnima away. Anger at Sumnima for leaving her behind.

Then she saw Niraj, faceless. Sumnima, on her knees, her mouth in a wide soundless O. She must have made a sound, because abruptly, she noticed that the Sano Raja had stopped mid-sentence with his mouth still open and was staring straight at her. She heard a high ringing sound in her ear, like the keening of a mosquito, and then, her legs gave way.

9

The Hole

'Eh Rita! Wake up! Wake up, Rita! Eh Rita!'
The voice was insistent.

A face floated before her, closing in, then backing away. Dark, even skin, features thick. Kali. Slowly, Rita looked around. She saw the far chair, piled with neatly folded clothes. A singular exposed light bulb, suspended from the ceiling.

'What happened, aabii?' the Madhesi woman was demanding, 'Eh Rita, are you all right? What happened?'

What was Kali talking about? Rita felt her throat scratch and it burned when she swallowed. What time was it? The room was cool and shadowed. But the window looked bright, awash with sun.

'Come on, get up.' Kali was dragging her up now by the arms, heaving her into a sitting position. 'You have to drink something. Dr Parajuli said to give you lots of fluids.'

Rita felt a sharp pain in her lower back that spasmed down into her legs. She was too warm in the covers. Kali brought a cup to her lips. Once again, she tasted the malty sweetness of Horlicks.

'Aabii!' Kali exclaimed again and Rita could not recall seeing the Madhesi woman this animated before, 'You gave everybody such a fright!'

Rita asked herself again, in a haze of confusion, what was Kali talking about? The only thing she remembered was a hole. A deep circular shaft covered in soil that came away in clumps and she was in it, at the very bottom. There, in the darkness, she could see nothing, but she knew there was something—or someone—with her. A thing alive, only a few paces away. She could feel it shifting—its muted scratching into the walls, the humid warmth of its breath, moving in closer and closer.

'What happened?' Rita asked feebly and her voice came out broken.

'You fainted! Right in the middle of the dinner party. You fell down and almost brought down the whole curtain with you. Aabii! We all thought the Jarsap would have a heart attack. Krishne and me, we carried you out of there double quick,' Kali's eyes grew large in her face, 'Then you started burning with fever and the Ranisab telephoned Dr Parajuli.'

Rita remembered now the Jarsap's son, sitting with his knees apart and his hands bunched into fists. *Infiltration*, he had said. *The counter-attack started before the attack had even begun.*

How much of what she told the two men from the health post caused what happened later? The two men had asked about the king. What did Manju Thapa and Niraj Rai think about the king of Nepal? Inside, she felt a scream rise.

Kali had a wet cloth now pressed to her face and was saying 'Shh, don't cry. Dr Parajuli said it is just a passing fever. It's the weather—lots of people are getting sick this time of year.'

Kali hauled her up to her feet.

'Come, if you are to get your strength back, you need to eat something.'

The bhanchaghar was empty.

'What time is it?'

'It's 3 o'clock in the afternoon,' Kali approached the stove, a pot in hand. 'You have been sleeping since yesterday. At least, the fever has subsided.' She closed and opened cupboards, filled the pot with water and lighted a flame. It occurred to Rita that she had never seen Kali at the stove before.

'Where is everyone?'

'Outside, the Sano Raja is leaving soon.'

Kali attended to the pot, her back to Rita, 'You know you were shouting in your sleep, like someone was coming to get you.' There was no surprise in her tone, no search for an explanation.

Right then, the main door of the bhanchaghar was flung open and Bajai stood frozen on the other side, her face covered with a network of wrinkles that all led to the pursed point of a thin mouth.

She thundered, 'Eh! What on earth do you think you are doing?'

Kali flinched but did not turn around. She continued to stir with a too-small spoon, her hand halfway into the pot.

'I am talking to you!' Bajai took a step forward, over the threshold, 'Who has given you permission to use the stove?'

'No one but god himself has given me permission to cook for a sick girl.'

'Ram! Ram!' Bajai gaped, 'But who told you to touch the stove? You touched the stove!'

'I will wipe it when I'm done.'

'The Ranisab is going to hear about this! And the Jarsap! Doing things as you like, without seeking permission first!'

Kali switched the stove off and carefully poured the contents of the pan into a bowl. Rita saw that it was jaulo, a mix of rice and lentils, a staple for anyone who was sick.

'Eh Madhesini, I am talking to you!' the old woman repeated, 'Have you gone deaf?'

But Kali simply handed Rita the bowl. And then she walked out the back door, slamming it shut.

That evening, all the servants gathered in the bhanchaghar.

'Ohho!' Krishne exclaimed, 'How Rita fainted!' he slapped his thigh, 'Up one minute, down the next with half the curtain ripped out! What a scene! Even the king turned around to look at what happened!'

'Shameful,' Bajai clucked her tongue, 'What a shameful spectacle in the presence of His Majesty!'

'That's what happens when a villager lays eyes on a king,' Krishne winked but Rita wasn't sure if he was teasing.

'How could she even think of doing something like that . . .' Bajai's voice rose to a screech, 'Must have been a demon that got into her!'

Krishne seemed to find this comment particularly funny, 'Yes! Yes! Maybe we should call a shaman, to find out what's going on with Bahuni here! Why do we even bother with a medical doctor? We must first drive out those pesky spirits!'

'Don't disrespect holy men!' Bajai's voice dropped to a low growl, 'You don't know their powers.'

'I know exactly what their powers are,' Krishne jumped up from the stool, 'look I will show you!' And suddenly, he sprung to the middle of the bhanchaghar, bending at the waist, a foot rhythmically thumping the floor. He closed his eyes as his mouth twisted and his hands beat an invisible drum. And then he was shaking and gyrating all over, leaping about like a crazed thing.

Rita had seen shamans in Rato Mato, with their big, feathered headgears and grass skirts, the terrifying beat of their taut drums. But even a shaman, she was sure, would not be able to drive out the clotted taste of mud in her mouth. *What have I done?* She wanted to ask out loud, her eyes stinging. *What have I done to Sumnima?*

Krishne quickly tired of the shaman act and started humming a popular tune. '*La hai*!' he sang out, '*Kanchi lai ghumaune Kathmandu sahar*!' And with that he was off—spinning, whirling, his voice high and feminine, his feet dancing like the god he was named after.

The room started to clap. Thul didi rose from her stool and started shaking on her feet, pumping her fleshy arms. And then another voice joined in, a voice deeper and richer than Krishne's, growing over them all. Rita turned in surprise to see Kali, squatting by the back door, her eyes shut, her voice pitched high, full of longing and memory. Rita had a strange sensation—as if in that moment, she was not alone but part of something larger. Something that touched the Madhesi woman singing in the corner, the Newari woman dancing in the middle, and even the Ranisab asleep in her quarters, brought to Kathmandu as a child. A deep, insatiable yearning but for what, she was not exactly sure.

After the singing and dancing, the servants ate leftovers from the party. Delicate strips of smoked wild boar, yoghurt marinated chicken, Bajai's peppered and fried potatoes. When she tasted the remains of the black forest cake, Rita realized she had never eaten anything so sweet or smooth before. It easily slipped down her throat and she forgot, in that moment, the tang of regret.

* * *

Over the next few weeks, early summer came to the gardens of the white house. Trees thickened, branches creaked and sagged. Rita counted plums, guavas and papaya. Under the shade of a tree, she read to the Ranisab. She was still working her way through the Ranisab's book collection, but now and then, she resorted to balancing out the myths and rhymes with snatches of news from the Jarsap's newspapers. The weekly read:

With most of the able-bodied men gone to find work in cities or abroad, Himalayan fields and farms are now almost solely run by women. One unlikely source of income that has emerged is marigolds. Marigolds from village fields are transported all the way to Kathmandu. This Dashain, many families in the capital will be wearing marigold garlands grown in the distant hills.

The Ranisab observed, 'Women have always been the guardians of the land.'

Rita thought of Aama, the way she heaved herself up, all but disappearing under the doko full of firewood. There were many things in her mother's life that could not be controlled, could only be suffered.

Rita moved on to the next article:

'Local politicians and foreign agencies alike are increasingly calling for the rebels to come to the negotiating table,' claims Dr Bhim Phedi. 'We are optimistic an agreement can be reached on constitutional reform.'

'*Hmph*!' the Ranisab snorted, 'Those greedy politicians. One day they say attack, the next day they say talk. As long as they create enough confusion so that in the meantime, they can line their pockets! Our so-called leaders have forgotten all their promises to the people. They have forgotten their duties, their faith. The only god they pray to now is the rupee!'

She sat back in her wicker chair, the parrot's head balanced on her knee and her eyes lit up.

'But if those cheats actually do hold talks, maybe, just maybe, there will be peace,' she looked down at Rita, sat upon the grass, 'And maybe you will be able to visit your village this Dashain.'

Rita glanced up. The thought had not crossed her mind.

'You have yet to tell me,' the Ranisab said, 'what is your village like?'

Rita hesitated. Then slowly, bit by bit, she described Rato Mato and the Dhire. She spoke of the fields, of goat herding and firewood gathering.

'And who do you have there?'

'My mother. And aunt. My uncle who's . . . ill. And,' Rita found herself hesitating again 'and my cousin sister used to be there too, hajur.'

'What's wrong with your uncle?'

'The . . . bottle, hajur.'

'Ah, a much too common curse. So, yet another household led by women, I see. And where is your cousin?'

'Hajur?'

'Where is your cousin sister?'

'She has gone. She has gone . . . away.'

'Where to?'

'She went away,' Rita felt herself on the verge of telling the Ranisab the truth but held herself back. 'She went away to get married.'

'Ehh! So, your cousin sister found her escape.'

And now Rita wondered if that was it. It had always felt like a betrayal, but is that what Niraj Rai had been? Like the guest house, an escape route for Sumnima, a way to construct a different future. She remembered what Neelam didi had said . . . the Rai boy could have studied his way out of the village one day. Guilt moved up, sluggish, filling her throat and stinging her nose. She picked up the next newspaper to read to the Ranisab, the *Nepal Sunrise*.

There, on the very first page, in black and white, was a photo of a string of youths sitting on the ground in ragtag clothes and flip-flops. Guns slung easily down their backs. Mixed faces, some of them women.

'What is it?' the Ranisab asked and Rita realized that the photo had shocked her into silence, 'What does it say?'

'It says . . .' Rita began, 'it says the rebels are made up of mixed ethnicities. And up to 40% of them are women.' Then she was quiet, her mind searching.

'Oh? Now that is something unexpected,' the Ranisab's voice piqued with curiosity.

'Hajur . . . before, in the villages, girls like these had nothing more than cooking ladles and sickles in their hands. And now they have guns.'

'Ahh, perhaps the goddesses have woken up.'

'Hajur?'

'Half the gods in this land are, in fact, goddesses, Rita. Shakti, power, itself is feminine. We even have the Kumari, a living goddess, worshipped by the three main cities. And yet, the flesh and blood females of this land have been left far behind.'

'Why do you think that is, hajur?'

The Ranisab shrugged, 'Fear, I suppose. Control. People start doing things a certain way for a specific reason and after a while, they forget why and forget to ask why. The one rule of life is that nothing stays the same. Time is always shifting, changing all around us. That is what, in fact, the goddess tries to teach us. That we must learn to dance with time.' Rita glanced again at the photo, bringing it close to her face. Half the youths in the photo had bandanas tied around their heads. In full colour, she knew, the bandanas would be bright red, embossed with a single white star. And yet, there was a camaraderie to the photo, an equality that jumped out. It did not seem to matter what caste, name or specific feature any of those faces held. It did not seem to matter if they were male or female.

The Ranisab sat forward in her wicker chair.

'Here, give me that, let me take a look.'

She took the paper in her small hands and squinted hard.

'Hmm,' she handed it back, 'Not all of those guns are even real. These two here, see,' she pointed, 'they are just sticks fashioned into guns. These youths are barely out of their childhood, and they are playing with toys.'

'Sticks, hajur?' Rita leaned again into the paper, peering closely.

'These youths have been driven to take up these guns, even if they are just sticks. That much is clear. But the question is, what will they actually achieve? So much destruction and for what, in the end? In the passion of youth, it is easy to be led astray by false promises.'

Anyone of those bandana-donning young women could have been Sumnima. Rita wondered if she was still in the vicinity of Rato Mato, hidden somewhere in the thickly forested hills, or if she was far away by now, in other forests on the other side of the country.

Suddenly, the front doorbell rang.

Rita and the Ranisab both looked out into the garden but Harke Bahadur, usually lingering out amongst the bushes, was nowhere in sight. The bell sounded a second time, insistent.

'Go, Rita. See who it is. Tell them to wait.'

Rita walked down the garden towards the car park, the sun hot on her neck, the photo in the paper still pulling at her mind.

Lining the top of the black metal gate were spear-shaped spikes and in the very centre, a pair of prancing peacocks held up a large half-moon clasp.

'Who is it?'

There was no answer.

She peeped through the gap between the gates but could see no one on the other side. Rita reached up, slipping off the half-moon clasp and took one step out on to the road. From where she stood, the road to the Seto Bangala passed by two other expansive compounds and a stretch of wide empty land. It couldn't have taken her more than a few minutes trotting to get to the gates from the garden. Who could have rung the bell and left so quickly? Rita peered over, into the empty weeds on either side. Unless, she thought, whoever had rung the bell had backed up and sped away in a car or motorbike. But in that case, wouldn't she have heard the rev of engine? She stood there thinking for a few minutes until she heard the voice of the Ranisab carry over the garden, 'Rita? Eh Rita!'

'Who was it?' Krishne was jogging down from the house now, meeting her on the garden path.

'No one,' Rita shrugged.

'What do you mean no one?'

'I opened the gates and there was no one there.'

'Oh! Probably those nuisance bloodsuckers asking for donations again!'

'Donations for what?'

'The cause,' Krishne waved a dismissive hand.

'What cause?'

'The revolution, of course.'

'What? The rebels are here? In Kathmandu?'

'Shh, keep your voice down, you want the Jarsap to get a heart attack? Of course, they are here. They are going from house to house, to shops and businesses, everywhere they can, collecting money. Eh Bahuni, do you think a revolutionary war can be waged without money? Kathmandu itself is feeding the beast that is going to devour us all.'

* * *

That evening, the Ranisab came down with a fever. Then Thul didi said the Jarsap's granddaughter couldn't swallow a mouthful of food. And in the servants' quarters, Harke lay moaning in his bed. A telephone call brought Gurung ji hastily back to the house even though it was a Saturday. Then he sped away in the Jarsap's jeep with strict instructions to find Dr Parajuli. When Dr Parajuli, tall and thin with thick greying hair, entered the Ranisab's bed chamber, Rita was reminded of Dhire dai. Dr Parajuli examined the Ranisab and gave the diagnosis of 'a passing virus'—common, especially after the rains. The first person to catch it, he surmised, was Rita a few days ago and the illness was now simply making its way through the household. He left a potion on the table and Rita did not leave the Ranisab's side all night. She worried as the old woman murmured in fitful sleep and watched her toss this way and that. She wiped the Ranisab's face with a constant relay of wet towels and from time to time forced her up, feeding her water from a cup.

At one point the Ranisab cried out in her sleep and Rita bent low over her, sweeping her hair back.

'Rita? Rita?'

'Hajur, I am here, hajur.'

'Ah Rita . . .' and then the Ranisab fell into a deep sleep.

In the morning, the fever broke. By noon, the Jarsap decided the Ranisab needed someone close at hand round-the-clock. Rita moved her belongings out of the bedroom she shared with Kali in the servants' quarters and into an empty room next to the Ranisab's. Standing there, three floors up, by an unfamiliar window that looked out beyond the compound walls, Rita had the same feeling that she remembered having up in Rato Mato. That there were others nearby—unseen and unknown. Staring at the moonlit outlines of the garden walls and the darkness beyond, Rita thought about ghosts.

10

Tudikhel

After three days of nursing the Ranisab by her bedside, Rita opened all the windows and brought the Ranisab's bedding to where the sun blazed in large geometric patches. The old woman remained weak, but her fever had completely subsided and her appetite had returned. Through the open windows, the house thrummed—Bajai banged about in the kitchen, the Jarsap's granddaughter threw up a wail that was matched by Thul didi's high-pitched admonitions, and from somewhere in the main house, the radio blared.

'Rita!' the Jarsap's voice rang from across the courtyard, 'Krishne! Go get Rita! Immediately!'

What could the Jarsap possibly want with her? Rita quickly screwed the cap on a bottle of massage oil and hurried down the corridors.

She met Krishne in the marbled hallway.

'What is it?'

'The Jarsap called for you. You have a telephone call.'

Rita had never before received a telephone call. The tea shop was the only place in all of Rato Mato that held a telephone. The owners of the tea shop, a short stern man and his portly occupied wife, guarded the contraption and made anyone who wanted to use it pay five rupees per phone call. Rita and Sumnima never had that kind of money. Neither did they have anyone to call. The most they had done as children was to sneak to the side of the tea shop and, with the owner and his wife bustling about inside, steal the receiver just to hear the dial tone.

In the baithak, the Jarsap sat on the velvet sofa, the daily newspaper spread out on his knees. Behind him, on the heavy wooden desk trimmed with felt and leather, Rita could see the Jarsap's personal mobile phone. How was she supposed to pick the instrument up and which end should she put to her ear?

She was so quiet on her bare feet that she had to hover at the edge of the carpet before the Jarsap looked up. In a moment of panic, she wondered if whoever was waiting on the other end of the line would hang up. For an instant, she thought of Sumnima.

'Oh,' the Jarsap looked up in surprise and then blinked, 'you are here. Go ahead. Dhire wanted a quick word with you.'

Of course, nobody in Rato Mato other than Dhire dai had an extra five rupees lying about. Nor would they have the wherewithal to make a telephone call. And then, Rita understood. This is how Dhire dai had been informing the Jarsap about his trees all along. This is how he had gotten permission, beforehand, to bring her all the way to Kathmandu.

She timidly approached the desk and lifted the contraption with both hands. She heard a faint buzz of static and brought that end to her ear.

'Hello? Rita? Rita? Is that you?' A far away voice.

'Dhire dai . . .' she whispered. Then a sudden shyness overtook her and she stopped.

'Rita? Are you ok? Is everything all right?'

'Yes,' she responded, louder this time, and wondered what her own voice sounded like. The Jarsap, reading his newspaper only a few feet away, could hear every word.

'Eh Rita. I wanted to telephone earlier. But I have been . . . busy. Everything here is ok. You should not worry about a thing. Not a thing, you hear me?'

Rita's mind went to Aama, her back bent like a sickle under loads of firewood. Kaaki, with an arm that couldn't be straightened out. Neelam didi, with the bad hip. How were they all managing?

'How are Aama and . . .' Rita ventured, but before she could say anything further, Dhire dai's voice came again, insistent on the other end of the line.

'Everyone here is fine. Your mother, your aunt, they are all fine. You shouldn't worry about them. You hear me?'

'Yes . . .' Rita said hesitantly, 'Ok.'

'I called because I have some news . . . about . . . your cousin.' He did not name her.

'Yes?' A vaulting against her ribs.

Rita knew that for Dhire dai to be having this conversation in the first place, one of two things must be happening. Either the tea shop was empty, the shop owner's wife busy with the dishes in the back and the owner loitering outside by the half-drunken carrom players. Or the tea shop was full, the shop owner's wife sizzling hissing jalebi in vats of oil, the shop owner shouting out orders over the noise and squeezing from one table to the next. Either way, he would be tucked away in a corner of the shop with the telephone wire uncoiled and stretched to its max. The village had many ears and Dhire dai was a cautious man.

'Someone from the village saw her . . . a few hills down. About two weeks ago. She is now . . . one of *them*. She is . . .' and here Dhire dai paused, 'she is *alive*.'

Rita felt her whole body pause. Not once had she considered the alternative. But every day, the newspapers carried stories of people disappeared, never to be seen again. In his leather sofa, the Jarsap made to move.

'I just wanted you to know that,' Dhire dai said, 'Take care of yourself.' Then the call cut off with a click.

'Everything all right at home?' the Jarsap asked off-handedly.

Rita felt her throat close up and she took a second to steady herself, standing by the desk.

'Hajur,' she nodded.

'Good, good,' he said as he put his glasses back on and stood with his hands clasped behind his back. He looked straight at her but his mind was elsewhere. 'Dhire said the trees are doing well too.'

That afternoon, Rita brought the Ranisab back out into the gardens. She sat the old woman in her wicker chair under a shady plum tree and before she had finished reading even a single page, the Ranisab had dozed off. She let the book rest and looked out into the green. Sumnima was alive. She was still out there, somewhere, in the hills. Overhead, crows-caw cawed loudly, jostling each other in the branches. Rita felt almost a dizzying lightness, a sense of things settling, piece by piece, in their place—she here, in this big house; Sumnima in the hills, safe; everything alright at home as Dhire dai had promised.

Then she picked up that day's *Kathmandu Post*. The front-page headlines shouted out, 'PM's Appeal for Peace.' The prime minister was appealing to the rebels to put down their arms and in exchange, the rebels would get full amnesty. The whole country could breathe a sigh of relief and finally move on. But the very next article screamed 'Opposition Leaders Agitate.' The opposition parties were already starting to say that the prime minister was failing to deliver a solution. At the gates, the doorbell burst into sound. Rita jerked her head up, remembering the incident from the previous week. Harke, she knew, was still recovering in his bed. Krishne would be somewhere inside the big house. One more ring and the bell would wake the Ranisab. She jumped up and jogged out to the gates.

Under the hefty metal gates, she could see canvas shoes, dirtied and laced. Two, no, three pairs, she counted.

She peered through the gap and saw on the other side, three young men in plain clothes.

'We have a letter,' a deep voice said, 'for the owner of this house.'

Rita swallowed hard.

'What kind of letter?'

'A letter of support. Support for our noble cause.'

'What cause?'

There was a pause. Then, 'Liberation,' the voice said.

She knew she should go call Krishne. But instead, she reached for the half-moon clasp and slid it off. The gate opened with a shudder.

'You must go,' she said, her voice barely above a whisper, careful not to betray her anticipation, 'the people of this house have no interest in your cause.'

All three young men wore faded pants above plain canvas shoes, tracksuit jackets and low-hanging baseball caps that shielded their eyes. Two of the men, she noticed, carried threadbare backpacks and stood with their feet parted. The man who spoke was the only one looking directly at her. And it shocked her to see that he was, in fact, not young at all.

'Just take this letter,' he said, his leathered face worn by the sun, 'that's all we ask for now.'

Rita hesitated.

'*Baini*,' he addressed her again, this time his voice a notch softer, the address informal, 'all we ask is you take this letter. And give it to the owner. That's all you have to do. We don't ask for anything else.'

Rita took the letter and nodded.

The man stepped back. All three of them turned their backs, readying to walk back up the road, and Rita felt surprised at her own sudden disappointment. What else was she expecting to happen? She slipped inside the gates reluctantly but just as she reached up to drop the half-moon clasp, a strong hand flew up through the crack from the other side, catching the gate firm and startling Rita. The older man's face was now right there, in the crack itself, just a few inches away from hers, his eyes holding hers in a steady unmoving gaze.

'And this,' he said, his voice so low it sounded like a rumble, 'is for you. Make sure you are alone when you read it.' A small envelope stuck out between the sheets of metal. Quickly, Rita pushed the gate shut and dropped the clasp. The letter fell to the ground. She waited till the footsteps had receded down the road before bending down to pick it up. The envelope was blank, without any address, almost weightless in her palm.

Back at the house, she handed Krishne the letter meant for the Jarsap.

'Will you give it to him?'

'Hya, you actually think I will give to him? And let the old man have a heart attack? This is not the first time this is happening, Bahuni . . . a letter, straight from the rebels, asking for his money. Can you even imagine the uproar if he ever read any of those letters? I may share a lot, Bahuni, but some things,' Krishne winked, 'I keep for myself.'

The second letter, the one meant for her, rustled, hidden between her belly and the seams of her leggings.

Later that night, before switching off the lights and crawling over the bed slats to her mattress in the empty room beside the Ranisab's, she carefully pried it open.

Meet me at the center of Tudikhel Park, Saturday at noon. I have faith that you will find an excuse. The park is close to Bir Hospital.

There was no address, no signature at the bottom. But Rita knew those curves, knew the way they rounded and hung from the lines like fat drops of rain clustered and clinging to roof edges. Sumnima had never been a good speller. Rita examined the note, then laid it aside. Then she picked it up again, reading it over and over. What had Dhire dai said? That Sumnima had been seen in the hills surrounding Rato Mato. How long ago had that been again?

She is here, Rita whispered to herself, her whole body shuddering. *She is here.*

* * *

A week later, Rita sat in the Jarsap's jeep as the vehicle inched along, stuck behind a small red Toyota car and ahead of it, a bus that looked like an overripe fruit, bulging at the sides and rusty with rot. It belched out clouds of smoke that seemed to swallow the red Toyota whole.

Gurung ji sat at the wheel with Rita in the seat next to him. She had never been in the Jarsap's jeep before. She hadn't been on the streets of Kathmandu since the tuk-tuk ride on the day of her arrival.

Up ahead, a sudden rev of engines overtook all sound and now motorcycles carrying men who held up large placards taped to sticks hurtled down the other side. The left-aligned political parties, currently outside of government, were seeking out ways to further destabilize the parties in government and their signs called for a general strike. It was meant to start at midnight and last three days. Rita could tell Gurung ji was nervous, his hands knuckled tight at the steering wheel, his moustache hiding the thin line of his lips. The roaring queue of motorcycles swept round the roundabout and powered back up the street.

The night before, just before the announcement of the general strike, the Ranisab had sat on the edge of her bed with her small feet dangling and listened intently to Rita. But Rita had been unable to look her in the eyes.

'When Dhire dai telephoned,' her voice sounded as if it belonged to someone else, 'he mentioned that my uncle has . . . taken a turn for the worse. Some of the villagers will be bringing him to Bir Hospital. With your permission I was thinking I could go and visit him.'

Rita felt a twang of guilt as she used her uncle for her excuse. She told the Ranisab that she would go in the morning and be back by the afternoon, and that she would take the local bus. But the Ranisab had summoned Krishne immediately. She instructed him that Rita was to be driven to Bir Hospital first thing in the morning.

Up the street, Rita could see a crowd of people on foot. Youths, marching with their fists in the air. The bus in front of them pulled ahead with a judder and the red Toyota rolled behind it. Gurung ji started the engine and they inched ahead.

In her mind, Rita played out all the things she would say to Sumnima. She would make things right. The truth was, what happened up on the Dhire, happened because she had wanted Sumnima to suffer. To pay for what they had done—Sumnima and the rebels, Sumnima and Niraj Rai. But then she thought of Sumnima, climbing step after step ahead of her up the Dhire as the rebel army approached. Sumnima, coming back, pulling her out of the bamboo grove. Sumnima had not left her behind. Even until the very end, she realized, the taste of mud back in her mouth, Sumnima had not left her. And now, Sumnima was here. Not even a year had passed since they had climbed up Dhire dai's trees and stolen his mangoes, but it felt like a lifetime.

From behind the car came the shrill call of sirens and a parade of police cars whizzed past, some closed vehicles fitted with men and others open lorries carrying police wearing thick padded body protectors, helmets and heavy batons. Gurung ji exhaled sharply.

'It's going to get ugly. Hold on!'

He swung around, slapping one hand on the back of Rita's seat as he scanned the street behind. Then he slammed his hand on the jeep's horn and with the blare of sound, Rita saw that the dull blue vehicle behind them was reversing. Gurung ji pumped with his foot, effortfully swivelling the steering wheel and with a sudden release, swung the jeep around, pivoting aggressively. Rita lurched to her right, smacking her head on the window as the jeep straightened out on to the road.

Gurung ji revved the engine up the main street and swerved into a narrow alley. Walls on either side hugged so close that she could see the outlines of bricks, aged cement and paddings of moss. Her fingers tightly held on to the seat. The jeep shot through the alley and up ahead, she could see a thin slice of daylight. Gurung ji hit the brakes and the jeep screeched to a halt. He pointed through the windshield.

'That building there, that's the hospital. I must hurry back. Can you manage on your own?'

Rita nodded, her stomach unwinding.

'I will come back at 3 p.m. and wait right here. But if there's any trouble in the streets, just stay put. Wait at the hospital.' Rita nodded and closed the door but Gurung ji was rolling down his window. 'Wait a minute!' He rummaged around before whipping out a piece of paper and pinning it on to the steering wheel.

'These days one never knows. In the worst-case scenario, if things get really bad and they block the roads before I can get here and the strike starts, follow this,' he drew a tree, forked with branches, 'Walk straight down this street, then turn right. Keep walking until you get on to a wide boulevard. At the end of it, you will see Singha Durbar palace. Hug the walls of the palace, turn right, then keep following the boulevard straight all the way until you reach the bridge. Across the bridge is Patan. Take the first uphill drive on your left. After that, you will be in the neighbourhood, at least, and you will know what to do from there. Right, right, then left. Got it? And make sure to avoid any gathering crowds.'

Rita took the piece of paper, folding it in her hands.

She watched the jeep drive away, the back of Gurung ji's head shrinking down the street. The building of Bir Hospital rose to her right, its bulk and wings taking over half the street. The oldest public hospital in the capital, even the villagers up in Rato Mato knew about it. It was where people sent the sick in the most daunting of cases, sometimes travelling for days on overcrowded buses down the winding hills. Behind her, across the street, stretched Tudikhel Park. Its length of plain grassy field sat in a large expansive oval, carved right out of the heart of the city and spanning the entire vertical length of the block.

When Rita stepped into the park, it felt as if she had stepped out of Kathmandu itself, its cacophony of honks and hurtling vehicles. She walked deep into the green, passing a small group of boys bent into the grass. Not more than six or seven years old, they were clothed in dirty rags, their feet bare. They were carefully stringing a kite, measuring the length of string on each side. It was still too early in the season for kite flying but somehow, these boys had managed to get their hands on one. Later, they would go begging out on to the main streets and sleep with their backs against the pavement at sundown.

Other than the boys, the park was empty. Somewhere in the distance, a siren rang past. Rita dropped to her knees and sat down, facing the sun.

All of a sudden, Sumnima was there, blocking out the light. Dressed in a jacket and pants, her hair shorn and tucked beneath a baseball cap. Sumnima, Rita thought, could easily be mistaken for a boy. In the moment, she forgot everything she had been preparing to say.

Rita felt a surge within herself—she wanted to throw her arms around Sumnima's neck, to laugh out loud and cry at the same time. She blinked and lifted a hand to shade her eyes. Sumnima flopped down beside her, her limbs loose, her movements borne of a confidence that was even more pronounced than Rita remembered. Their knees touched.

'So!' Sumnima started as if no time had passed between them at all, 'How are things? In the big house, I mean.'

'How . . .' Rita began, her throat dry, her limbs tremulous, 'how did you find me?'

'Easy. We have eyes and ears everywhere.'

'But you left the village. Nobody knew where you were. Nobody had any contact with you. Dhire dai said . . .'

'Hya! I don't need to be *in* the village to know what's happening there, or anywhere else for that matter. Like I said, we have eyes and ears everywhere. Our people are everywhere.'

Despite her giddiness at seeing Sumnima, Rita felt a smacking irritation at that phrase, 'our people.' How quickly Sumnima had shed who she had once been and plucked up another identity, another sense of belonging, a new sense of destiny. Nothing, Rita realized suddenly, was as it had once been.

'They are treating me fine,' Rita replied, then immediately regretted the lack of conviction in her voice, 'and how is your new life treating you?'

Sumnima rolled up her jacket sleeves and lay back upon her elbows. Her forearms were roped, her fingers long and slender. Beneath her, the grass, newly fed by the rains, dazzled green, an arrogance of vitality.

'There is only one word to describe it,' she picked up a young green stem and stuck it playfully at the side of her mouth, '*Possibility*. Everything is possible.'

'So . . . you are one of them now? A rebel?'

'I am a *revolutionary fighter*. And that's not all. They have just promoted me to commander. I now lead a group of thirty men and fifteen women.'

She said this casually, but Rita started.

'Even women can be commanders?'

'Sure. In our movement, we say that men and women are like earth and sky. Both are equal. I was simply faster and better than all the rest.'

Sumnima shrugged as if it wasn't a big deal. In the mango forests up on Dhire hill, if Sumnima started running, she could run the entire hillside without stopping once and without slowing her pace. But Rita remembered now what the Ranisab had said, that many of the fighters were just children, playing with toys.

'What do you do . . .' Rita ventured, 'as a fighter?'

Sumnima tipped her head back, her face open to the morning sun and her cap inclined away so that Rita could see her eyes, long and heavily lashed, half-closed.

'Oh, every day is different. Most days, it's just about lessons and preparation. Practice and some more practice,' Rita could feel herself loosen, but then Sumnima continued, 'And then some days, we put that practice into use.'

'Have you . . .' Rita ventured, tremulous at the thought, her voice careful not to betray it, 'have you seen an actual fight?'

'Sure!' Sumnima said it so easily that Rita felt again as if she were in reverse, her feet pointing away from solid earth, her mind brushing against a subterranean reality, 'my platoon has been involved in quite a few skirmishes.' In Rato Mato, the rebels and their capacity for violence was something that was feared but here was Sumnima, fully embracing it all, even after everything that had happened. What was it that Neelam didi used to say? Rita found herself asking. That Sumnima was *too much*.

'Have you . . . shot at anyone?'

Sumnima laughed, her mouth wide open against the blue sky and Rita thought that she could swallow the sun.

'How else do you think we fight?'

'Have you . . . killed anyone?'

Sumnima shrugged. As if taking a life meant nothing more than plucking a stem from this vastness of available green around them.

'We usually shoot down from the hills into the highways below. It is not always possible to tell exactly where a particular shot has landed from. But I am told I rarely miss.'

Rita felt herself shiver, a chill running up her arms and down her spine. She remembered what they had seen up on the Dhire that day. What she had been unable to look at, above Niraj's lifeless hips. She found that she had nothing more to ask.

'So . . .' Sumnima filled the silence for her, 'tell me more, how are the people in the big house treating you?'

Even though their knees were touching, Rita felt a distance open up between herself and Sumnima. Rita wanted nothing more than to forget what had happened up on the Dhire. But here was Sumnima, going back, threatening to repeat it all over again. What if what happened to Niraj happened to Sumnima?

'Good . . . I cannot complain.'

'How much are they paying you? For your . . . work?'

'I eat well, I have new clothes, I have my own bed.'

'So they don't pay you?'

It had never even occurred to Rita that she should be paid. Even if it had, how could she have ever asked? She searched desperately now for a way out of where Sumnima had pinned her, upside down.

Sumnima looked straight at her but her surprise, Rita could tell, was feigned, 'Not even one rupee? All our fighters get paid. I have stashed away a tidy sum already.'

Rita decided to change the subject. 'So . . .' she broached, 'what are you doing in Kathmandu then?'

'After they promoted me, they sent me here for training and to learn other means of . . . public agitation. *The rise of the masses*!' Sumnima pointed towards the far corner of the park beyond which Rita could now hear a faraway rabble. As if a crowd of people were marching together, on the next street or the street beyond that, their voices rising.

Sumnima seemed to be quoting someone but Rita did not know who. Then abruptly, Sumnima lifted herself and sat upright, grazing Rita's knee in the process, her legs folded beneath her. She turned, her eyes studying Rita's face.

'Tell me, what are your plans? Where will you go from here?'

'I don't know,' Rita shrugged, 'I will stay here until the fighting is over, I guess. That's what Dhire dai said. But I don't know how long Aama and Kaaki can go on. Without anybody to help them.'

'The fight is only just beginning. It will be a long time before it's over. Soon, we will bring the fight to Kathmandu city.'

The finality of her words was cold and factual, as if Sumnima were in possession of the future.

'So, tell me, what will you do?'

Rita shrugged. Her life had never been a series of actions, planned and willed into place.

'Does Dhire dai know you are here?' Rita asked. It seemed easier to be the one asking the questions.

'No.'

'You didn't make any contact before you left?'

'It is safer if they don't know anything about me. Safer for them.'

'How . . . how are they?'

Sumnima shrugged.

'They work harder than ever. Life goes on.'

Rita was quiet.

Then she said, hesitantly. 'How much did you know? Up on the Dhire, how much did you know about what was going to happen?'

'I knew,' Sumnima looked away. She spoke softly now, 'I knew they were planning something.'

'Then why did you not go with them? Why did you come with us up to the Dhire?'

The question was finally out, in the open. But even as she said the words, Rita had the nagging feeling that she was missing something.

'It was never supposed to happen like that. The rebels were meant to gather above Rato Mato, up on the Dhire, and then descend in the night. The attack was supposed to be swift. A surrounding and a surrender. No real fight at all. But somebody betrayed us.'

Overhead, the distant cry of a hawk. Rita felt herself pulled back again to Rato Mato hill, to the courtyard, the two men from the health post who asked her question after question as the clouds gathered.

'Who . . . who betrayed you?' the question came out a whisper.

Sumnima shifted, looking down at her canvas shoes, the silence lengthening.

The moment stretched and spread, beyond the park, beyond the growing din in the distance. Rita felt her mouth go dry, her heart so loud against her ribcage that she was sure Sumnima would hear. How would she explain the feeling that had come thundering towards her, the images that barrelled down, assailing her all the way down the Dhire just as the sandy soil came rushing up. Sumnima and Niraj Rai. Sumnima and the rebels. Sumnima leaving her behind. The anger and the fear that came before it, that threatened to consume her whole.

But then Sumnima said softly, 'I don't know.'

Rita blinked.

'Sometimes,' Sumnima continued, 'it's those we trust most who betray us. Someone who knew our movements exactly. *When*, *where*. One day, I will find out who.'

Rita felt the guilt again, rising like a slow tide of wet earth. The moment had come. The moment to tell Sumnima everything. To make things right. But how would Sumnima react? What if she lost Sumnima all over again?

Sumnima reached up and adjusted her cap. The distant din seemed to be surging and crashing, like angry waves against river rocks.

'By the way, my people say that the old woman in your big house has more jewels than anybody else in Kathmandu. Is that true?'

Rita shrugged, her mind still on what she should say to Sumnima. What reason would she give for what she had done? And if she said nothing, would Sumnima find out anyway?

'Have you ever seen them?'

'What?'

'The jewels . . . have you ever seen them?'

'Oh . . . once . . . or twice.'

'So it is true.'

Rita shifted on her haunches, her mind a mass of confusion.

'Tell me about them,' Sumnima's gaze was locked on her face, 'tell me about the jewels.'

Rita's mind turned slowly to Sumnima's question and she wondered, vaguely: *What did Sumnima know about the Ranisab? What did she know about the ox cart, the great fire, the kamlari woman, the parrot inside*?

'Remember, you are not one of them. You are just a poor village girl. You are expendable to them. To be used and cast aside,' Sumnima's eyes were lightless.

'The question to now ask . . .' she spoke pointedly, and Rita could hear the undertone in her voice—the same taunting tone Sumnima would use whenever she would challenge Rita—'what is your future? What is it that *you* can do? How can you help the cause?'

Rita closed her eyes. And for a second, the field of grass was gone, Sumnima gone with it. Instead, she saw the groves of mango up on Dhire hill. Their leaves lush, long and pointed. She smelled the sweetness of their fruits. She bent down and felt the richness of the red earth, coming away in her hand in thick knotted clumps. Beyond, a vista of hills, hill after hill undulating as far as the eye could see.

As children, the only toys Rita remembered playing with were ones that she and Sumnima fashioned themselves—a *chungi* ball made out of curls of rubber bands tied together, a faceless doll made out of a discarded bit of cloth, a V-shaped branch reworked as a sling shot. Every new toy was Sumnima's idea, every new game played at her direction. And every time Rita became good enough at bouncing the rubber ball on the side of her foot for a count close to Sumnima's or approached the target better and better with her slingshot, Sumnima abruptly changed the rules of the game or changed the game itself. But at night, it was Sumnima who pulled Rita's *dolai* blanket up to her chin, who sat up and drummed her fingertips, light as feathers, upon Rita's head until she fell asleep.

Rita opened her eyes.

'Why did you come with us? The rebels were marching, you could have easily gone with them. No one would have stopped you. But instead, you came and hid with us.'

So far, Sumnima had deflected the question. But Rita needed to know.

'Because of you. Because I did not want to leave you behind.'

'What do you mean?'

Sumnima seemed to hesitate, her eyes now looking out to the far line of trees.

'They wanted me to join. But I was too worried, worried that if I went away, then by the time I returned, you would be married off already. To another village just like ours, a possession to a total stranger, worked to the bone. And there would be nobody to stop that from happening. A woman in this country has no place, no voice, no meaning. You and me, we never had any options.'

'But . . .' Rita stuttered, 'but what about Niraj Rai? Weren't you going to marry him? You were planning on going away yourself.'

'Who told you I was planning to go away?' Sumnima shifted, her zippered jacket rustling.

'But you were spending all your time with them. With him.'

'I would not have gone away.'

Rita swallowed hard. She remembered how tightly Sumnima had grabbed on to her arm up on the Dhire, hauling her through netted stalks of bamboo in the rain.

'But if we are to change things, truly change things, for people like us, we have to *do* something. We have no choice but to *force* change. You see, the action we take is for ourselves. For you, for me, for our mothers. This, you understand, is our only way out.'

Rita found herself searching, her mind pulsing, her heart reaching forth and yet holding back.

'The jewels. Where are they kept?'

'In . . . in the bedroom.'

'Where, in a wardrobe?'

'Yes.'

'Who has the key?'

'The Ranisab.'

'Which means, you can easily get to them. How many jewels are there? Have you ever seen them?'

Rita nodded but her throat knotted and her eyes started to prickle.

'The old woman won't even notice if one goes missing. Don't be afraid, there is never any use for fear.'

But it is fear that keeps us safe, Rita thought.

'But . . . the Ranisab is kind to me. How can I steal from her?'

'Why wouldn't the old woman treat you well? You serve her hand and foot, don't you, all without getting paid a single rupee for it. You don't belong in that house, you never will. Do you think the big people in that house will ever be loyal to you? Ever pay you back?'

Sumnima's voice softened. 'One day, you and me, we will be back in the village. We will claim what is ours. We will no longer be living hand-to-mouth. I have always told you, have I not, that we are meant for more?'

And then Sumnima's voice was rising again. 'Life is not only about survival. About blaming our karma and not doing a thing about it. Life is about living to our fullest. Life is about *possibility*. And about striving to fulfil that possibility.'

The clamour in the distance seemed to fragment and scatter. A faraway unison of sirens. And then silence.

Sumnima stood up, wiping the seat of her pants.

'Remember that guest house we used to talk about?' she said suddenly, 'In Bandipur, just outside of Kathmandu, I saw one just like it on my way into the valley. If they can do it, then why can't we? We, too, can do anything we want! Remember . . . each of us has a part to play. Now, you must do your part.'

And with that, Sumnima turned her back and Rita felt a sudden panic rising up to her throat.

'But . . . but how will I find you again?'

'Don't worry, you don't have to find me. *I* will find *you*.'

'But how do I . . . I mean . . . how do we communicate?'

Sumnima started to walk away, her shoulders strong and squared.

'Leave a note!' she called out, 'in the wall.'

'What . . . which wall?'

'The one by the gates.'

Her back still turned, Sumnima lifted a hand in a half-wave and picked up her pace until she was jogging down to the tree line, in the direction opposite to the park entrance. Then, with a clean leap, she was over the park fence and was gone.

When Rita exited Tudikhel Park, the streets were completely empty. *What time is it?* She wondered if the curfew had started already. There had definitely been trouble on the streets. What had Gurung ji said? She dug around her tunic pocket and pulled out the piece of paper with a scribbled tree and branches. She walked up the silent street, then turned right.

Strewn across the next intersection were shattered bottles, broken bricks, someone's lost shoe and a discarded bloodied shirt. At the very centre, smoke plumed out of a large charred tire like an expended ghost. She saw an abandoned plain red bandana flung in the middle. She wondered if it belonged to a rebel or to a protestor from one of the democratic parties. How could one tell? The rebels were trying to take advantage of the instability, infiltrating protest crowds. They were, as Sumnima had said, everywhere.

Rita looked down at the scribbled paper in her hands, checking for Gurung ji's instructions and turned right again. The street curved around a bend and opened into a wide boulevard. From where she stood, at a gentle rise, Rita could see the sweeping gates of Singha Durbar at the end of the boulevard. This is where the Ranisab had grown up—once a Rana palace, now a sprawling building holding offices of the Nepal government. As she approached the great palace, the white columns on either side of the gate grew into thick colossi of carved concrete and lamp posts reared up like guards. She quickened her pace, remembering the story of the bird that one day rose in the middle of a great fire and soared into the night sky. Back at the house, Krishne, Kali and Thul didi all flapped about her. The Ranisab meanwhile railed against Gurung ji for leaving Rita behind with trouble brewing in the streets and questioned Rita about her uncle. Rita avoided the Ranisab's gaze and lied through her teeth. And through it all, the only thing Rita could think of was Sumnima. How could she ever make up for what she had done to Sumnima?

11

Murder

A week later, Rita sat on her new bed in the empty room next to the Ranisab's, propping up her pillow. Kali had helped her remove the old moth-eaten mattress and Rita had laid out her own assigned mattress upon the bare wooden slats, but the bed still looked sparse, the mattress too thin and narrow with gaps of slatted space on either side.

She had piled her new clothes on a shelf by the wall—a pair of slip-on shoes, carefully selected from an assortment of the Jarsap's daughter-in-law's hand-me-down things, a new woven sweater given to her by the Ranisab, and the pretty tunics. She had stuck the cloth bag from Aama, with the Mahendra Malla book inside, in a corner.

She thought of it now, the vestiges of a previous life. Had things really been that bad, as Sumnima said? She remembered the familiarity of the village, the rhythms of tasks from morning till evening, the freedom of running down the hills and carved out terraces, the wind in her hair. But then, for all those years, where had she been running to? She thought of the jewels, stored within the steel cabinet right next door, in the Ranisab's bedroom.

But whenever she thought of what Sumnima had asked of her, Rita felt a heaviness that weighed down her legs, clamping them to the ground.

'Krishne!' the Jarsap's voice, guttural, broke from an open window across the courtyard, 'Krishne!'

Somewhere a door banged. Why would the Jarsap be calling at this hour? Rita hurried across the room to the set of windows that faced inward to the courtyard and yanked the curtains aside. From the servant's quarters, a figure hobbled out, crossing the length of patterned brick with jerky movements. For a moment, Harke Bahadur reminded her of the small three-legged dog that had followed her the first time she set foot in Kathmandu.

And then she heard the Ranisab call.

'Go see,' her face was gaunt under the bedside lamp, 'go see. Something has happened!'

In the main house, she could hear voices. The Jarsap, throaty and confused, Krishne's pitched crescendo that sounded like a woman. And then somebody let out a shrill yowl that made her blood go cold. Bajai.

Inside the sweeping bedroom, the Jarsap was stooped over his mobile phone, gripping the instrument with bleached knuckles.

'And the queen?' Rita heard him ask.

Krishne was kneeling by the Jarsap's side, his eyes trained on the mobile phone and Bajai was bent double beside him, as if someone had just taken a swing to her stomach. Kali was pressed against a wall—a long, slackened shadow.

'The queen too,' the shock in the Jarsap's voice was blunt, a tumbling fall.

Bajai let out another yowl and staggered back. Rita could hear sounds outside the corridor and Gurung ji bounded into the room now, followed by Harke Bahadur, panting hard. Harke must have run across the whole garden to go call him.

'Hmm, hmm,' the Jarsap was grunting, his eyes squeezed shut in concentration. 'And the Princess? Yes. And the Prince too? Ok, Ok.'

At those words, Rita noticed the blood leave Krishne's face.

'Are you sure?' the Jarsap was asking now into the phone, 'Are you absolutely sure? Are you sure it was him?'

Despite his small stature, the Jarsap had a commanding voice, full of authority and privilege, but the weakness in it now made Rita fear it even more.

The Jarsap stood up and blinked.

'His Majesty, the king . . . and Her Majesty, the queen . . . Their Majesties have been . . . murdered.'

At the words, Bajai sent a high ululation straight up to the gods. Thul didi gasped and sat down with a fat thump right where she stood, taking up the entire doorway.

Rita felt the warmth drain from her face and neck, a tingling at her fingertips. She heard Sumnima's words: *we have to change things from inside out. Our people are everywhere.*

'By whom?' Thul didi was trembling, 'How? What are you saying, hajur?'

The room went silent. Then Rita heard her own voice.

'Was it the rebels?'

Their faces turned to her now, all of them pale and she could see the fear. The same fear she had felt, all those months ago, up in Rato Mato.

'No, no. Their Majesties were murdered . . . by the crown prince.'

Rita thought she had misunderstood.

'Nonsense!' Thul didi challenged the pronouncement, spittle lacing her lip. 'That cannot be. It cannot be!' There was a savagery in her words, her countenance stripped of its kindness.

'The call came from Birgunj. From the Sano Raja himself. It has come from . . . from the highest authority. The crown prince shot his family, then turned the gun on himself.'

The Jarsap seemed to shrink within himself. Without any perceptible movement, his shoulders went limp, his legs feeble, his skin sagged. He stretched out a hand, reaching, to no one in particular.

Rita remembered the crown prince's face from the photos in the school building up in Rato Mato. He had the same rounded face, the same small eyes and solid moustache as his ancestors. How could a son ever murder his own father?

'Jarsap hajur!'

Krishne, now standing next to the Jarsap, snapping them all to attention.

'Jarsap hajur, you must go to the hospital. You must go see for yourself. You must hurry, hajur. Hajur what will you . . . what will you wear?'

Krishne sprung to a wardrobe, digging his head deep inside and emerged with a bright white suit in a sheer plastic casing. 'Maybe this,' he said, quickly laying it on the bed. 'Or maybe this one,' and then he sprung back to the wardrobe, this time emerging with a woollen green. Rita recognized the thick woven leafy uniform of the Nepal Army, above its breast pocket parallel lines of squares glinting in polished bronze and dyed colour.

'Jarsap, hajur,' Krishne rushed on, 'the white is suitable for a state funeral but . . . but, if you go in white, you will be the first to acknowledge that His Majesty is no longer there. Maybe hajur, maybe you should wear military green instead. It would be respectable without being presumptive. Yes, yes, green would be good but . . .'

'Hajur Jarsap,' Rita spoke suddenly, out of turn, but the fear and indecision in the room threatened to choke her, 'should I go call the Ranisab?'

The Jarsap looked at her as if he didn't know who she was. 'What? Yes . . . In fact, yes. Bring my mother. She will know what to do.'

Rita took to her heels, her mind spinning, her heart thundering ahead.

* * *

The stick with the parrot head entered the Jarsap's bedroom first, tap-tapping against the carpeted floor.

'She has told you?'

'She has.'

The Ranisab turned to Krishne, still standing in the middle of the floor with the white suit in one hand and the green uniform in the other.

'Son,' the Ranisab's voice rang out strong. 'You are not on active duty anymore. And this is not a military matter. This is a private matter. You must dress accordingly. Krishne!' she ordered now, 'get the traditional national suit out.'

Krishne blinked—he had not thought of that alternative and for a moment, he seemed to doubt himself. Then, as if compensating for the oversight, he leapt across the room into another wardrobe and sprung back with the daura suruwal in his hands. The last time Rita had seen the Jarsap wearing it was at the dinner party. Just over three weeks ago.

'And pack the white suit as well. Take it with you. And Bajai, pack him some food and water. Gurung ji, go prepare the car!' the Ranisab commanded.

The Ranisab turned a small sweep around the room. She stopped at the doorway and reached for the doorframe, steadying herself. Rita hurried to her side and as they proceeded down the hallways, the Ranisab did not turn back once.

Television captured the aftermath of the murders. Women collapsing on to pavements, old men streaming tears. Young men with their heads freshly shorn in ritual mourning, in respect for the father they had just lost, the father the entire nation had lost.

All night, Krishne sprang back and forth between the telephone and the baithak. Gurung ji confirmed that the Jarsap was spending the early hours at the hospital. The doctors were on double duty and reinforcements had come in through the night. But nothing could be done. The Jarsap would change outfits at the hospital, wearing the white ceremonial uniform. And then Gurung ji would drive him directly to the funeral grounds.

The Jarsap's cousins who would have barely acknowledged him otherwise, now sought out Krishne. *Hajur, what should I know?* Rita heard him pause at the telephone before launching into a recapitulation of every sordid detail. In turn, Krishne never put down the receiver without finding out more. *Hajur please do tell me what you know*, he chirped, *hajur*, *hajur*. And then he came to report everything to the gathered room. This cousin said . . . that nephew heard . . . this Major claims . . . that Doctor Saheb said . . . Cousin's brother-in-law, aunt's nephew, niece's husband—Krishne knew every relationship, title and name in the sprawling repertoire of the Rana family. And he recounted for them all exactly what happened the evening before.

The royal family had all gathered at the palace for a Friday evening dinner. The evening had been very ordinary, until the crown prince came down from his apartments dressed in full military fatigue, acting drunk. He had been sent to his room to sleep off the effects and then had shortly returned, this time fully armed. He aimed first at his father.

'No man could do this to his own family, his own father, his own mother. I don't believe it,' Thul didi, sat on the carpet, shaking her head in denial. The large jovial woman Rita had known all these months looked reduced, shrunken.

'It was him,' Krishne insisted, 'the survivors have corroborated it. Definitely him.'

'For a woman? All for a woman?'

'The king and queen would not accept his choice of wife. They gave him an option. Either the woman or the throne. But the crown prince . . . he would have both. And nobody would stand in his way.'

Rita thought of the monarchy, the feudal system it headed, the system that Sumnima and the rebels wanted to bring down. But then she remembered the image of the first Shah king in her Mahendra Malla book, his index finger lifted high, jabbing the air. One country, one people. Principal sir always said that the king was a unifying force, holding them all together, like a handful of grains, from the far-flung Himals down to the deep jungles of the flat south. What would happen now that the fingers fell away, the hand went limp? Would they all fall out, grains rolling helter-skelter?

The Ranisab had said little the whole morning, but now commanded Rita: 'Take me to the telephone.' Krishne looked up, and he seemed to know something Rita didn't.

He followed Rita and the Ranisab out to the alcove under the stairs. The house telephone sat on a tall table. Krishne pulled forth a chair and then, from under a pile of carefully stacked magazines, he dug out a heavy leather-bound book. Rita leaned forward. She watched as he flipped through the pages, then pointed with one finger into the book and with the another, punched into the telephone. He looked up and caught Rita's eye. 'The queen mother,' he mouthed.

Rita stood next to the Ranisab and listened as a long line of clicks came from the other end of the receiver. Krishne, in the highest form of Nepali vocabulary, requested to be connected to the queen mother's residence. Another long line of clicks. Then, suddenly, Krishne handed the receiver over to the Ranisab. The Ranisab spoke.

'He Ram,' she said, then she asked, 'Is it true, about him?' From the other side, only silence. The Ranisab, with the receiver held close to her ear, closed her eyes and crumpled. A lone tear travelled down the craters of her face. 'He Ram!' was all she said. 'Oh God, He Ram.' And then, without another word, she put the receiver down and Rita had the urge to pick her up, gather her frail bones, grasp her small paw-like hands.

She remembered now, among the things in the Ranisab's empty rooms, one photo in particular. The Ranisab as a young woman and standing next to her, another dewy faced young woman. Rita had felt many times, looking at that photo, something familiar about the other woman, and now she knew. All these weeks, she had been looking into the face of the mother of the king.

That evening, Rita put the Ranisab to bed early. The servants gathered in front of the television. They watched in silence as the royal bodies lay upon pyres in Pashupatinath, the holiest temple in the land. Behind them spilled a landscape of temple structures, brick made lions, white stone stupas. Lined up in rows were government officials in traditional national costumes and a scatter of military uniforms in thick white brocade. Bald priests in loincloths hurried about—beneath them, the waters of the Bagmati river lapping at the stone steps.

'*Eh hut*!' a voice called and a military band started playing the national anthem in a clang of brass. Rita remembered the feeling of confluence where earth met sky, but now the anthem felt empty, a clanking echo.

At the pyres, the priests came forth with lighted flames. Suddenly, she heard a shot and flinched as a gun salute reverberated in complete silence. It struck her that the king, revered in life as a god, was an ordinary man in death. The flames consumed his body, the river waited to carry his ashes. She thought of Niraj Rai. What had they done with his body? Had his family been allowed to collect it, to wail over it, to cremate it down by the Marsyangdi or higher up at one of its tributaries? The camera zoomed in and there, filling up the whole television screen, still positioned in a sharp salute, was the Jarsap. The room took a sharp intake of air. The Jarsap's round face was creased and shining wet. His magnified eyes behind the spectacles looked into the distance. Soundlessly, he wept.

In the days that followed, the city mourned. Singular wails rose and fell through neighbourhoods, each individual sorrow mirrored in the collective. In the white house, everything came to a standstill. The kitchen, with its banging pots and Bajai's voice, shrill in command or chastisement, lay quiet. In the hallways, tabletops lay untouched, covered with thin layers of sandy dust. Out in the gardens, grasses and weeds grew free.

In the quiet, Rita roamed the many empty rooms in the Ranisab's quarters. She felt a dull ache when she thought of the dead king and the ache turned sharp whenever she thought of Sumnima. What would happen now?

Then her mind wandered to Rato Mato. The blue-roofed buildings of the district headquarters and the local police station, squat and waiting. How small and defenceless they would have looked from above, like toys ready to be plucked clean off the earth. Dhire dai had said that the rebels had been planning their attack by encircling the district headquarters from above. A shot at the district headquarters, with its village representative selected by Kathmandu, would have been a shot at the capital itself. The rebel army, hidden by the forests skirting the Dhire, would have waited before sneaking down under the cover of nightfall, surrounding the plateau of blue roofs before the sun was up and anyone sounded the alarm.

Her thoughts kept coming back to Sumnima. Someone close, Sumnima had said, had betrayed them . . . someone who knew the details exactly . . . *where, when*. And suddenly, it occurred to Rita. The two men from the health post—she had told them too much; things she never should have said. But who had told them that the rebels were planning an attack?

The next day, Rita brought the tea tray up to find the Ranisab in a contemplative mood. The old woman shook her head, 'Look, how much has been laid to waste! In this country, everyone wants to be king. One after the other, they have come and they have gone. They have taken, and then taken some more. But the day will come when . . .'

She stretched out a hand.

'Take me downstairs, I want to show you something.'

The Ranisab slowly weaved through the empty rooms, 'This here, look. This marble statue was gifted by an Indian prince. It survived the great earthquake. Toppled right down the top of a high shelf and not a scratch. And this,' she revolved around the room, stopping and examining one object after another, 'this is a gift from the crown prince of England. And this here, from the Egyptian Ambassador in New Delhi . . .'

Rita could feel a new energy, vibrating beneath the Ranisab's thin frame.

'This here, is the photo of the last Rana prime minister of Nepal, my husband. A dictator, they called him. And this here, is the deceased king's grandfather. A Shah king, the one who ended Rana rule and first brought democracy to the country. And this one here, the first democratic prime minister of Nepal. Beloved by his people. But do you know what all three had in common?'

Rita looked from the faces of the three men to the Ranisab, her bright black eyes.

'The truth is, each of these men represented institutions that ultimately, over time, only wanted one thing: power. You see, the Rana maharajahs had all the authority for a while, but they were never kings and never had the mandate of the heavens. The Shah king, meanwhile, had just returned from India, bringing democracy with him. But he was king only in name—he had no army and his reign was short-lived. And then, the prime minister. The country's first democratic prime minister was later imprisoned by the son of the very king who had first brought democracy to the country. Later, the various successors of democracy forgot their promise and devolved into squabbling over money and whose turn it was to sit on the prime minister's chair. We went from one king to many kings. Do you see?' The Ranisab put the last photo frame back down. 'Now we have the rebels and the revolution they are fighting to bring about. Do you think they will be any different?'

Rita had always thought power was a birth right for the limited few. But it was not, she saw now. It was transient. Something that could never be taken, could never be truly possessed.

'You see, history is being written every day. Each new day, we get to write our own history. Now, look at this.'

The Ranisab gently rapped the wood beneath the weight of the photo frames. Rita looked down at a thin-legged table, its surface discoloured in streaks.

'It is nothing much to look at, is it? But this table came from Singha Durbar palace. Before the great fire. Before the time of the late maharajah, and his father before that. You know how much this table has seen? How many lives, how many moments? How much it has heard? These things, Rita. They stand in corners, year after year. But they are not just things. They are *alive*. They are alive with our lives, our thoughts and deepest desires. Here, put your hand here.'

She took her hand off Rita's arm and guided it towards the table. 'You see the print that it just made? Years from now, when you and I are both gone, this table will still hold the memory of us. Nothing is lost. These things, these walls—they are made of our lives. They are made of the present, the past and the future. Do you understand?'

It seemed implausible, that this big house would remember a village girl, but standing there in that vast room, Rita felt strangely as if anything were possible. As if time itself were opening up to her, blossoming. She thought of Niraj Rai. *Just because he is a Rai, his life doesn't count?*

Four days later, with no heirs remaining, the deceased king's younger brother was crowned the new king. Rumours ran rife and angry crowds gathered in the streets. The government conducted an official investigation into the royal murder but people said it was not good enough—many said that the brother of the dead king was involved in the whole sordid affair. After all, he was the only member of the royal family not present that night at the royal dinner.

In the bhanchaghar, friction between Krishne and Gurung ji escalated to a boiling point. Krishne said that the culprit was definitely the crown prince—every surviving member of the family who was witness to the events of that night had corroborated the facts. But Gurung ji said that there were other strange events that night—the sounds of multiple helicopters hovering over the city skies that evening, the fact that the palace servants were rumoured to have seen not one but two crown princes . . . one real, the other an imposter in a mask that only looked like the crown prince. Out in the hills, the rebels staged more attacks against district headquarters across the country. The prime minister—faced with the backlash of the royal massacre and the mounting insurgency—resigned. 'Democracy in Crisis!' the newspapers headlines screamed, 'Peace Talks Now!'

A few days after the coronation, Rita slipped out of the house and headed towards the garage. There, by the gates, she studied the walls. She scanned the creepers that ran up and over, blanketing the compound walls in a thick carpet of green and searched with her fingers in thinner spots, feeling aged brick, their edges crumbling away. And then she spotted one particular spot that was balder than the rest and when she tugged, the entire brick slid out, wet with dampness and moss and a flurry of scattering silverfish. There, in the sunless gap, was a carefully folded chit of paper.

Recent events have meant a change of plans. I will be heading back to the hills, to our district. But I will be back before long. In the meantime, I know you will find your courage.

Rita found Krishne by himself in the bhanchaghar, slumped against the shelves.

'Eh, Bahuni,' he nodded when she walked in. His voice sounded deflated.

'The newspapers say this king is much tougher than his brother. They say that if there is no ceasefire, he is going to bring the fight to the rebels. Is it true?' Rita found herself worrying the end of her tunic, twisting the cloth tight around her fingers, 'What is going to happen now?'

Krishne pulled in his knees and shrugged.

'Anything is possible, Bahuni. Look, how much has happened since you came to this house. A live king. A dead king. A new king. It feels impossible, doesn't it?' Krishne closed his eyes as if in a state of reflection, but his mouth kept moving.

'I suppose that is the nature of life. Things always change. If the events of the past months have taught us anything, it is that. All this, look,' he swept a hand, 'all this one day will end. This big house, these big parties, how long can it go on for? This life, too, will end.'

'What do you mean?' Rita looked at him, his beautiful face and long, soft lashes.

'That cupboard,' Krishne pointed across the kitchen floor, 'you know what that is filled with? Alcohol. Imported with 200 per cent tax from abroad. All these parties, fuelled with five-star hotel cakes and desserts. The Jarsap is continuing to live like it is still his father's time. Where is the money coming from?'

'Where?' Rita echoed.

'Land. And jewellery. He is selling it all off. One by one. Until one day, there will be nothing left to sell. And the parties will have to stop.'

She could not imagine it, all this ending one day. The white house felt separate from life outside. Time stretched out through its hallways and spilled out into the gardens. He turned to her.

'The lands that Dhire manages up in your village. How long do you think they will last? One day, the Jarsap is going to sell those mango forests too.'

'But Dhire dai's family has managed those forests for generations!'

'They might have. But they've never owned the land. The Jarsap can sell it all at any time. The land, the forests, the mango. It can all be gone, the whole lot, just like this.' Krishne snapped his fingers.

'But what will Dhire dai do?' Rita felt a sudden rush at the indignity.

'What will any of us do, Bahuni? What will I do? What will you do?'

His eyes held hers. Then he shrugged and stood up, 'Time is a demanding agent, Bahuni. Before we know it, the future is the present, and the present is history. What is our own history to be?'

That evening, when the servants gathered in the bhanchaghar, Krishne stole in suspiciously. His shirt was untucked and he approached Gurung ji first. He winked and cleared his throat and only then did Rita notice the outlines of a bottle, pressed against his chest. A peace offering. Gurung ji reached for his cup and downed it, then tucked his chin into his neck as the cup filled with thick froth instead. At the stove, Bajai busied herself, then walked over to drain a large pot in the sink. Then she left the bhanchaghar, slamming the screen door. Krishne jumped at the opportunity. Quickly, he filled his own cup before handing Harke Bahadur and Thul didi a cup each. Then he offered some to Rita but she shook her head.

He pinched his fingers, his eyes shining, 'Only a little,' he whispered.

Bottles reminded Rita of her uncle but Krishne grabbed her cup and poured into it. Hesitantly, she touched the steel cup with her lips and the froth tickled her nose, the taste suddenly bitter. She felt her face contort and for the first time since the king's murder, there was laughter in the room. They could hear Bajai's footsteps approach from the courtyard and Krishne quickly dipped whatever remained in the bottle into Rita's cup before shoving the bottle up the front of his shirt. Then he winked at her and said out loud, 'So how does Kathmandu water taste, Bahuni?' and the room burst into laughter again.

That night, Rita felt lightheaded as she crawled into the too big bed next to the Ranisab's bedroom. She did not dream. Sometime between night and morning, she woke to a sound. Coming from somewhere overhead, an intermittent scraping. It could be mice or pigeons in the attic or other things, nameless, bumping around in the dark. She sat bolt upright and swung her legs over the slats, her entire body listening.

A thump, loud and distinct this time. *Don't be a darcherua.* She forced her mind to narrow itself to the logical. Every night before she turned in, Rita locked the door that led from the main house to the Ranisab's quarters. She was sure that she had locked the door last night. But then she remembered the bitter taste from the bottle. What if she had forgotten?

Who else would have access? The Jarsap surely had a separate set of keys. Also, there was a front entrance door to the Ranisab's quarters, but it had not been used in years. What if someone—an outsider, a thief—had managed to enter through the unused main door? Anything was possible these days. Rita had never ventured to the attic. She imagined suitcases full of statues and vases, photo frames embossed in silver. Then she thought of the Ranisab, small and frail, asleep by herself next door. She stood up, tiptoed across the carpet and opened her door a crack.

Outside, the corridor tunnelled out to the left and to the right. She considered shouting out, but what if no one heard and instead she woke the Ranisab? She focused her gaze, making out the silhouette of the staircase at the far end that led to the attic and, beyond it, the roof with its balcony. Weak light from the back window illuminated the metal railings. Rita felt stiff, every muscle readying to make a dash when suddenly, appearing at the top landing of the staircase, she saw a figure. It was bent over and seemed to be struggling, tugging at something on the floor.

Thud, something rolled over, falling down a step. A large sack. Then *thud*, it fell down another step.

Rita slipped out the door. She pressed herself against the corridor wall, barely breathing. At the stairs, the figure grunted, tugging. The sack let go, rolling all the way down the stairs and on to the corridor landing. Then the figure straightened up and leapt down after it in long smooth strides. Suddenly, Rita yelped.

The figure turned, suspended against a slat of cold blue light.

'What are you doing?' she asked out in a loud whisper.

'Bahuni? Shh!'

And then there was Krishne by her side, yanking her arm until they both sat down in the middle of the corridor, their backs against the wall.

'Before I tell you anything, you must promise!' in the semi-darkness, she could only see the whites of his eyes, 'You must promise never ever to tell anybody about this!'

'I won't,' Rita murmured 'but what are you doing? What time is it?'

'Remember what I told you earlier? That one day, all this is going to end. It can't go on, Bahuni. And when it stops, where will we go?'

'But things won't end tomorrow!'

'They will end faster than we think. If these past days have taught us anything, it is that. Look at this house. How long can it run on the fuel of the past? And what skills do you have? What skills do I have?' Krishne grunted in the dark before continuing.

'The only skill I have, Bahuni, is being a servant. And I would rather sell my soul than become a servant to a newly-minted merchant, or worse, a greasy politician. Before, in the Jarsap's father's time, loyal servants like me would have been given tracts of land. *Bakshish*, a gift. For our service. But now, what do we have? Pennies to our name.'

'What is in the sack?'

A sharp intake of breath, then Krishne was quiet.

'That isn't a sack, Bahuni.'

'Then what is it?'

'It's an old tiger pelt. Half eaten by moths. Nobody even remembers it. It was shot accidentally by the Jarsap's father. A female. He hadn't meant to shoot the female. He had meant to shoot the male but, in the confusion, up on the elephant, they hadn't realized there were two tigers in the grass that day, not one. The Jarsap told me the story himself. Nobody wanted to hang her up on the walls, and later, they forgot about her.'

'But what are you doing with it?'

Krishne sighed.

'I'm going to sell it, Bahuni. Do you know how much a tiger pelt is worth? Tiger skins are rare these days.'

Rita stared in the dark. Loyalty was a thing that could be measured, and now it was running short.

'What I have been asking myself is, is it stealing if people have forgotten the thing stolen? If they never wanted it in the first place?'

Rita thought of Dhire dai. Imagined him being turned out of the land his family had guarded for generations. Loyalty was running short with him too. She felt it hit her like a wave, the tenuousness of it all. And suddenly, she thought of Sumnima: *You will never belong to that house.*

They sat there in silence, side by side.

'I understand that we all must do what we must,' she said finally. Then she stood up, entered her room and shut the door. She waited behind it, listening to Krishne roll the pelt down the stairway to the hallway below. Who was he going to sell it to? But she didn't care. A shuffle sounded along the distant marble, then faded away.

12

The Jewel

(*Sharad Ritu*, Early Autumn, 2001)

Early autumn came and the winds started to pick up again. Up in Rato Mato, Rita and Sumnima would fly kites this time of the year. Sumnima always battled hungrily, expertly tugging at her roll of string at the precise moment, slicing through the string of the other kite. Then Rita would race after the floating kite that had lost, catching it mid-air and raising it high above her head as a prize. Sumnima won every time.

The Jarsap emerged, after many weeks of mourning, and made an announcement. What had happened was unforgettable and traumatic for the entire nation. But the time had now come for the nation and the white house to move on. Next month, the white house was going to host a dinner. 'Something small to start with,' he said, 'family and close acquaintances only.' Once again, the silver was brought out to polish and every forgotten corner was dusted. But while the white house took on a hectic, harried air, somehow things felt changed, as if the house itself knew what had come to pass.

In the gardens, Rita moved her mouth to words by Lekhnath Paudyal, this time a poem titled 'The Himal'. But in her heart, she felt a flutter of trepidation about things unknown, swirling and unsettled.

A scarf of pure white snow
Hangs down from her head to her feet,
Cascades like strings of pearls
Glisten upon her breast . . .

Beyond the boughs of the trees overhead, she could see them now, suspended between earth and sky—the Himals. These same Himals would be watching Sumnima, up in the hills. What was she doing? She had said she would be back soon. All these many weeks Rita had kept checking the walls but there had been no message, no sign of a return. *Where was Sumnima?*

For ages past she has watched over Creation,
And now she stands smiling, an enlightened ascetic,
Our blessed Himalaya.

The Ranisab dozed in her chair, the carved parrot nestled face-down in the folds of her shawl and Rita put the book down, flitting instead through the week's papers, freshly arrived. The headlines shouted out, 'Where Are We Headed?', then 'Peace at Last?' and finally, 'Rebels Agree to Ceasefire.' Rita felt her chest squeeze and then let go, a great gulp of air rushing in, entering the very pit of her belly. Around her, a breeze played at her hair, her tunic. But just as she flitted through the pile of papers at her feet, a sudden gust sent the whole stack fluttering with a thin scrappy weekly rolling out into the grass. Rita leapt up and chased it down a few paces before pinning it with a stamp of her foot. And there, below the paper title of the *Spectator* was the very first article: 'Women's Jail Break.'

The women's district prison in Tanahu district has seen a major jailbreak with up to twenty prisoners escaping the prison overnight. An undertaking of exceptional daring and fortitude, the convicts dug under the prison construct itself. Police officers were alerted by locals after a large hole appeared in the neighbouring field the morning after the escape. The suspects remain at large and are believed to include multiple female cadres of the Revolutionary Liberation Army.

Rita heard a pulsing sound in her ears and around her, the wind gathered itself, slapping the *Spectator* flat to her belly so that she had to pry it off to read the article again. *An undertaking of exceptional daring and fortitude.*

Standing there, with the world starting to whip about her, thinking that she should take the Ranisab back inside, Rita remembered her dream. She felt again the *thing*. She felt its clawing against earth, its digging through the darkness, ripping towards the light. And Rita had the vague notion that in her dream, it was *this* hole she had seen. This hole she had just read about. It was as if she had known of its existence all along. As if she had been down there herself, deep inside its walls of soundless night.

In the next few days, Rita forgot to screw back the cap on the bottle and spilled a dollop of thick massage oil on to the Ranisab's carpet. She forgot the Ranisab's medication. She misplaced the Ranisab's favourite khasto wrap and found it later in Kali's wash pile. Once she caught the old woman watching her, the stick with the parrot head by her side, his curved beak jutting out in unspoken reproach. She found a quick excuse to run out of the room and catch her breath outside in the corridor.

In the gardens of the white house, Harke Bahadur's marigolds came into full bloom, the yellow and orange buds synchronizing their dazzling arrival. And yet, Rita was starting to see things that had not been apparent to her before. The creepers that ran up the garage walls circled the whole compound, thick and lush but holding, hidden underneath, crumbling brick. The skirting that looped around the house, once swollen with monsoon dampness, now sagged, cracked at the seams and peeling.

Inside, she saw all the things that Kali only ever dusted before a party. She saw the places where things had chipped or rusted or lost their shine. She wondered how much Krishne had gotten for the tigress' moth-eaten pelt. She looked at the wealth laid to waste around her, the extravagant preparations for yet another dinner party and thought of Aama and Kaaki up in Rato Mato. Their tenuous existence, beholden to someone else's whims and the weather. Then she thought of Dhire dai, his aged baggy knees and bare feet dappled in forest shadow. What would he do if the Jarsap decided to sell all the land—to sell the entire hill? Dhire dai had no claim. None of them did.

A few days later, Rita entered the Ranisab's chambers to find it empty. The Ranisab was in the prayer room.

'Eh Rita,' she called, 'come here. Tell Harke to bring me some marigolds, the best flower heads he can find. *Aiaa*,' she reached out to grab Rita's arm, handing over the parrot walking stick, then steadied herself before painfully sinking into a cushion seat.

'If we weren't growing so many of them right here in our gardens, we would be importing them up from the hills, wouldn't we?' the Ranisab was smiling but Rita looked at her blankly and blinked. Then she remembered the newspaper article about villages run entirely by women, exporting marigolds to Kathmandu for a living. And it struck her, that entire livelihoods were being measured by a week's worth of blooms.

Rita fetched the copper jug with clean water, hollered out from the courtyard for Harke to bring the flowers, arranged the sweet-smelling incense sticks for the Ranisab's prayers. With everything prepared, she shut the door of the prayer room leaving the Ranisab and the parrot-headed stick inside and stepped into the empty bedchamber.

The keys were where she expected them to be, on the bedside table, together with the Ranisab's medication and a half empty glass of water. On the other side of the room, the steel safe stood waiting, a wintry greenish grey. The bunched keys felt fat and heavy under her fingers.

Her fingertips brushed against the table surface and momentarily, she felt her hand withdraw. How could she do this? Around her, many eyes were watching—the Lord Brahman, Naaga the serpent god, a winged Garuda, the all-seeing lotus of Goddess Saraswati. But then another instinct—sharper and deeper—prodded at her. *Don't be a darcherua*. She had to do this for Sumnima. This would be her own act of daring, her own assertion.

Rita knew exactly which box to take. The black one, at the very bottom. Inside its velvet inlays—a necklace, bracelet, and a ring studded with bright blue stones. Sapphire. An unlucky stone for her horoscope, the Ranisab had said. As she put the box back, snug in its place, and locked the safe door, Rita thought not of Sumnima, but of Aama. For a fleeting moment, Rita missed her. She saw her mother now, lowering the doko slowly against the mud-swept porch, taking her time to painfully unfold her own body. All her life, Aama wordlessly waited out the whims of these very gods that watched her now. She had just placed the keys back on the bedside table when she heard a sharp rap at the door. She leapt to open it, her heart in her throat, only to find Harke Bahadur outside, his hands full of bright marigolds.

Over the next few days, Rita went about her duties as she always did. But there was a heaviness that accompanied her and she found that she could not look at the Ranisab's face. She avoided the parrot on his stick. She slept lightly, waking to the smallest sound. Once, in the middle of the day, she heard the Ranisab call out to her from her bedroom but when she entered the room, she found it empty, then remembered that she had left the Ranisab out in the garden. As she made her way swiftly back downstairs, it was as if there were eyes watching her go—the hung pictures, the white walls, the windowpanes and carved chairs, the house itself.

In the outer wall, she left a message with the day of the week and time. By the next Saturday, when the bell at the gates rang, she was ready. Rita ran to the sound before anybody else could get to it, the jewel bumping against her thigh deep in her tunic pocket. She had wrapped it in a piece of cotton, then folded it into an old shred of newspaper. Underneath the gate, she could see two pairs of shoes covered in dust. Two boys stood in low hanging baseball caps. Quickly, Rita moved along the compound wall and in between knotted vine, yanked out the loose brick. On the other side, one of the boys copied her movements and she could see his zippered jacket, similar to the one Sumnima had worn, through the hole. She pulled the carefully folded newspaper out of her pocket and shoved it into the hole before putting the brick back in its place. The boy whispered, 'You have done well, bahini.' But it was not a voice she recognized.

That evening, Rita was brisk with her duties for the Ranisab. She cleared the dinner tray, ministered a handful of coloured medicines, unwound and brushed through strings of greyed hair and then kneeled beside the bed, oil in hand, the Ranisab's thin-veined legs stretched before her. Just as she bent to start the massage routine, the Ranisab said,

'Something is bothering you.'

Rita felt herself twitch.

'I am ok, hajur.'

'Something has been bothering you since you came back from that hospital trip.'

'Hajur,' Rita nodded, her eyes carefully averted, 'everything is fine. It's just . . . a lot has happened recently.'

'And there is nothing else?'

'Nothing else, hajur.'

'You know, Rita, I have lived a long time. The one thing I have learned is that it is better not to carry around things you don't need. Things that don't serve you. Thoughts, you know, have their own weight. Some are heavy enough to bury you. It is important to remember that even the heaviest ones are just that. Thoughts.'

Rita felt the colour rise to her cheeks but did not look up.

She tucked the Ranisab into the layered sheets and left the room, walking past the gods and goddesses up on the walls. Each in a different pose, each a unique expression of something larger. As she passed through the door,

Rita's mind went back to Aama. Except for the story of Sumnima's birth, there was not a single thing Aama fought against. It made her angry now, the easy excuse of fate that painted over everything with a false neutrality that Aama simply suffered through. At least, Sumnima acted. And now, so had she.

The next morning, voices rose and fell through the white house, a high-toned volley emanating from the baithak.

'Bastards!' the Jarsap hollered, 'What is our government doing? The incompetent fools! Not a damn thing they can do! Even the Americans are calling these godless rebels terrorists, and what are our politicians doing about it?'

'Yes, hajur,' Rita heard Krishne's voice whinny in agreement, 'Not even one thing they can do!'

Krishne held on to the tail of the conversation and brought it into the bhanchaghar.

'Another attack,' he announced, 'up in the north.'

'What?' Rita put down the teacup she was holding with a rattle.

'The rebels. They have attacked a police post *and* an army barracks.'

Rita felt a prickle run up her spine.

'But I thought . . . the newspapers were talking about a ceasefire!'

'And you believed them? You seriously believed the rebels would lay down their arms?'

What had Sumnima said? That the fight was only just beginning. That the fight would be brought here, to Kathmandu.

'At least,' Krishne dropped his voice, 'now, because of this attack, our useless politicians will *have* to act. They will have no choice. There is a rumour that an ordinance will be passed. The new prime minister will call for a state of emergency. And finally, the king will release the army!'

'But what . . . what does that mean?' Rita felt a catch in her throat.

'It means, this country is finally going to be fighting the rebels not only with our police force like it has done so far, but with the national army itself. We are entering a dangerous period now, Bahuni. A civil war. The army is going to rake through this whole country. They are going to wipe out the rebels, every last one of them. And god help all those who have harboured and aided the rebels, or associated with their cause. Nobody is going to be safe. Not in the city. And not in the villages.'

In the hallway, Rita struggled to catch her breath. Her feet moved of their own accord, echoing down the lengths of marble.

Outside, the gardens were empty. She found the farthest tree and curled up in the foetal position against it. What would happen to Sumnima? What would happen to Aama and Kaaki and Neelam didi? Her mind volleyed to Dhire dai. What if someone had seen and reported them? Dhire dai, smuggling Rita, a close associate of Sumnima, a proven rebel, out of the village. Would the army go after him? Would they go after Aama and Kaaki? Rita gasped for air, the world around her tipping and spinning out of control.

In front of her, above the roof of the white house, something caught her eye. An oblong piece of paper. Thin and green, leaf-like, swaying in currents as it slowly approached the ground. The kite had the same kind of tail that Sumnima and Rita would make as children. Scraps of old newspaper, twisted at carefully measured points to give the kite the right kind of weight and steady it against the strongest of gusts. A poor child's kite.

It hovered before her, suspended in the air. And then a strange thought came to her. She saw Sumnima, in the middle of Tudikhel Park, standing with a kite wheel in her hands, a length of string caught taut. Sending a kite, this kite, all the way here, to her. A spark of memory, a thread of belonging, a link that needed no words but stretched forward like a shared dream. The kite dipped, bowed, ripped forward right towards her and flew straight into the tree overhead. The sudden rustle of leaves made Rita jump up to her feet.

Rita left her slippers side by side, at the base of the trunk. The bark was rough but somehow familiar under her skin. The kite was stuck right at the top. Branch by branch, Rita crouched and stretched, not knowing what exactly was propelling her but it was there, an urge to grasp and hold still the world around her.

The higher up she went, the thinner the branches got, the further apart they twisted and spread. She climbed along a thick fork but at its highest point, Rita saw that she would have to swing herself on to a separate vein, a thinner one that held the kite. She stood up slowly and reached but the branch was too far away. She wiped her damp hand against her tunic, grasped tight on to the branch she was still on and stretched her free hand as far as it would go. She was now only a few centimetres shy.

Rita knew what she had to do. She had seen Sumnima do it many times before. She started swinging the branch she was on, pushing hard with her feet and letting go, swaying back and forth until when she reached again, she touched bark. The next swing, she was able to wrap her fingers fully around the branch. She gripped with all her strength and suddenly, her body splayed open, the branch she was standing on retreating quickly back. In a split second, it occurred to her that she would have to let go and leap on to the branch that held the kite. She felt the brush of breeze against her face. Just before she jumped, she heard the walloping of her heart, the sounds of the kite's tail, briskly fluttering.

* * *

When Rita opened her eyes, it was to a man's face hovering over her. Thin and aged but soft, lined with thick hair. For an instant, she thought of Dhire dai. The man leaned back and she knew she had seen him before. Pain came stabbing now, shooting up her elbow, down her side, right down to her knees. Rita realized that she was propped on her back in a small cool room—the room she had shared with Kali when she first arrived at the white house.

'What do you suggest, Dr Parajuli?' a voice came from the doorway.

Rita ran her eyes along the length of the room and saw the Ranisab sat on a stool by the open doorway, one hand extended out, grasping her walking stick. Her brows were knitted together, her face pained in concentration. Next to her stood Kali, her bright orange tunic a loud contrast against her dark skin.

The man beside Rita made a movement and Rita saw that he had lowered his stethoscope round his neck.

'Nothing is needed for now. The painkillers will leave her groggy for the whole day. We will have to X-ray that arm. I will fix an appointment.'

Rita reached for her throbbing elbow.

'No!' Dr Parajuli swivelled around and gently pinned down her arm. 'Don't touch it. Best not to move it at all.'

He was looking down at her quizzically.

'What is a grown girl your age doing climbing a tree?'

Rita winced, her mind blank.

'You are lucky, you know. A few bruised ribs, a sprained arm and a big bump on the head. It could have been much worse. I don't think you have anything broken. But you could have. We will have to check.'

Rita felt her hand shoot up to her head but Dr Parajuli batted it away too.

'What did I just say?'

'Dr Parajuli cleaned that cut,' it was Kali, talking suddenly, out of turn, 'There was so much blood, aabii!'

'Enough!' Dr Parajuli was admonishing Kali now, 'There is no need to frighten the patient. The bump is big but the cut was small. I have applied some strong creams and left some medicines. The swelling will be gone by tomorrow.'

Rita made a move to sit up and Dr Parajuli motioned for Kali. Together, they lifted her into a seated position.

'Here,' he reached into a plastic bag and brought out three multicoloured packets. 'You must take these. This one, two times a day with food. And this one, first thing in the morning and this one, at night before you go to sleep. Do you understand?' And then, turning to Kali, 'Make sure she takes them.'

Rita felt herself nod, the movement painful, and looked down, examining the bandage around her arm, feeling the dull compression on the side of her head.

Dr Parajuli stood up and collected a large leather satchel by the foot of the bed.

'No more climbing trees for you!' He wagged his finger before turning around.

'Aabii!' Kali could not contain herself, 'She was climbing that tree just like a monkey! A langur in a forest!'

And suddenly, the room filled with guffaws. The Ranisab's small face opened and she laughed until she was reduced to tears. Rita felt her cheeks grow hot. She remembered now the tree, the kite that came right up to her, the roughness of bark. But what had she been thinking, climbing to retrieve it?

'Go, Kali,' the Ranisab said, 'go give Dr Parajuli some tea in the main house before he has to leave.'

The Ranisab remained, seated in her chair, the parrot's carved face hidden deep in the folds of her sari, as if he, too, were spent with laughter.

'Hajur . . .' Rita started, but the Ranisab shook her head.

'Don't talk, don't make too much effort.'

The Ranisab was silent for a while, watching. Rita wondered if she had ever been down here before, in the servants' quarters.

'When Harke found you, he came running as fast as he could. Poor thing. No one could understand what he was saying or where he was pointing to. Finally, Krishne and Kali followed him out to the garden. And you know, when I saw that kite, you know what I realized? That you are still a child. By the time I was your age, I was married and with child already. And yet here you are, still chasing kites.'

That is what Aama would say to them, to Sumnima in particular. Aama would have scolded her and twisted her ear and then spent the whole night hovering over her. Rita bit her lip, trying to control herself in front of the Ranisab.

'But hajur,' her voice cracked, 'how did you see the kite?'

The Ranisab laughed, a soft chuckle, then unveiled a hand and pointed. There, propped against the set of drawers, was the green kite, its twisted tail limp against the cool tiled floor.

'They found you flat on the ground with the kite in your hands. You must have made it right to the top before you fell.'

For the next two days, Rita moved between her bedroom and the bhanchaghar slowly, her entire body a bruised and aching bundle, a thick wad of bandage around her left arm. Kali made sure that she was well-fed. Bajai grudgingly made Rita a special jaulo meal and Horlicks, Kali standing by the door and blocking out the light until she finished. Kali hounded her about the medicines, asking two, three times whether she had taken the right ones. At night, she slept in Kali's room, in her old bed, while Kali took her mattress upstairs and laid it on the floor in the empty room next to the Ranisab's.

On the morning of the fourth day, Kali hovered at the bedroom door.

'Do you think you can read?'

Rita nodded. The throbbing in her head had subsided, her jaw felt stiff but workable. Then Kali disappeared and came back with a stack of newspapers.

'Here,' she said, 'these are fresh, just came in new. She's waiting for you.'

In the Ranisab's chambers, Rita sifted through the papers. 'The New Prime Minister's Gamble,' a title in the *Nepal Sunrise* read, 'Rebels Call for Constitutional Reform,' another shouted out, 'Power Play,' said a third. And then, the most recent one: 'State of Emergency Announced.'

Rita felt a vague pounding at her temples and had the sudden urge to shred them all. To lift every single paper and tear it apart. On her chair, the Ranisab was twirling the parrot about, the slick black stick spinning, the bird flitting in a dizzy whirl. Rita peeled her eyes away from the headlines and instead focused on the various advertisements jumping out at her in garish colour.

'Kathmandu Nursing International,' she read down a dented side column, 'now established with the affiliation of Bir Hospital. Offering three-year Proficiency Certificate Level (PCL) nursing program with 50 seats per batch.' Rita stopped and swallowed. Her throat was so dry, it itched. She considered asking the Ranisab if she could go get a drink of water when a large figure appeared, filling the doorway.

'Ranisab hajur,' Kali spoke, 'Krishne asked me to pass you a message. Dr Parajuli is ready for the X-ray on Sunday morning.' Rita felt a small apprehension rise. She didn't know what an X-ray was. She imagined a stab of pain and her blood went cold.

The Ranisab blinked, the parrot momentarily catching himself. 'Good. Ok, that's enough for today, Rita. Go rest.'

Kali accompanied her downstairs and left her in the courtyard, but Rita did not return to her room in the servants' quarters. Instead, she headed for the slip between the white walls, passing through the archway that led out to the gardens.

From a distance, Rita assessed the height of the tree. The tree was large, one of the largest in the garden. Cautiously, she approached it. She stood under its extended branches, staring up at the veins that thinned and scattered into the sky. How had she done it? How had she done what she had never done before and only Sumnima could do? The only way she could have had the kite in her hands was if she plucked it clean from the very top.

She lingered, and then slowly made her way to the car park. The Jarsap's jeep was in the garage. Above it, the sound of the radio percolated down an open window from Gurung ji's quarters. Rita passed the gate and walked along the compound wall, studying the growth of vines until she found the loosened brick. She tugged at it, firmly, instinctively. Rita looked up, making sure Gurung ji was not at his window and pulled out the note, neatly folded and waiting for her.

Meet me by the peepal tree in front of the house. Saturday at 1 p.m.

On Saturday, Rita slipped out of the house exactly ten minutes before 1 o'clock. The Ranisab had just settled in for her afternoon nap, as had the rest of the household and Rita had taken her time in the bhanchaghar, clearing her plate until she was the last one left. She crossed the grass, checking over her shoulder. The garage was shuttered, the parking lot quiet, Gurung ji had left to visit his family. She reached up and struggled with the half-moon gate clasp, manoeuvring it with her good hand while her whole body groaned in pain. Then she squeezed through the gap in the metal and crossed the empty field, keeping away from the road.

At the very end, where the road diverged in two, stood the peepal tree, surrounded by a small brick ledge and a clean circle of earth. Someone had tied a red prayer flag around the widest part of its trunk and applied an offering of red and yellow flowers. Neelam didi had once explained to her that a peepal tree was a living passage to the world of the spirits. A peepal tree never lost all of its leaves—when one fell, another grew elsewhere in its place. It birthed and rebirthed, perpetually carrying on the cycle of life.

Rita sat on the brick ledge and waited, her bandaged arm jutting out and set awkwardly on her lap. Sumnima came without a sound. She simply appeared and squatted under the tree. But this time, an arm's length away from Rita.

Rita turned to look at her, wincing from the pain caused by the movement. Sumnima wore the same jacket, cap and canvas shoes as the last time she had seen her, but something about her was changed. The jacket was looser against the nape of her neck, as if hollowed out and filled with nothing but air. The cap was pulled low over her head, shading her eyes and her hands were stuck deep inside her pockets.

Sumnima spoke first.

'What happened?'

'A fall.'

'From where?'

'A tree.'

Sumnima snorted, her voice dry.

'Is that the truth?'

'It's the truth. I fell.'

Sumnima looked down and seemed to contemplate her cloth sneakers, dirtier than before and frayed at the toes. But with the cap shading half her face, it was difficult to really tell.

'What were you after? Fruit?'

'A kite. It was stuck at the very top,' Rita offered, a glimmer of expectation.

Rita thought Sumnima would laugh out loud or slap her knee. But she did neither.

Instead, she said, 'We found a buyer. He paid handsomely. All the proceeds have already been disbursed to the cause.' She cleared her throat.

Rita felt a snap of irritation.

'You mean to the pockets of your leaders?'

'The proceeds will sustain many fighters. A single jewel is worth a month of food.'

Rita opened her mouth for another retort but decided against it. Sumnima shifted her weight from one leg to another. Her boy's jacket rustled, her hands dug deep and searched inside the pockets. It disturbed Rita, that she could not see Sumnima's eyes.

'The papers were talking about a peace deal. There was hope. And then, your leaders, they went and broke everything with that attack, didn't they?'

'Like I said before, the war is only just starting. The peace deal was just an excuse. The army will now be released. We will be facing a new enemy in the battlefield.'

'What will you do?'

Sumnima shrugged her shoulders, more angled than before.

'Exactly what I am doing right now.'

'You will continue to fight?'

Sumnima kept looking down at her laced canvas shoes, her face averted.

'Tell me one thing,' Sumnima changed the topic again. 'The son of the big house, the one posted in Birgunj, responsible for the southern front. When is he coming to Kathmandu next?'

In her mind, Rita saw the Jarsap's son, his broad, square shoulders, the way he looked at her the night of the last king's dinner all those months ago.

'Why are you asking?'

'We need to know things about our enemy. Who is moving, when, from where to where. What roads they take. Who do they travel with. How many guards, bodyguards. No detail is too small.'

A sudden gust blew and low-hanging clouds scuttled along swiftly over the empty land ahead.

'Why do you need to know all that?'

'Like I said, the army is going to be released. And we need to keep precise tabs on our enemy. We need names, numbers, minutes and seconds. Everything counts. The only way to be one step ahead of the enemy is to know what they are going to do next.'

Inside herself, Rita could feel something growing now. Something hot and heavy, churning.

'This is *different*, don't you understand?' Rita scampered up to a kneeling position, her arm twisting in pain, her voice rising to a cracking whine, 'The army is going to rake through the entire country. They will leave no stone unturned. Lots of people are going to get *killed*!'

But Sumnima did not move a muscle.

'There are always casualties in any struggle. Some of them innocent. But the struggle must go on.'

Her tone was mechanical, flat. It reminded Rita of the times Sumnima would memorize the Mahendra Malla before the exams. Line by line, repeating after her. But if Rita asked her a question a week later, Sumnima could not recall a thing.

'But this is the *army* we are talking about! The rebels can never win against the army!'

'Do you think we are not prepared to fight against the army?'

Rita stared at her.

'How can you be so selfish?' she felt herself suddenly spitting out. 'You think of nothing, nobody, but yourself!'

Sumnima swivelled around, her eyes just visible below the shade of the cap, rounded and black. In them, something Rita had never seen before, but what was it? Beneath her eyes, blue half-moons dripped down like bruises to her cheekbones, even more pronounced than before. Rita took a sudden intake of breath.

'*I* am selfish?' Sumnima's voice lashed, 'You think I am *selfish*? Do you know where I have been while you were sitting comfortably in your big house in Kathmandu?'

Rita blinked.

'I have been fighting for *freedom*! With nothing but my bare hands. You know what they did to me? They threw me in prison. That's what they did. No struggle comes without sacrifice! I dug myself out, with my own fingers.'

She motioned, her hands straining against the fabric of her jacket pockets but as yet, hidden deep within them.

Rita felt the blood rise now, throbbing up to her cheek bones.

'You were in prison? I . . . I read about it. The prison escape. That was you?'

She remembered now, the hole, the *thing* inside. Dhire dai's words, the way he had spelled them out. *She is alive*.

Sumnima exhaled, turning her face away, to the plain field ahead. And all of a sudden, she seemed to deflate, as if the wind that filled the contours of her jacket was being sucked right out.

'Yes, it was me,' she said, almost a whisper.

'But how did it happen? How did they catch you?'

A shiver had taken hold of Rita's body and she could feel every part of her tremble. Sumnima was the strongest person she had ever known. There was a physicality to her, a vitality of conviction, an enormity of will. She would have known all the hills and valleys of their district, every ravine and each hidden pass. How had she managed to get caught?

'I got caught . . . because of my own mistake.'

'This whole thing is a mistake! What you are doing is a mistake! You could have gotten killed! You still can get killed!' Rita's voice was climbing, turning into a high whine. 'You . . . you don't have to do this.'

'I do, *we* do, because we *must*. We must do this for our own survival, do you hear me? And we will prevail. We *will* prevail! All the sacrifice is worth it. All of it.'

Rita felt her eyes start to prickle, her voice finally crack. 'I miss the way things used to be,' she said. She would give anything to change this topic, this reality.

'The way things used to be,' Sumnima said, her voice sounding tired, 'was never sustainable.'

Then slowly, almost carefully, Sumnima stood up.

'I am counting on you,' she nodded beneath the shaded cap, 'You did well with the jewel. And I know you will do well with this next task too. Report back to me everything you hear. Remember, no detail is too small.'

And without another word, she was gone.

* * *

By Sunday, the streets were open but traffic was sparse. Gurung ji was careful to drive only along the largest avenues. In front of the hospital, a heavily pregnant woman was being slowly led in by an older man who held her firmly by the arm.

'Follow me,' Gurung ji said and strode inside.

Rita entered a tiled network of elongated hallways and everywhere, there seemed to be people. Some stood, some squatted on the floor. Small clusters gathered in corners, speaking in serious tones. On a bench, a man stretched out asleep, his belly protruding from a shirt buttoned halfway. From down one corridor, she heard a long loud moan. She quickened her pace.

Gurung ji turned and she followed him down a long corridor until at the end, they came to an open door and inside, bright lights and the whirring play of shadows.

'Welcome!' Dr Parajuli waved her in and pointed to a chair. He did not smile, but his eyes were soft. On the ceiling, a fan whipped by, its blades reminding her of the helicopter she had seen up on the Dhire. It moved so slowly that she wondered why it was there at all.

Dr Parajuli told Gurung ji to wait outside and shut the door behind him. Then he sat on his chair behind a wide wooden desk.

'Ok,' he said promptly, 'let us begin. Tell me some of your details. Full name. Age. Have you had any medical issues before?'

Rita watched with a mixture of apprehension and awe as he flicked his wrist and scribbled into a notepad. Her answers came in monosyllables, and he seemed to be writing more than she was saying.

'Nurse!' he called out suddenly.

Rita felt her apprehension rise.

'Doctor sahib, what will happen to me?'

Dr Parajuli looked up, his pen suspended mid-air. He did not come from the same upper echelons of Kathmandu society as the Ranas did, she knew, but still he was an important man. Someone who was not questioned very often.

'You will be taken to an X-ray machine in a special room. You will be placed in front of the machine. Then, the X-ray machine will take a picture of your arm. After it is done, the nurse will come to collect you again.'

'Nurse!' he called out again.

'The machine will take a picture of my arm?'

'No, the machine will take a picture of the bones inside your arm. The picture will determine whether you have any damage to your bones.'

Dr Parajuli went back to his notepad.

'Why do I have to be by myself in the room?'

'Because the X-rays can be harmful if exposed too many times.'

'But it won't be harmful to me?'

'Not if you're not exposed too many times.'

'But how can the machine take a picture of what is inside my arm?'

Dr Parajuli put down the pen.

'Do you always ask so many questions?'

Rita felt herself blush. She knew she should not be asking so many questions of this important man, but somehow, under the slow beat of the fan in this white tiled space, it seemed permissible.

Suddenly, a door at the back of the room opened and a woman stepped in. Dressed in a pale sari with a white apron, she wore a pair of green plastics over her shoes and her hair was also tucked tightly under a green plastic cap.

'This way, nani,' she said, using the endearing word to address Rita. The woman's arms were bare and smooth, her eyes neither young nor old. She carried an air of efficiency. Rita followed her out, down the corridor and they stopped outside a door. The nurse rapped a quick staccato knock and then, waving at Rita to join her, sat on a bench outside the door.

'Your turn will be next,' she said.

They sat a while in silence and then the nurse turned to her.

'How long have you had the bandage for?'

'A week.'

'Was it a fall?'

'Yes,' Rita responded but stopped short of telling the nurse she had fallen out of a tree.

'Will the X-ray hurt?'

'Not at all,' the nurse smiled briefly, and suddenly under the halo of the green plastic cap, she looked like a younger woman.

'There is nothing to worry about. Out of all the procedures we do here, X-rays are the ones that hurt the least. In fact, you don't feel anything at all.'

'Oh,' Rita nodded, 'during those other procedures, it must not be easy to see patients in pain.'

'Well,' the nurse shrugged, 'one gets used to it.'

'Have you been a nurse for long, didi?'

'More than ten years.'

'That's a long time,' Rita sniffed. 'You must really like helping people to do this job for so long.'

The nurse smiled.

'Partly. And partly because the world will always need nurses. It's a sure employment. Both my jobs are sure employments.'

'Both your jobs?'

'Yes, between shifts I am also a tuition teacher.'

Rita's eyes widened. Except for the NGO health workers up at the health post in Rato Mato, and the straggle of teachers at her school, she had known very few women with actual skilled and paid employment. And now this woman here had two.

The door in front of them sprung open. A young man hobbled out, one leg of his pants rolled up halfway, a sliver of bandage peeking out above his knee. Slowly, he shuffled down the corridor.

'Come,' the nurse was up on her feet, 'your turn now.'

The room was long and sparse. The nurse took her to a metal table on the far end and Rita watched as she expertly unwound her bandage and stretched out her arm, placing it against a thin metal sheet. Rita was shocked to see how thin her arm had become in only a few days of being wrapped in tight gauze, the skin a shade of milk.

'Don't worry,' as if reading Rita's thoughts, 'it won't hurt, I promise.' Then the nurse disappeared behind the door, calling for Rita to hold still. From somewhere came a loud cranking noise and Rita braced herself. Nothing happened. And a few minutes later, the nurse was back in the room.

'You see? It didn't hurt at all did it?'

Rita blinked confusedly. She hadn't in fact felt a thing.

The nurse took Rita back to Dr Parajuli's office and was told to wait outside. She sat on a chair and thought of the time Kaaki had sliced her palm with a sickle. The gash seemed to shed a limitless amount of blood and they had taken her down to the health post. Rita recalled a single room, with a long line of people waiting outside and a tired healthcare worker had taken one look at all the blood and ushered Kaaki to the front of the line. Kaaki's hand was cleaned and bandaged. Later, Rita kept the used bandage and practiced it on Sumnima's arm, Sumnima wincing every time she brought the safety pin out.

After a while, Dr Parajuli opened his door.

'Here, look,' he handed her a thick sheet of plastic. It was smooth and black and heavy to the touch.

'Lift it to the light.'

Rita lifted the sheet.

'Make it flat,' Dr Parajuli said, 'against the light.'

And suddenly, she saw them. The long ghostly white of bone, the smaller bones at the end that shaped into digits and spread out into fingers. A small sound escaped her mouth.

Dr Parajuli broke into a laugh that made Rita jump. Rita had not thought him a man capable of laughter. Then he looked at her.

'It's amazing, isn't it? That is exactly why I decided to become a doctor. Because of how amazing it is. *Achamma*!'

Rita looked at him and nodded in agreement. It felt to her that being a doctor must feel as close to the gods as being a king. And being a nurse, like the woman who had taken her to the X-ray room, was only one step removed. A rush of strange excitement flushed through her body and on the drive back to the white house, she felt giddy at the prospect of possibility. A different kind of possibility, one that opened up and offered itself only through true expertise and service. *Achamma*, she silently played the word over and over.

It was evening by the time they got back. The compound was steeped in darkness, none of the outdoor lights switched on, and Rita wondered why. Harke was waiting for them, a shadow sprung amongst the bushes and he ushered them with flapping arms towards the house.

The hallways were barely lit, dim faces floating high up on the walls, and the baithak door was left open. Inside, the whole household seemed to have gathered in a tight, little circle. All the servants were there and the Jarsap was seated behind his desk, only his desk lamp on. Lamplight bounced off a stack of white glossed paper on the desk, the Jarsap's spectacles, a gold-tipped pen and three slender boxes, stacked one on top of the other. The Ranisab's jewellery boxes. Rita felt her heart stop, her body drain.

The Jarsap's face was ashen as he spoke.

'I have called you all here,' he announced but the command in it was somehow punctured, 'because I have made the most unfortunate discovery.'

He now pointed his spectacles at the stack of boxes.

'This morning, I had reason to take these boxes out and here,' he reached for the box at the very bottom, the black one, 'and I discovered . . .' The Jarsap stopped mid-sentence. His face took on a deeper shade. 'I discovered . . .' he opened the box with a sudden impatience, 'I discovered a ring missing. A very valuable ring.'

A sharp inhale from the gathered group of servants. Rita's stomach fell.

There, in satin inlay, was the set of beaten white gold necklace and bracelet, and above it, the empty tray where the blue sapphire ring had lain.

Nobody said a thing. Rita remembered Krishne's words. One by one he was selling them all. That was how the Jarsap was sustaining the house, the household, the dinner parties.

'There is no way the ring could have left the box by itself and little chance it had fallen out accidentally,' the Jarsap continued, 'but still, to be sure, Krishne, in my presence, combed the entire room.'

The Jarsap stopped now. He took three deep breaths, then sat back in his chair, depleted, and nodded in the direction of Krishne.

Krishne stepped forward. He stood with his feet slightly parted, his hands clasped behind his back, his gaze held to the back wall. His face was grave as he spoke in an even low keel.

'We have determined that there are two people in this room with direct access to the boxes, but that doesn't mean somebody else could not have accessed them from the outside.'

Rita couldn't look at Krishne, couldn't look at anybody in the room. Her eyes fell to the thick weave of carpet, her barely visible toes.

'However, let us first start with the two people in this room who could have accessed the boxes. The first has been with us for many years now. Kali,' and at the mention of a name other than her own, Rita looked up at the Madhesi woman, half hidden in shadow, standing immobile opposite herself, 'is someone the Ranisab trusts. But we all know, the Ranisab is now getting along in age. She is an easy target. Most recently, it is Kali who has been spending the nights with the Ranisab.'

Kali gaped, her eyes shot white, not a sound escaping her. Then her hand flew straight to her heart and watching her, Rita felt a pulsing, right at the top of her head.

'Aabii!' Kali exclaimed, 'I know nothing . . . I cannot understand . . . I don't know . . .' She stuttered, her words coming thick and fast, sticking to each other in a tumbling fall.

'I have always said,' a sudden hooting broke from the crowd, 'I have always said, have I not, that these Madhesis could never be trusted?'

Bajai took a step forward. She was a tall woman. As tall as Kali.

'Bajai!' the Jarsap interjected from his chair with a wave of a hand, 'Let Krishne finish.'

'The other person who also has access,' Krishne continued, not a muscle twitching, 'is Rita. The newest member of the household . . .'

At the sound of her own name, the pulsing turned into a thundering and Rita felt herself wilt. Her breaths came out in short hiccups, sweat crowding her face, neck, armpits.

'Aabii!' Rita looked up as Kali now stepped forward, standing shoulder to shoulder with Bajai, 'But she is just a child!'

'She is young, yes,' Krishne did not twitch, 'but maybe not too young to know the value of the contents of these boxes.'

'It is not possible,' Kali's face solidified into something oblique and formidable, 'for such a young girl to plan something like this! She has not even been in this house a year!'

Krishne continued undeterred,

'We must therefore first determine if either of these women could have accessed these boxes for dishonest reasons.'

'If you have to blame anyone, hajur,' Kali looked past Krishne and addressed the Jarsap directly, 'then blame me. Only I have recently handled those boxes. I don't know how, but maybe the ring fell out, hajur. Hajur, I am sure, the child is not to blame.'

Rita felt herself fold, into smaller and smaller pieces until she could disappear altogether. Kali, who came from nothing and had nowhere to go, was taking the blame for her. And then, a voice, somewhere deep inside her. *Darcherua.* Rita thought suddenly of Sumnima but no, this voice sounded different, a scratching whisper that was growing louder and louder until it was screaming. *Darcherua.*

Outside the baithak, across the courtyard, a familiar call.

'Rita!' from across the courtyard, the Ranisab summoned, 'Rita?'

'Jarsap,' Rita stepped forward, her voice a whisper, 'Jarsap hajur, the Ranisab is calling for me.'

The Jarsap looked at her, exhaustion in his eyes. 'Ok, go,' he breathed in permission then slumped against his seat as Rita ran out of the room.

She found the Ranisab halfway across the hallway.

'Where is everyone?' the Ranisab's stick smacked against the marble, 'What on earth is going on?'

'Ranisab hajur, you must help Kali . . .' Rita began but her words were tripping over each other, 'Hajur . . . you must help . . . Kali is . . . in trouble.'

'Where is she?'

'In the baithak, hajur.'

* * *

The baithak door pushed open and the sleek parrot entered first, its carved eyes catching the lamplight, its beak a horned curve, pointed and sharp.

'Explain to me,' the Ranisab's voice came next, roaring into the room, before the Ranisab herself stepped fully inside, 'What on earth is going on?'

The Jarsap exhaled slowly before responding.

'Mother,' he addressed her, 'a ring is missing from one of these boxes. I am afraid . . . I am afraid it has been stolen.'

The Ranisab stood stock still, both hands clasping the stick before her.

'How do you know it was stolen? And who are you saying stole it?'

The Ranisab moved forward. Her sari caught the lamplight and lit up a pale gold. Her eyes were transfixed on the sitting figure of her son.

The Jarsap made a movement, as if to stretch out his legs under the desk, but it only made him look smaller.

'Mother, the ring has always been there and now it is not. It is nowhere to be found in the safe, or around it.'

'So, who are you saying took it?'

'Krishne . . .' the Jarsap started and then hesitated. 'Krishne and I have gone through all the possibilities. But it can only be someone who has close access to the keys.'

Rita felt the prickle of tears now, stinging and blurring everything inside the room. She blinked and they rolled down her face, gathering at her chin. She had betrayed Sumnima once. Now she had betrayed the Ranisab and turned her into a simple fool. And somewhere, in undefined places deep within, where caste or circumstance of birth or ownership did not reside, where freedom and equality were constructs of the outside and not within the self, Rita knew the truth. She had betrayed herself.

'Which ring?'

'The blue sapphire.'

The room held its breath.

Then the Ranisab swore, 'For the gods' sakes! You idiot!'

In his chair, the Jarsap blinked.

'All this fuss over that unlucky sapphire? I gave that damn ring away! That's why it is not in its box!'

'You gave it away?' the Jarsap sat up, his face bleached.

'Yes, yes, I gave it away.'

'To whom?'

'To that godforsaken astrologer who told me it was unlucky in the first place. Who wants to keep an unlucky ring?'

Still standing to attention, Krishne twitched.

Then the Ranisab tapped the parrot, patting it on its head, almost congratulatory. Rita watched, blinking back her tears in confusion, as the Ranisab shuffled, made to turn around. 'Eh Rita,' she called and stretched out a hand, 'come, enough of this nonsense. Take me up to my room. I am feeling tired. And next time, son, check with me before you go frightening the entire household. Don't forget in whose name all these things still remain. And I'm far from gone yet. Now, let the servants get back to their work!'

With that, the Ranisab and the parrot stepped back out into the hallway, Rita slipping out behind them. The baithak door groaned, then closed with a muted thud.

Over the next few days, the Ranisab made no mention of the incident with the missing ring. And Rita tried hard to imagine that it was someone else who held those keys, who fitted the folded newspaper snugly into brick. She thought of the cause, but whose cause was it anyway? The fight was never hers to begin with. Then she thought of Sumnima.

Sumnima, running down the southern face of Dhire hill. The smallness of life that threatened to catch them, hold them fast. The anger born of powerlessness. But where was Sumnima running to? In moments of silence, Rita heard from somewhere deep inside herself, a voice. More than once, she found herself sitting still, trying to listen to what it had to say.

Slowly, day by day, her arm healed. The bandage was now replaced by a long-sleeved tunic top that covered the receding bruises.

The appointed date of the Jarsap's dinner party was almost upon them and in the bhanchaghar, Bajai's voice pitched to a dizzying crescendo. Meanwhile Krishne and Gurung ji continued to debate various conspiracy theories. An unvoiced truce seemed to hold them off the topic of the king's murder and instead, they debated about who was really behind the rebels' rise. Gurung ji blamed the white foreigners and NGOs for giving air to leftist propaganda, while Krishne echoed the Jarsap and said it was all India's fault. India, he theorized, wanted to keep its smaller neighbour weak by undermining its institutions and its very foundation. Neither of them ever mentioned places like Rato Mato.

Two days before the dinner, the Ranisab sent Rita on an errand to the main house. In the hallway outside the baithak, she slipped off her shoes at the bottom of the carpeted stairs and made her way up. At the top landing, she heard a male voice. It was low, a murmur. Rita stopped in her tracks.

'How bad is it?' The muffled voice was coming from beneath the stairs, in the alcove that held the telephone with the long twisting wire that stuck out from the wall.

'Can cars pass through? Hmm . . . hmm . . . but then how will you get here? Hmm . . . when? Tomorrow instead of Friday? Eh, ok. Yes, yes, I won't tell. Understood. Can't be too careful. Yes, I am conscious of what's happening. Such things must be kept quiet, these days. *Huncha*, ok.'

She heard the receiver being gently put down.

Then, the Jarsap's voice emerged in the hallway, booming now.

'Krishne! Krishne!'

Rita ducked down and sat on the top step. Below her, she could see the bald spot on the Jarsap's head, the mound of his belly, leading the way.

Down the hall, a swift patter of eager footsteps.

'Hajur Jarsap?'

'Tell Bajai to expect the Sano Raja tomorrow.'

'Tomorrow? I thought Sano Raja was coming Friday morning?'

'Yes, but there has been a landslide. Panchak highway is closed. He will be taking the Barahi road instead. They will be travelling early, leaving the barracks at five in the morning. We should expect them by early afternoon. And don't . . .' the Jarsap paused, 'Tell Bajai to prepare, but don't tell anyone what I have just told you. Do you understand?'

'Eh . . . lau!' Krishne sniffed, 'Hajur, I will tell Bajai right away.'

As Krishne's footsteps pattered down the hall, Rita thought of what Sumnima had said. No detail is too small. Movements and minutes—where, when, who, everything mattered. Still hidden behind the balustrade, she slipped soundlessly across the top landing and down the corridor.

That evening, Rita read to the Ranisab, her last shift before dinner time. Her folded legs buzzed beneath her weight and her hands felt like they should be doing something other than holding on to folds of paper.

'Ranisab, hajur,' she looked up, 'everyone is saying the army is going to be released soon. The army is going to be fighting the rebels.'

'Hmm,' the Ranisab's eyes were at the window, 'it seems that is now the only alternative left.'

'If the army is released, will the Sano Raja be fighting the rebels directly?'

The Ranisab blinked, her gaze finding the room again, 'Given his position, I doubt he will be in the front lines. But his men will be.'

'So, his men will fight the rebels.'

'One must do what duty calls for. Fighting is what soldiers are meant to do.'

'The army is much stronger than the rebels.' Rita thought of Sumnima's hands as she spoke. She remembered slim long fingers that could hold with a vice-like grip as easily as they could gently comb through hair or deftly knot a braid.

The Ranisab paused.

'That is true. But the army is made up of soldiers, men. And those men, they don't come from the city. How strong will they be when they are sent back up there? To their own villages, to fight their own brothers and sisters? Remember the Mahabharata—even the great warrior Arjuna wilted in the face of fighting his own blood. What will be the resolve of our soldiers?'

She had not thought of it, but the Ranisab was right. Most soldiers hailed from villages not dissimilar to Rato

Mato. At the end of the day, what was the difference between soldier and rebel?

'Are you worried for the Sano Raja, hajur?'

The Ranisab shrugged, then looked out the window again.

'We each have our own destiny. And we each have our own duty, our own dharma. He has chosen his.'

But even as she said the words, Rita knew the truth. Nothing livened the Ranisab more than the sight of her grandson, the broad-shouldered man with the years rolling away as he approached her apartments, bouncing into her room like a boy.

'Tell me,' the Ranisab had turned to her now, a curious expression on her face, 'tell me, what is it you plan to do after?'

'Hajur?'

'The fighting will one day end, Rita. One day this situation, too, will come to its conclusion. So, what do you plan to do after?'

Rita had never thought of *after*. The insurgency felt like something that had crept up on her, slow and insidious, like misting rains that fell endlessly through days and nights and then, unannounced, swept away entire hills. She only knew the before and then, a slow perpetual sliding that consumed it.

'Will you go back to your village?'

'I guess, hajur. My mother will need help.'

'You will till the fields?'

'Someone will have to.'

'Hmm,' the Ranisab reached for her stick, gently clasping it at the base of its neck. She seemed to be deep in contemplation, her brow furrowed.

'But will you go back to school?'

'I don't know, hajur. I'm not sure if the school is even open. I hear many schools in the villages are too afraid to stay open these days.'

The Ranisab was watching her.

'Would you like to go back?'

Rita shrugged. She knew what she should say. She should go back, be a good daughter, help the women left behind. But the truth is, she did not want to. The village felt now like another lifetime, the house too small, the life too cramped. Its breadth and width defined only by lack. A lack of possibility.

'You know, when I was your age, there were no schools. Except for one or two institutions opened later in Kathmandu, they simply didn't exist. You could get a guru. But very few girls ever got one. It is a waste, they said, to educate a girl. I was an exception, one of the lucky few. But these days, they say going to school is a fundamental right, for girls as much as for boys. And it seems to me, once something as fundamental as that has been won, one should never give it back again.'

Rita looked up at the Ranisab and felt a vague sense of unease. Village life, this war, becoming a servant in this house, none of these things were done by choice. Having a choice, that, she could agree, was a privilege.

'After all my years on this earth, what I have come to realize is this, Rita. All of us have a path in this life. You are a smart girl. I am sure there are few girls or boys who can read like you in your village. Someone like you won't remain a servant for long. But what is your true purpose? You must search for it, find it.'

The old woman had a strange look on her face, a mix of curiosity and knowing. Rita thought of responsibility; its measurements, weight and definition. But what the Ranisab was talking about was something else. The Ranisab was talking about possibility, about having a dream. Nobody before Sumnima, and nobody after her, had spoken to Rita about dreams. She remembered how once it had been the only thing that mattered.

Rita leaned forward and picked up the familiar *Nepal Sunrise* from the top of the pile. She ran her eyes over a large Pepsi Cola advertisement in brassy ink that took over half a page, then three entire columns dedicated to the drooping face of the new prime minister.

On the next page, in black and white, was a building. Rita stopped. She peered at the picture, the oblong rectangle that sat on a levelling of earth, the small cut-out windows, the sole entry door. Crowning the whole image, a corrugated black tin roof that the photographer, in real life, would have observed as bright blue.

The title read, 'Ghost Village: The Aftermath.'

Nearly two months have passed since the case of the school principal at a school in Rato Mato village in the district of Tanahu. An estimated thirty to fifty rebels are said to have stormed the local village school, kidnapping the principal and tying him to a nearby tree. At the time, witnesses claimed that the principal was beaten with sticks, his legs broken at the knees. Locals claimed that the principal had refused to close the school despite numerous warnings from the rebels to do so. Some said that the rebels demanded money, money which the school did not have to give. The school has remained shut since the incident. Now, children remain out of school and it is not known when or if, they will return to their studies. The village of Rato Mato itself has become a shell of its former self, a ghost village. What little the village had by way of infrastructure has been destroyed and the way of life of its people has been altered, perhaps irreversibly. Of its population, those who could, have left. Meanwhile, this reporter has learned that the principal of the local school put up a brave fight but eventually succumbed to his many injuries and passed away last Sunday night.

Rita gasped but her breath came short.

For a moment, Rita saw Principal sir, the way he had been, at the school assembly. His arms by his side, his glasses glinting in the morning light, his mouth shaping to the words of the national anthem. God, king, country. A man with the best English in the three hills but a hole in his jacket large enough to fit a fist through it. A man, as Sumnima had said, without the ear of Kathmandu. A harmless man.

Rita flung the paper back down and suddenly jumped up.

'I will bring your food now, hajur,' she said even though she knew it was still too early and rushed out of the room.

She headed towards the far side of the garden, to the wall by the garage. Tears sprouted fast, streaming down her face and she swiped at them with her sleeves. Gurung ji's window was lit and the radio was on. A smell of spices and incense lingered in the air. Rita slipped in behind the tree line and closely hugged the wall.

At the same spot, she pulled out the loosened brick and fitted in the scribbled note. Small, angry letters.

Arrival expected Saturday evening. Leaving at 9:00 a.m., via Panchak highway. Two cars. Five passengers total.

As she turned back towards the house, she imagined the rebels going down to Panchak highway, only to find that the road had washed into the river. The error would cost them time. She imagined Sumnima's reaction. Her knowing that the error was not by mistake. That Rita had decided not to tell her the truth. This time, the betrayal was purposeful and calculated. A turning, somewhere deep within herself.

The next day, in the post-lunch silence of the house, Rita slipped to the alcove beneath the stairs. The leather book, she knew, sat at the very bottom of a stack of magazines. She had seen Krishne flip through it many times and now she riffled through the stiff glossy paper, her fingers moving page by page. She went through the whole book, didn't find what she was looking for under the letter 'D', reversed back and found the name under 'P'. The names and addresses were not written in Nepali. But Principal sir had left his legacy and she could follow the words in halting, laborious English.

Doctor Parajuli.

She picked up the receiver with one hand. With the other, she checked the number twice, her finger hovering, before punching each individual button. She was crouched down low in the alcove, hidden under the ribbed frame of the staircase. She wondered what she would do if she got one of the numbers wrong or if the wrong person picked up. How would she explain herself?

There was a loud long tone, then staccato beeps. A whirr in the wire, then a dial tone and before she knew it, a woman's voice on the other end.

'Bir Hospital, Dr Parajuli's office?'

Rita swallowed.

'Is . . . is this Dr Parajuli's office?' She thought she recognized the voice but couldn't be sure.

'Yes, Dr Parajuli's office,' the woman repeated, a hint of impatience, 'How can I help you?'

Rita paused. She had rehearsed the words to herself again and again. But now that the moment was upon her, they slipped and ran right through her teeth.

'I . . . I,' she could hear her own stutter which only made her stutter more, 'I . . . am calling from . . . from the Seto Bangala.'

'One moment,' the woman responded immediately. Mere mention of the white house was still enough to unlock most doors in Kathmandu, 'I will connect you to Dr Parajuli.'

'No! No!' Rita almost shouted out 'I am not looking for Dr Parajuli himself . . . I am looking . . . for you, didi.'

On the other side, a silence followed by confused hesitation, 'What? What did you say?'

'My name is Rita and I . . . I came to the hospital a few weeks ago.'

'What did you say?' the woman repeated herself, the confusion turning quickly to dismissal. Rita thought the woman would hang up on her any moment now.

'I came with a sprained arm,' her words rushed out, 'You gave me an X-ray. I work here, at the Seto Bangala, for the Ranisab.'

'Ehh,' recognition finally on the other side, 'nani yes, I remember. Are you okay? Is there any problem with the arm?'

'No, no, the arm is ok. I am calling because . . . because I have a question.'

'Oh?'

'When I was at the hospital, you told me that you had two jobs. A nurse and also . . . also a tuition teacher.'

'Yes?'

'Didi . . . I don't . . . I can't go to school anymore. But I would still like to learn. I would like to become . . . like you one day. I was thinking . . . maybe I could ask for your help.'

At the other end of the line, a long silence. Rita could imagine her, with her plastic-wrapped shoes and her plastic-encased hair, leaning against the office wall, under the slow whirring fan.

'So, you want me to teach you?'

'But I don't . . . I don't have any money.'

'Have you told anyone in the big house about this? Have you asked for permission?'

'Not yet. But I'm pretty sure . . . I'm pretty sure the Ranisab would agree.'

Rita thought she could hear a lengthy calculation being silently conducted on the other end of the line.

'I could teach you,' the woman's voice answered, 'But I cannot teach you for free. However, because you are keen and because you come from a big house and having a student from a big house is always good for business, I will teach you at half price. Do you think you can manage that? You can discuss it with the Ranisab.'

Rita said that she did, even though she could not imagine how.

'But you must get top marks, you understand. You must help me market myself as a good tuition teacher,' the voice on the other end of the line continued in measured pace, 'For this arrangement to work, what I will need to determine is your potential.'

Throughout the conversation, Dr Parajuli's assistant only ever addressed Rita as 'tapai,' a formal, more respectful version of 'timi,' or *you*. Rita was not sure anyone had addressed her as tapai before. It made her feel suddenly grown up, more than just a servant girl. It felt like finding this *potential* that Dr Parajuli's assistant had mentioned, was of utmost importance.

Just before hanging up the telephone call, Rita realized that she had, in fact, never asked for the woman's name.

'What do I call you, please didi?' she asked, suddenly embarrassed by the awkwardness.

'My name is Rai,' the voice said on the other side, 'You can call me Rai Miss.'

* * *

That evening, Rita sat apologizing before the Ranisab and the parrot head, explaining herself.

'The school in the newspaper yesterday, hajur, was my village school. The man they mention, the principal, he taught me.'

'Hmm,' there was no surprise in the Ranisab's voice, 'Who decides to take a life? Who decided to take his?'

'They say he was punished.'

'Dharma and karma, both are to be fulfilled in this lifetime. They may know the former, but men fool themselves into thinking they know the latter as well. Who is he to decide to take the life of another?'

'I was thinking . . . hajur,' Rita ventured, 'I was thinking since there will be no school left when I go back to the village, maybe I could continue my studies here. In Kathmandu.'

The Ranisab propped herself up in her bed, 'Oh?'

'Only until the SLC exams. After, I could find a way to pay you back, hajur. To pay you back for . . . for . . .

everything.' Rita felt it again, the weight that pulled at her. She wondered how much the blue sapphire had fetched. She would never be able to pay the Ranisab back for it.

The Ranisab laughed, a chortle that shook her tiny frame. What precisely she found so funny, Rita could not tell.

'And how would you pay me back?'

'I could . . . find work, hajur.'

'But aren't you already working here?'

'Hajur, I could find . . . paid work. Part time, of course.'

Rita felt a deep blush burn her neck. The Ranisab's eyes watched her.

'And what sort of part time work would you be interested in doing?'

Rita thought of Dr Parajuli, the way he had lit up, almost shouted out the word 'achamma'.

'Maybe I could become a nurse, hajur. Work at the hospital.'

The Ranisab looked at her for a while.

'Maybe it's time my son included you in the household budget or pay you in kind. For your work here. What do you say? Here,' the Ranisab stretched out a hand, 'Lift me up and hand me my stick.'

As she reached for the black walking stick, she saw the parrot's face in bright relief. His carved eyes, his hard-rounded beak. By the cuff of his neck, the bone was carefully chipped into even lines—a ringed collar. Alive, his beak would be as red as the earth up in Rato Mato, after the rains. His feathers as green as Dhire dai's mangoes. His call would ring around the hills and swoop down into the valleys below, lifting and echoing into the sky.

Rita was summoned to the baithak and inside, Krishne was already there, standing to attention beside the Jarsap's desk.

'My mother wants Rita to start attending school here, in Kathmandu,' the Jarsap announced, taking off his spectacles. 'Rita, I understand you want to continue your studies?'

'Hajur,' Rita acknowledged, careful not to look directly at the Jarsap. From the corner of her eyes, she could see Krishne twitch.

'Krishne,' the Jarsap now turned to him, 'can you look into it? Are there any schools here, close by? Maybe Rita can attend for a few hours a day, so that it does not get in the way of her duties.'

Krishne sniffed.

'Hajur, if I may,' Krishne's eyes switched, 'we are going to let a young woman from this house attend an outside institution? There may be implications of . . . of mixing with the locals.'

The Jarsap's eyes widened.

'What implications?'

'Hajur, Rita has been left here in trust by Dhire. She has been trained well in this house and is a good worker. But outside of this house, there may be other influences that . . . that we cannot control.'

He had been the first one to ask her about *after*, and yet here was Krishne, Rita realized with an empty feeling, tempering ambition other than his own. Was it because he didn't want anyone else to get ahead of himself? Or was it because Rita had borne witness to a side of him that Krishne wanted no one to see?

'Yes . . . yes you are right. A young woman, no matter her background, ought to be . . . carefully supervised.' The Jarsap's round face pinched in distaste.

'Also,' Krishne continued, 'a day school would get in the way of Rita's duties. The Ranisab depends on her now. And a night school . . . well, they only take place after dark.'

'What!' the Jarsap barked out, 'What sort of nonsense is a night school!'

Rita could feel her palms grow wet, the moment slipping away from her.

'Hajur, Jarsap,' she spoke up, her voice just audible enough to be neither presumptuous nor feeble, 'perhaps I could take . . . tuition lessons. Here. I wouldn't need to leave the house.'

'Tuition?' The Jarsap turned to her. Children of the Kathmandu elite took tuition classes after school to bump up their report cards. Even the middle classes were starting to follow the trend, and the newspapers were rife with tuition advertisements. Rita could feel Krishne's eyes bore into her.

'Hajur . . . there is someone . . . in Dr Parajuli's office. The Ranisab said . . .'

'What does Dr Parajuli have to do with any of this?'

'Not Dr Parajuli himself, of course, hajur. But his assistant.'

'Oh?'

'She is a nurse and also . . . a tuition teacher.'

The Jarsap's eyes widened further, his brows arching high into his thinning hair line. Rita was not sure what surprised the Jarsap more. The budding plan or the fact that she had one. Rita took a step forward.

'Hajur, the Ranisab suggested maybe Dr Parajuli's assistant could teach me.'

'Krishne, what do you think of this?'

Krishne's eyes narrowed but the plan was backed by the Ranisab. The repercussions of pushing back on the old woman's desires could be manifold and unforeseen. 'I suppose . . . I suppose that could work.'

'Hmm, yes, yes,' the Jarsap sighed and reached for his spectacles, 'it is Dr Parajuli after all. And Dr Parajuli's nurse should be alright.'

'She said she would teach here for half price, hajur,' Rita chipped in.

'Oh?'

'Hajur, she said that only because it is the Seto Bangala. She said it would be her honour to teach someone in this household, hajur.'

Rita was surprised by the smoothness of her own words, but after these many months, she had learned. From the corner of her eye, she could see Krishne give her a slant-eyed stare. The Jarsap's face softened. The Ranas might no longer hold political power but the power of status was still theirs. Incidences like these, she knew, were delicious little reminders of their glorious past. And to this day, the Jarsap was living off his glorious past.

'Ok, Krishne will do the necessary,' the Jarsap recovered himself and waved a hand in dismissal.

13

Rai Miss

That Friday, a day before the Jarsap's dinner party, Rai Miss strode down the garden path dressed in a starched light pink sari and a black blazer. Her hair was twisted into a slick knot on the top of her head and her feet, in medium-height heeled shoes, made no effort to proceed unheard. A large canvas satchel hung down her shoulder. She walked past the bustle out in the gardens—the borrowed help, the delivery boys, an electrician, a carpenter. The Jarsap's original guest estimate had exceeded threefold. She entered the echoing hallway and if she were startled by its vastness—its sweeping ceilings and unbound adornments—she did not show it. She clipped across the polished marble and Krishne's eyes shifted as he led her through the house, Rita trotting behind them. Krishne sniffed the air, swerved towards the Ranisab's wing of the house and halted by the man-sized pair of tusks at the base of the staircase.

'Your shoes,' he announced, his irritation obvious, and Rai Miss paused, swiftly kicking off her heels. The heels were well used, Rita saw, chafed and lopsided.

When they reached her room, Rai Miss stepped in in thinly socked feet. Rita could tell that everything about this visit must be unfamiliar, yet Rai Miss looked undaunted. Without further direction, she headed straight to the two cushions Rita had laid upon the floor.

'I am being paid by the hour and given there are only sixty minutes in an hour, we don't have a minute to waste!' Rai Miss lowered her satchel and, crossing her legs, sank on to a cushion next to it.

Krishne lingered at the door. 'Do you have everything you need?' he asked.

Rai Miss looked up. 'Oh yes, bhai, if you could only get me a glass of water.'

Krishne's long lashes fluttered and Rita knew what he was thinking. Rai Miss should have addressed him as 'dai' not 'bhai'. Given it was impossible to tell who was older and who younger, the courtesy of a stranger, and a female one at that, would have assumed to give the man the deference of age. But with one word, Rai Miss had elevated herself over Krishne. Rita considered jumping up and getting the water herself, but without a word, Krishne nodded and disappeared down the corridor.

'Now, before we start, tell me Rita. What class have you studied till?'

'Class seven, Miss.'

'Complete?'

'No, Miss. We had only just started.'

'Hmm,' Rai Miss dug into her enormous satchel 'Here, in that case these are the ones we will start with,' she slapped one book after the other on to the carpet, 'We will start with Nepali, then proceed with maths, science and English. We have some catching up to do, you understand.'

Rita nodded, barely believing that this was happening—the nurse with the plastic cap and plastic shoe covering was now here, her very own guru.

Sitting cross-legged on the cushion, Rai Miss started the very first lesson by slapping open the Nepali book, a clean, crisp version of the Mahendra Malla, pinning it down with one hand and whipping out a foot-long plastic ruler from the depths of her satchel with the other. Rita felt herself flinch, the memories of Principal sir lashing at Sumnima and Tsering Lama coming back to her. But throughout the lesson, Rai Miss never lifted the ruler once. She simply used it to keep pace, tap-tapping on her own knee as Rita read the first chapter out loud.

'So,' Rai Miss did not interrupt her until she had reached the end of the poem, 'what is the poem about?'

'A parrot,' Rita replied, 'A parrot trapped in a cage.'

'And how does the parrot feel?'

'Sad and . . . and desperate. He misses his parents, still out there in the forests. He misses the fruits he used to eat and the life of freedom he lived.'

'And what else?'

Rita stole a glance at Rai Miss, focused on the open page. She had a small face but the skin was smooth, taut, closely lining her jutting jaw, the rounded swell of her forehead. Her eyes were slanted slits with thick skinned lids. She had the same eyes as Niraj. And it suddenly gripped Rita now, the irony. It could have been him. Niraj Rai—a good student, one of the very best Rato Mato had ever seen—could have come here to Kathmandu, could have become a tuition teacher. Could have been sitting right here, tapping his knees, had the outcomes been different. But instead, he was gone, his ashes swept by the river.

'The poet Lekhnath Poudyal,' Rita focused on her words, 'is describing the suffering of a caged bird. But on another level, he is using the parrot to describe the state of the country. The parrot trapped in its cage is a parallel to the entire nation trapped under the dictatorial Rana rule.'

Rai Miss did not say anything, as if she were expecting more.

'The poem,' Rita pressed on, 'is an allegory. It has two layers, a deeper meaning hidden under the obvious one.'

'Yes,' Rai Miss looked up, her eyes on Rita's face. 'It is an allegory. You are right. But the poem could have more than one interpretation—a third layer, if you will. The first layer is what meets the eye, a parrot locked in a cage. The second layer is the country itself, locked under a dictatorship. What could the third layer be?'

Rita blinked. She did not know.

Rai Miss waited patiently for a while before proceeding to answer her own question.

'The third layer,' Rai Miss spoke slowly, each word weighed individually, 'speaks to the spirit. The parrot, you understand, is representative of the soul. What happens when a person is caged in this life, in this body, never recognizing his soul? When he does not know who he truly is. Why is he here? What is his purpose? Or rather, what is *her* purpose?'

Rai Miss looked at her, and her eyes were still.

'The only thing the parrot wants,' she continued, 'is to do what she was born to do. The parrot wants to fly.'

Rai Miss looked at her watch and ended the lesson with a 'Well done,' but it sounded perfunctory and she seemed, suddenly, in a great hurry. She hadn't, Rita was pretty sure, found that *potential* she had come looking for. Rita would have to do better next time.

Rai Miss jogged down the stairs, her satchel straining against her shoulder and while she stopped to squeeze her toes into her shoes, Rita asked, 'Are you late Miss?'

'I am *almost* late, but it all depends on how bad the traffic will be.'

'Do you have far to go? Will you be going back to the hospital?'

'No,' Rai Miss was now clopping down the hallway, 'I am going to my local chapter of the Women's Rights Committee meeting. Today is an important day. We are drafting the wording of an amendment we are going to propose to the parliament.'

'Oh? What is the proposal, Miss Rai?'

'Have you heard of the Muluki Ain? The national code?'

Rita shook her head.

'Well, the amendment is going to change parts of the civil code. It will allow women to retain parental property even after marriage. Right now, women can only inherit if they are over thirty-five and unmarried. The amendment, if it passes through parliament, will finally recognize daughters as equal heirs.'

'Do you think the amendment will pass?'

'I am pretty confident that it will. Never underestimate the power of purpose-driven civil action, Rita.'

They could hear a commotion coming from the main house now, voices rising and resounding through the hallways. Rai Miss stopped mid-step and asked, 'Has something happened?'

'Oh,' Rita had almost forgotten, 'it's the Sano Raja, the Jarsap's son, he must have just arrived. The house is throwing a dinner party tomorrow.'

Rai Miss looked at her and blinked.

'A party?' she said, 'With everything that's happening in the country right now, I would not think it is the right time to be throwing parties!'

And with that, she turned sharply on her heels, clipping towards the entrance door. Rita watched her leave, thinking about what Rai Miss had just said. She thought of Aama and Kaaki, the ghost village Rato Mato had been reduced to. Who was grazing the cattle and who was tilling the fields? Who was carrying back water from the village tap? And had they managed to hide away their winter stores of food before the rebels arrived? Meanwhile, in the bhanchaghar, Rita knew Bajai was cooking copious amounts of mutton for over fifty people, prepared in three different ways.

* * *

In her chambers, the Ranisab was waiting.

'So? How is she?'

'A bit frightening,' Rita moved towards the bookshelf.

The Ranisab chuckled, 'Next time she's here, bring her to me. I would like to see this woman for myself.'

'Hajur, you want to see her?'

'Yes, why not? She has your future in her hands, doesn't she? Besides, I had better check out what it is I am paying for.'

A few days later, Rai Miss was back, suspiciously eyeing the remnants of the dinner party—extra gasoline drums being rolled back down the garden, garden lights looped back from the trees, a cacophony of pots and pans in the bhanchaghar.

'So, did you have your dinner party?'

'Yes, Rai Miss. It was supposed to be a small affair but there were so many cars the line went past the peepal tree out front.'

'Hmph!' Rai Miss grunted and kicked off her shoes at the stairs.

'And your amendment, Rai Miss . . . is it now with parliament?'

Rai Miss looked at her sharply, as if she had not expected Rita to remember.

'It is. We suspect they will bring it to motion in a few months' time.'

Rita hesitated, 'The Ranisab has asked to see you first today before we start.'

'Oh? What does the Ranisab want with me?'

'She . . . would just like to meet you, that's all.'

'Well, we don't have much time as it is. Let it be quick.'

Rita noticed a small hole in Rai Miss's sock. They were brown, knitted with a loose weave. The winking hole reminded her of Principal sir. Rita felt her apprehension rise.

'This won't take much time,' Rita said quickly, 'She is just down the corridor.'

At the door to the Ranisab's room, Rai Miss' eyes roved the walls, the larger-than-life images of gods and goddesses, the vast carpet inside that sprouted sofas and armchairs, the large canopied bed at the far end. Then her eyes lingered momentarily over the fortified steel cabinet in the corner and suddenly, Rita felt her face flush. Rai Miss, she was sure, would not steal a thing in her life. She would earn it.

'Ranisab, hajur,' Rita announced at the door, 'Rai Miss is here.'

The armchair swivelled and revealed a bundle of khasto blankets and peeping through, a small wrinkled face and sharp black eyes. From behind, an electric heater threw a fluorescent orange glow.

'Come in,' the Ranisab brought out a hidden hand and motioned, 'come in, let me see you.'

With the other hand, she laid the parrot against the armrest.

Rai Miss took three steps into the room.

'Rita here seems so taken by you, I wanted to see you for myself,' the Ranisab chuckled, 'Tell me, Rai ji, what is your full name? Where do you come from? How did you end up working for Dr Parajuli?'

Rai Miss took a moment to collect herself, straightening her shoulders and parting her feet. Then she said, 'You have asked, so I will tell you.'

Rita jerked her head up. Rai Miss had not used the word 'hajur' to address the Ranisab but had used the word 'tapai'—a customary official address, but one far beneath what someone like the Ranisab was used to. Rai Miss, Rita realized, had just addressed the Ranisab the same way she addressed Rita herself.

But the face half hidden in wraps did not blink, and the black eyes firmly held Rai Miss.

'My name is Nilima Rai. I hail from a village in the east. I came to Kathmandu to continue my studies.' Rita could hear the pride behind her words, 'Then, after finishing my SLC exams, I went to nursing college and Dr Parajuli hired me.'

'Ohho!' the Ranisab exclaimed, 'A woman so far from Kathmandu completing college! That is unusual.'

'I had a father who was ahead of his times. He believed in educating his daughters, you understand.'

'Hmm,' the Ranisab nodded, carefully considering this piece of information, 'And you have always wanted to be a nurse?'

'Yes, I have.'

'And I suppose you have wanted to pass on your learning to other young girls, hence becoming a tuition teacher?'

'Yes, that is part of it. But I also wanted to be independent, earn my own money.'

'Hmm,' the Ranisab nodded again, 'and which village are you from?'

Rai Miss blinked, the question unexpected.

'A small village in Sindhuli, far from here.'

'Ehh, Sindhuli. Well, I come from even further than you. I come from a village close to Biratnagar.'

Rita knew it was the last thing Rai Miss would have expected. The Ranisab, a vastly wealthy Rana woman of another generation, sitting here and speaking of far-flung villages.

The Ranisab did not wait to fill in Rai Miss's silence.

'So, are you going to take Rita here on rounds of the hospital one of these days?'

'What do you mean?'

'Well, I think she wants to be like you one day. A nurse. Don't you, Rita? She still must complete her studies, but in the meantime, why not show her what you do? Get her familiar with the hospital, let her see first-hand what it is she will be getting into. Only recently, we read about a nursing course offered by the hospital. Didn't we, Rita? Well, maybe by getting her foot in the door, Rita here can get a head start.'

Rita was surprised the Ranisab had remembered the advertisement.

'I guess . . . I guess that could be arranged. But we will have to follow the due process and get the necessary approvals.'

'I can put in a call to Dr Parajuli to get his permission.'

'There is more to it than just that. Even for members of big houses like the Seto Bangala, the correct procedure must be followed, there can be no exceptions.' Rita Miss stuck her chin out, a challenge.

'Of course,' the Ranisab smiled, 'Rita here is a girl from a faraway village. Just like us,' Rita felt herself start at the use of the plural, 'And like you and me once, she is a girl with a dream. I'm sure you will be able to manage all the relevant procedures and get her permission, won't you, Rai ji?'

'I will . . . try.'

'Good!'

The Ranisab picked up the parrot and the chair turned back around, blocking the heater and with it, the iridescent glow of electric light. Rai Miss had been dismissed.

14

Patient Ward

The patient ward in Bir Hospital reminded Rita of the carpet factory she had visited with Sumnima and Neelam didi when the three of them had climbed up to Pemba Monastery. Inside, seated at each loom, had been a woman, a northerner dressed not in a sari or a tunic with leggings like those further down the hills, but in a robe and a bakhu apron made of coarse yak wool. The women's hands had flown up and down along stretched lengths of yarn and the room had risen in endless chatter and swirling dust. The hospital ward was just as airless, light breaking into the long room through high, squared windows below which beds were arranged in rows, one after the other. There was a constant din of moans and grunts, conversation from visiting family members crowding one bed or the other, the bustling movement of nurses coming and going.

Rai Miss was walking with Rita from bed to bed, naming each patient by number and ticking them off her notepad, 'This one is recovering from a particularly heavy case of typhoid and number seven there has acute gastroenteritis.' Rai Miss was known as 'sister' here, as were all the other nurses, but Rita still called her 'Rai Miss'. She, Rita could tell, held an elevated position to the other nurses as they all dipped their heads when she passed and she was the one with the checklist.

'The duties of a nurse are varied,' she spoke as she walked, 'It depends on each individual case. And sometimes the pain is not physical, it is mental—those cases can be the hardest. And then there is the family and visitors that need to be dealt with. One can never know, one day to the next, what exactly the task required will be.'

'But how do you deal with pain that is not physical?'

'Well . . . first we try and engage with the patient. Try to get them to talk in a safe and secure environment. And then, if we succeed in getting them to talk, we listen. You will be surprised how many people just need a listening ear. Some patients will come with physical symptoms that can be medicated, but the real underlying issue will be mental or emotional. The most difficult cases, of course, we are not equipped to handle. Those we refer to the specialists.'

'Does Dr Parajuli come and see all these patients every day?'

'No, not every day. He also has a private practice so he only comes to the hospital once or twice a week. And that's why these are so important,' Rai Miss tapped the board that held the checklist, 'We note down every detail into these progress reports. Each patient is profiled and their progress carefully monitored.'

'Do you also work at Dr Parajuli's private practice?'

'No,' Rai Miss shook her head. 'The money would be much better if I did. But if I did, then who would look after this place?'

They passed by bed number nine and a young man raised his hand, reaching into the air.

'Sister!' he called, 'One minute please, sister.'

'What happened?' Rai Miss barked, authority in her voice.

'Please sister, one minute of your time only!'

As Rai Miss approached, the young man pinched two shaky fingers at her, 'Just one shot, please, just a small one.'

Rita wasn't sure what he was talking about, but his eyes looked crazed and she noticed deep red scratches all along his arms. He was shivering, his entire body convulsing.

'We have talked about this already. You know you just need to wait some more.'

'Please sister!' the young man lunged forward, reaching for Rai Miss and she batted him back with her clipboard. Then she quickly handed the clipboard to Rita and held the man firm by his forearms, pressing them down. A struggle ensued and Rita could feel the fear growing in her, she darted her eyes around for help but all of a sudden, the young man let go. Now he curled up, whimpering back into the bed. Rai Miss waited a full minute by his side before leaving him and continuing down the row.

'They found him unconscious,' she explained matter-of-factly, 'drug overdose. Hadn't eaten in days, he was almost lifeless when they brought him in. Lucky for him, it was a call from high up, a politician, otherwise we wouldn't have had a bed to spare. Half the beds here,' she tossed her head, 'are taken, thanks to a *connection*. If you don't know people in this city, you go nowhere. We had to keep him on saline water for the first few days. Now he is starting to feel the symptoms of withdrawal. As he grows in strength, he can become dangerous now, to himself and others. Tomorrow they are going to remove him, move him to a different ward.'

Rita's eyes widened and she turned back to look at the young man curled up like an infant on his side, the covers framing his face. She could see he had been strong once, his jaw powerful, his hands wide, his limbs long. How could someone like that find himself in a situation like this? She understood what Rai Miss meant. Many of these scars seemed to run deeper than the eyes could see.

Rai Miss completed her round of the ward, noting neatly and diligently into her notepad, Rita watching her every move.

Across the room, at bed number fifteen, she saw a patient with a wad of bandages sticking out, almost covering half the body.

Rita craned her neck, 'What happened to that one?'

'Ah . . . a victim of one of the protests. There were more before, but only this one is left now.'

'What happened?'

'Petrol bomb. Fell right next to her, burned half her side. She hadn't even been part of the protest. She was just caught in the wrong place, at the wrong time.'

Rita winced.

'Come, I will show you.'

The young woman was asleep, her face layered with long hair. Sticking out under the cover, Rita could see her entire right thigh and side wrapped in wads of bandage. The woman was paying the price for something that had nothing to do with her, a cause that was not her own. Rita felt a dull anger now and it lingered with her the rest of the afternoon.

That evening, Rita crouched on the carpet in her room like she did every day, copying down entire chapters from the tuition books until she memorized them whole. Soon, it would be the Ranisab's dinner time. She could hear Kali come upstairs, bringing a pile of the Ranisab's fresh laundry and with it, the smell of the winter sun. She lingered at

Rita's door, watching quietly. Rita looked up, quizzically, but Kali brought a finger up to her lips and just stood.

'Kali didi, come!' Rita motioned and hesitantly, Kali entered the room.

'Here,' Rita handed her the pen, 'Do you know how to write?'

Kali shook her head.

'Do you know the alphabet?'

Again, Kali shook her head.

'Don't worry, Kali didi. Come, I will teach you. Let me show you how to write your name first.'

* * *

The next week Rita was back at the hospital, entering the maze of corridors, catching pungent smells from open doors. In Dr Parajuli's office, Rai Miss waited with a pinched brow and an air of distraction.

'Dr Parajuli just called,' she spoke quickly, 'and said he is going to be here within the hour. I was only expecting him later in the afternoon!'

Then she took Rita by the wrist and led her to the row of chairs that lined the wall outside the office.

'Just sit here. You mustn't get in the way, you understand. Dr Parajuli is a busy man. And a very demanding doctor. Just wait here!'

Rita sat quietly, surprised to see Rai Miss, usually so contained, in this state of flustered efficiency. Here was a chance to observe not only Rai Miss, but perhaps Dr Parajuli himself. His patients started trickling in long before Dr Parajuli arrived. One of them was a bent old woman and Rita wondered how she had made the journey here alone. But then she noticed a boy squatting on the floor nearest to the office door, hidden by the row of chairs. His face, strikingly like the old woman's, told her that the boy had brought his grandmother to the hospital. She recognized the blank daze in his eyes—a villager, unused to the pace and complexity of the city. She had been that boy, once. Rita rested her back against the chair and her head softly bumped the wall behind her.

Out in the intersection of corridors, she watched visitors wandering past, nurses briskly moving in and out of view and a middle-aged man slowly ambling along, dressed in a hospital gown and holding on to a metal contraption that rolled along in front of him. Then Rita noticed a small group of plain-clothed people walk to the centre and halt. There were three of them, all with cropped hair and low hanging baseball caps, pants and thin zippered jackets. In the middle of the group was a woman, short and wide hipped, mounds of breasts standing up behind the layer of jacket. The other two were young men. The trio stood there and seemed to be debating something. Then they turned towards the exit, heading down in step.

Dr Parajuli strode down the hallway without looking left or right, directly into his office. He did not notice Rita sitting among the patients. One after the other, the patients entered his office. Then finally, after the last of the patients had exited, Rai Miss left the door open wide. Dr Parajuli came walking out in a hurry. He had a knee-length white gown thrown over his shoulders and a stethoscope draped around his neck and looked up in surprise at Rita, 'Oh, you are here?' Then he walked past and as if in afterthought, threw a glance over his shoulder, 'You can come with me on my rounds of the ward if you want.'

Dr Parajuli marched down the aisles, ignoring everything but the patients and the notes that Rai Miss dutifully handed him at each bed as Rita hurried to keep pace. Ornamenting the rows of patient beds were colourful dolai blankets brought from home, large steel tiffin containers of food cooked by relatives, plastic bags full of clothes left lying about that nurses pushed away with their feet.

The typhoid patient seemed to have improved significantly—he was sitting up in the bed playing a game of cards. Like an obedient student in the presence of a teacher, he put the cards away the minute Dr Parajuli came to stand at the foot of his bed. Dr Parajuli scanned the note sheet and listened carefully as Rai Miss supplemented it with more detail. He asked, 'Are you strong enough to walk?' The patient nodded. Then Dr Parajuli addressed Rai Miss, 'Prepare the patient for discharge,' and without another word, moved on to the next bed.

Up in the hills, Rita knew, most of the people in these beds would hardly have survived the night. The patient in bed number seven was asleep despite the din, a long tube stuck under the skin of his arm and travelling to a bag that hung from a steel rod. A woman sat by his feet, slowly kneading his blanketed legs. Dr Parajuli tapped the note sheet with his pen. 'Let's increase the dosage,' he said to Rai Miss who quickly scribbled into her clipboard.

Then they came to bed number nine, but the young man was no longer there. Rita felt her throat catch. She knew nothing about him. He had as yet looked the healthiest among all these patients and yet, she knew, his fight against his own addiction would be one of the hardest. In his place was another patient, sleeping on his side with his back turned to her and a hospital blanket pulled up to his ears.

'This is the one I spoke to you about over the telephone,' Rai Miss explained as Dr Parajuli studied the note sheet, 'She came in this morning. The symptoms are abdominal pains, vomiting, weight loss and fever.' Rita looked from Rai Miss to the bed. *The patient was a woman?*

'When is the blood sample coming?'

'Not before a week, we've been having delays.'

'Any coughing, shallowness of breath?'

'Nothing. No pulmonary symptoms at all.'

'Hmm, let me examine her. Turn her over please.'

Rai Miss called out and another nurse appeared. Together, the two nurses moved to opposite sides of the bed, rolling the blanket down to the patient's chest and gently hauling her over. The woman was so thin, Rai Miss needn't have called for assistance. Rita watched, her eyes travelling from the bony appearance of veined arms beneath a hospital gown to the deep hollows around the patient's neck, up to the protruding jaw. And suddenly, her heart stopped.

'Sumnima!'

Dr Parajuli whipped around.

'You know this woman?'

Rita's heart was beating with a force that made her tremble all over.

'Yes . . . Dr Parajuli, she's . . . she's from my village.'

Sumnima's face, once beautiful, was crested and shadowed, her eyes closed, the sockets lined with bone and too large for her face. Her mouth was parted, shallow intakes of breath whistling through parched peeling lips.

'What's wrong with her? What's wrong, doctor?'

Sumnima's chest looked so light, as frail as a weathered leaf, that for an instance, Rita doubted herself, studying her again. Her shoulders, still wide, were rounded, collapsing in on themselves. Her defined nose now stood out too large in her sunken face. Her hair was the same cropped hair she had worn outside the Seto Bangala, but thinner, dulled. Rita felt a pair of hands on her shoulders. Softly, they guided her a few steps back.

'We don't know what's wrong with her yet,' Rai Miss's voice spoke in her ear, 'Are you sure this woman is from your village?'

'Yes . . .' Rita realized that she was sobbing, gasping for breath but her eyes stayed dry, 'yes . . . but she looks nothing like she is supposed to.'

'I know,' Rai Miss's voice's now turned reassuring, a gentle undulation, 'She has lost a lot of weight. We have started giving her saline water,' and only now did Rita notice the same contraption with the bag hanging from a rod behind the bed, 'And in the past few hours, there has already been some improvement.'

She had seen Sumnima under the peepal tree . . . how long ago had that been? She remembered Sumnima's too-loose jacket, the bruise-like stains under her eyes. But still, physically she had seemed fine—thinner and perhaps more tired, but fine. This person was nothing like the Sumnima as she had always been before—stronger, faster, bolder than anyone else, her limbs sheathed in muscle.

Dr Parajuli sat on the edge of the bed, listening to Sumnima breathe in and out through the stethoscope. Then he pulled the blanket all the way down to her thighs and Rita was shocked to see hip bones stick out like wings, clasping in their midst, a mound of belly, rounded and swollen. Up in Rato Mato, Rita had sometimes seen children with bellies like this, and the hungriest child always seemed to have the most rounded belly. Dr Parajuli cupped a hand and felt around her ribs, her stomach and down her abdomen.

'Let us immediately start her on a course of antibiotics,' he stood up.

'You have a diagnosis, doctor?' Rai Miss raised her eyebrows.

'We cannot be sure until we have the blood results. The diagnosis is a difficult one. It could be almost anything. But looking at the state of this patient, I suspect it is, in fact, tuberculosis.'

'But there are no pulmonary symptoms at all, doctor!'

'TB usually strikes the lungs, but not always. In this case, I think it may have gotten into the digestive system. TB is very tricky, it's a disease that knows how to mask its symptoms well. At least until we get a proper diagnosis, let us start on the antibiotics. Sister, please arrange for urine tests and an endoscopy as well.'

Dr Parajuli handed back the note sheet, took two steps, then stalled at the foot of the bed.

'Has the patient had any visitors? Any family?' the question seemed to be posed at both Rai Miss and Rita.

'None, doctor.' Rai Miss glanced at Rita. Rita stood, still trembling, her eyes on Sumnima's wasted body. Her mind unable to formulate a sentence.

'Who brought her here?'

'I was told some youths left her at the emergency entrance.'

'Hmm,' Dr Parajuli rubbed his chin then turned to Rita, 'she is lucky then we had a spare bed. Given the patient seems to have nobody else, if you would like to visit her for the next few days, you can do so. After all, you are from the same village. I will let the Seto Bangala know.'

15

Sumnima

(*Hemanta Ritu*, Winter 2001)

Rita fed Sumnima with a spoon. Her parched lips took slow sips, her eyes elongated slits, and Rita felt herself hurt just watching her. In the hospital corridor, kerosene heaters were placed at each intersection, but still the winter cold seemed to seep through the walls and reach up the cemented floor. Rita wrapped Sumnima in extra khastos and dolai blankets salvaged from the white house and sat, momentarily shivering, in a woollen high-neck under her tunic with a nurse's apron thrown over it. Small tin cups of water placed atop the heaters humidified the air and the square windows overhead turned pallid with steam.

When Rita had finished feeding Sumnima, she read out loud to her. Once, mid-sentence, Rita looked up to see Sumnima's eyes wide open, staring at her. In them, a splinter of recognition but no surprise. Then she turned away, facing the grey green walls, the steel bedside table that held a bottle of ice-cold mineral water and a bowl of unfinished broth.

'Dr Parajuli says that people catch the kind of TB you have only in the worst of living conditions,' Rita spoke as if no time had passed between them, 'In his entire career, he has only seen two other cases.' There was no point hiding things from Sumnima. Even in her condition, it seemed somewhat disrespectful to soften things for a fighter. And Sumnima had always been a fighter. 'If you ask me,' Rita continued, 'I think you must have caught it in the prison. Dr Parajuli says these things take time to show. It would have started with abdominal pains, vomiting, unexplained weight loss. Then fever.'

Sumnima did not respond. She tilted her head and looked out, across the rows to bed number fifteen opposite her, now empty of its occupant. Rita had forgotten to ask Rai Miss what had happened to the woman injured in the protest. Then Sumnima looked over at the small steel table, eyeing the unfinished broth in the bowl. Rita raised the broth again to her lips. Kali had made the broth fresh that dawn. She had awoken long before Bajai, stolen a small piece of chicken from the fridge and boiled it with a few herbs until the soup ran clear, layered with thin grease. Then she had put everything back in its place exactly as before so Bajai would never know.

'Guess what I have brought you,' she said now. Rita pulled up her old copy of the Mahendra Malla, placing it higher up on Sumnima's lap. She could see Sumnima roll her eyes down in its direction, briefly, then look back up again. 'It will be like just before the exams. But this time, I will read and you just listen. Let me start with my favourite poem. "The Caged Parrot" by Lekhnath Paudyal.'

There, sitting on a stool by Sumnima's bed and slowly swaying back and forth to the cadence of her own voice, Rita felt as if they were back again on the swept red earth of the porch outside their house, Dalle baying in his shed, the chickens clucking and scratching in the vegetable yard. Sumnima took a few more sips of the broth and then her head rolled on the edge of the pillow, her eyes shut, her breath steadier than the day before.

Rita put the book away and sat quietly. Sumnima breathed out in long low rasps, drifting into sleep. And then Rita braced herself for what she would find. Slowly, she lifted the blanket and ever so lightly sought out Sumnima's hand, raising it. She held it, the wrist shrunken, the palm pale and wrinkled, the fingers slender and weightless. Then she turned Sumnima's hand over and started. There were no nails, all blunted to the quick, raw, red flesh in their place. Sitting there with Sumnima's hand in hers, Rita felt something surge inside her. A mingling of rage and loss, a sensation of resistance that jolted and rammed up against her ribs, pushed its way up to her face. She felt a spurt of hot tears, large and loose, and her teeth were biting down so hard that their echo thrummed under her entire skull. What had they done to Sumnima? The police and the rebels alike, what had they done to her?

Rai Miss said that the antibiotics would take effect immediately and Rita thought she could see it. By the fourth day, Sumnima's skin started taking on more colour, and she looked a little more like the person she used to be.

By the end of the week, Sumnima's appetite improved. Every day, Kali went out of her way to wake up before the rest of the household and make the chicken broth fresh. Then one day, Rita entered the bhanchaghar, a used plastic bag ready to carry the soup container when Bajai suddenly burst in.

'Eh!' she roared, standing at the threshold, her face flush at catching them red-handed.

'I knew it would be you! You dirty Madhesi! You thought I wouldn't find out?'

Kali's hands jumped, but they continued stirring the pot.

'Who gave you permission to touch the stove?'

Kali did not reply, her back turned, her shoulders hunched in on themselves.

'I did!' Rita suddenly heard herself shout out, 'You are not the only Bahuni around here. And if you have a problem with that, I will report you straight to the Ranisab!'

Bajai stood stung at the doorway as Rita poured the soup quickly into the thermos container, slammed it shut, then rushed out, yanking the spring door with a resounding bang.

In the days that followed, Sumnima slept most of the time. The blood results came in and confirmed Dr Parajuli's diagnosis: primary intestinal tuberculosis. Dr Parajuli said that the patient would take at least six months to recover. She would have to take a full course of anti-TB antibiotics. She would need healthy food, exercise and fresh air if she was to make a full recovery. The fever came in waves and Rita waited for it, a moist towel in her hands. She had brought other things in a bag from the Seto Bangala—a soft muslin khasto pillowcase, a second thermos bottle of Horlicks, a rubber hot water bottle that would keep Sumnima's feet warm under the covers. Rai Miss had made her wear a nurse's apron, so that the other visitors didn't think she was getting special favours by staying after they all had to leave. She had also insisted that Rita wear a thin paper mask that linked her ears and covered her mouth.

Given you are sitting so close to her and feeding her, it is better, safer for her, she had said. Outside the high windows, the sun sank and the floor of the ward stretched out into silhouettes. Soon, Gurung ji would be waiting for Rita at the reception.

Rita heard the scrape of a shoe and turned around to see Rai Miss bustling over with a small cup full of colourful medicines.

'These are for tonight,' she said brusquely before placing the cup on the steel bedside table. Then she paused a moment, lingering.

'She is slowly getting better, but this patient's journey will be long. Soon, we will have to move her elsewhere. The hospital will need this bed back.'

'But where will she go?'

'Somewhere where she can rest and slowly recover her strength. What about your village, can she go back there?'

Rita shook her head.

'The village is not safe. Especially not now, not for her.' But the moment the words left her mouth, Rita bit her tongue. What if Rai Miss realized who and what Sumnima really was?

'Oh?' Rai Miss looked at her quizzically, her eyes small and bright.

'My village has been . . . impacted by everything that has happened. There is nothing left. It is nothing but a ghost village now.'

Rai Miss did not respond, her eyes travelling from Rita back to Sumnima's sleeping figure.

'Well, we will have to figure something out,' she said after a while. Then she hurried over to the other beds.

Rita got up from her seat and just as she reached down into her bag, pulling out the Mahendra Malla, she heard more footsteps and a deep voice behind her.

'Sister! Namaste, sister! How is the patient?'

Three people were walking up to Sumnima's bed and Rita recognized them instantly. These were the same youths she had seen loitering around the hospital corridor the day Sumnima was brought in. Two men and one woman, in low-drawn baseball caps and laced canvas shoes.

Rita looked at the man who had spoken and saw that he was in fact middle-aged. His face creased and burnished by sun. With a startle, she recognized the same face that had spoken to her outside the gates of the Seto Bangala. The face of the man who had handed her the letter, Sumnima's letter.

'Hello, sister?' the question directed straight at her. Rita felt herself instantly withdraw. This same man had looked her straight in the eyes not even six months ago. Surely, any second now, he would recall that moment.

'Hello, sister?' an underlying impatience.

The man was standing only a few feet away from her. Waiting for an answer. Slowly, it dawned on Rita that although his eyes were looking straight at her, there was no light of recognition in them. Her nurse's apron, her face mask, her hair pulled away into a tight bun, the four walls of this hospital ward. She was, Rita realized, in the perfect disguise. But what had Sumnima said? *Our eyes and ears are everywhere*. Would that still be the case now that the country was in a state of emergency, now that every single rebel fighter would be needed out there, to regroup and face a new enemy?

The man took one step towards her, his face darkened into a frown.

'Sis—,' he began but before the fear could take hold, Rita felt a sudden surge of resolve within herself.

'Be quiet!' she snapped, 'Can't you see the patient is sleeping?'

'Sorry . . . sorry, sister. We just wanted to know how she was doing,' he softened his tone.

'Well, how does she look like she's doing?'

The three remained where they were, hands in their jacket pockets and shuffling their shoes. Rita felt her cheeks grow hot. In the moment, she wanted to lash out at them, shout at them to leave. With all her might, she hated them. Hated them for taking Sumnima away from her, for what had happened to Sumnima, for what she had become. The short wide-hipped woman took a step forward. She took her cap off and addressed Rita, her manner apologetic, her voice sugary.

'Sister, we know how hard you work here, we don't mean to disturb you, we are just concerned for our colleague here.'

Rita knew that voice and suddenly she was staring into the large expressive eyes of Manju. Her head bow-less, her hair shorn to a stump that clumped around her ears. But Manju, nonetheless.

Manju stood, waiting for an answer.

'Your colleague is no longer going to be of use to you.'

'What do you mean, sister?'

'She has caught a severe case of TB,' at the mention of the disease, Manju's eyes widened. She took a step back. Up in the hills, the dangers of TB, the pulmonary kind, were well known. It started with chills and fever, pain in the joints and then a hacking incessant cough. One person started coughing and before long, the whole household was coughing, the disease infectious, its patients slowly wasting away.

'The patient has TB?'

Rita felt the veins at her temple pulse. She thought back to Manju flouncing up the stone steps to their house in Rato Mato. How effortlessly she had convinced Sumnima and taken her away. And now here was Manju again, circling Sumnima even as she lay in a hospital bed. This time, Rita would not let them win.

'That's what I just said. It is a very serious case. The doctor says it could take months until full recovery. Even then, this young woman will never be quite the same. Nothing is certain.'

A sharp intake of breath. Manju turned around and exchanged looks with the middle-aged man.

'She is one of the best we have, sister.'

'The best you have for what? I'm not sure what use this patient is right now. For anything at all. She needs rest. Nobody should disturb her.'

Manju's eyes wavered and now she was studying Rita, running her gaze carefully and curiously over Rita's bundled hair, her masked face, her loose hospital apron. Rita felt herself flinch. Over the past year, she had shot up, grown thicker around the waist. But now her confidence flagged. Surely, any minute, she would be recognized.

'Are you sure it is TB, sister? Can we speak to the doctor?'

But here was Rai Miss now, brusquely striding back down the floor, this time with a catheter in a tin tray.

'Is there a problem?' she asked, her movements born of authority, her voice clipped.

'I was just telling these people . . .' Rita felt hot, sweat teaming against the cool cloth that stuck stubbornly to her, 'that the patient is in a very serious condition.' Rita looked at Rai Miss, her eyes pleading, her heart in her throat, 'And that she should be left alone.'

Rai Miss glanced sharply at Rita, then looked at the three youths and narrowed her eyes.

'That's right, this patient will be transferred out in the morning.'

'Transferred? She will be leaving here?'

Manju's face rippled, thick brows herding a shiftless gaze.

'To the TB hospital up in Teku. It's too dangerous for this patient to remain in this ward. She is infectious.'

Without a word, Rai Miss had understood. And now, Rita realized with a rush of relief so strong that it stung at her eyes, she was playing along.

'If I were you,' Rai Miss continued, 'I would not get one step closer. The blood results only just came. If we had known earlier, we would never have admitted her into this hospital in the first place. I am not sure this patient will even make it. This is a critical case.'

Manju exchanged looks with the older man.

'Now,' Rai Miss glanced at her wristwatch, 'visiting hour is over. You must leave.'

The three wavered.

'But sister . . .' Manju's eyes switched, her voice thinning and rising.

'Visiting hour is over,' Rai Miss snapped, 'we make no exceptions to policy. We have patients here who need their rest.'

'Namaste sister, thank you for your help,' it was the older man who spoke now, 'We understand.'

Manju took one last glance at Sumnima. Then without another word, she turned on her heels and the trio swiftly departed down the corridor. At the entrance to the ward, Manju turned around once again to look, her eyes still searching, but Rita pretended not to see. She lifted the cup of medicines as if to administer them, her motions swift but her hands shaking so hard that the cup trembled in them. When she finally looked back up, Manju was gone.

* * *

When they entered the gates of the white house, Gurung ji manoeuvred the jeep into the cemented parking space and halted momentarily to let Rita out. She firmly shut the door and walked towards the tree line, agitated by the events of the evening. Manju and her entire family had escaped the village immediately after the counter-attack by the armed police force. Manju's father was a wily man, able to extract money out of stone, someone who was 'as bent as a sickle', as Neelam didi had put it—someone who, going into every election, always managed to canvass for the winning party and get paid for it. And now, Manju was in Kathmandu, still in the rebel movement—but, Rita was sure, unlike Sumnima, Manju had never been in any harm's way.

Beyond the boughs of pine, the gardens held the last vestiges of a watery light, the lawn a sparse green. Crows noisily nestled into trees and a small black bat darted around the windows, lit on the inside.

Krishne was at the entrance door.

'Eh Bahuni,' he said gently, almost apologetic, and it reminded her of the old Krishne, those first days when his teasing manner had put her at ease, 'the Jarsap would like to see you. He is in the baithak.'

'See me? What for?'

'Something has happened, Bahuni. He will tell you himself.'

A quickening of pulse.

'Is it the Ranisab?'

'No, no. He is waiting for you, in the baithak.'

A large kerosene heater sat in front of the Jarsap's desk, but the room was still cold. The last time she had been called here, Rita had almost been caught for a thief and now she wondered, her heart starting to hammer, if the Jarsap had finally discovered who the culprit really was.

'Eh, Rita, come in,' the Jarsap stopped what he was doing, then took his spectacles off and leaned back behind the desk. 'How is the woman from your village . . . the one in the hospital? My mother mentioned it to me. First your uncle, now this woman. It seems Bir Hospital is getting busy these days.' For a second, Rita did not follow him, and then it came to her, the very first excuse she had used to leave the white house, ironically turned out to be close to its mark.

'She is getting better, hajur. It will take some time, but the doctor says she will recover fully.'

'That's good. That is good news indeed.'

'And how are your lessons going?'

'Very well, hajur. I could not be more grateful for this opportunity. Rai Miss is very pleased with my progress.'

'Good, good.'

The Jarsap stood up. He shuffled behind his chair and neatly tucked it under the table. Then he remained standing where he was, as if trying to make up his mind. He raised his hands off the backrest of the chair, then let them drop back again.

'Look, Rita, there is no easy way to say this. And I know you are still . . . of a tender age. But I will just come out and say it. This afternoon, I got a telephone call. From Rato Mato.'

Rita felt the hairs on her arms and neck rise, her whole body tensing.

'Dhire used to call me occasionally. About once every two–three months or so, so I thought it was him. Instead, it was Mr Chandra, the owner of the local tea shop. I believe you know him?'

Rita nodded, swallowing, her throat burning dry. The tea shop owner was a small busybody of a man, a constant presence at the heart of Rato Mato.

'Rita, I am very sorry to break this news to you. But Dhire is no longer there. He passed away in his sleep. He was, as you know, already quite an old man.'

Rita did not move.

'There,' she could hear the Jarsap's voice, 'just sit down. Just seat yourself on that seat.'

Rita sank down into the depth of cold leather. The Jarsap turned around now, abruptly, and with his hands clasped behind his back, stood and faced the window. Outside, a cacophony of nestling birds sounded from the far trees. The small bat whizzed past the windowpane, erratically chasing its own echo.

'Dhire was a good man,' the Jarsap spoke, his voice softened, 'his family has been loyally taking care of my family's lands and forests for generations. But he leaves no one behind. No progeny. No one to pick up the mantle and carry on.'

The Jarsap remained at the window, waiting. She remembered how Dhire dai had brought her to this house, walked her over these very carpets. The smell of earth and khaini that lingered, layered with the sweetness of mango. She thought of Neelam didi, imagined how she would have run, limping, downhill for help, how later she would have sprawled out on Aama's porch, tearing her own hair out.

'I . . . I will have to decide,' the Jarsap continued, 'what to do with the forests. And the land. Now that there will be no one to take care of them.'

'Hajur, will you sell the lands?'

She could tell by the Jarsap's stiff neck and shoulders at the window that he was not expecting a question back from a servant, or at least, not from her, in this moment. But he did not turn around.

'Yes, Krishne has already telephoned a broker this afternoon. And then . . . then there is the question of you. My mother is very happy with you. She says you are a good worker and a capable girl. She would like you to stay here, in this house, for as long as you wish.'

Again, the Jarsap waited, his back still to her. As if he were giving Rita time to process the words without the burden of witnessing its various physical and emotional manifestations. But her mind was elsewhere. She had seen something. A flicker of light. It came and went, teasing in chinks. She stretched towards it.

'Hajur, you don't have to sell the lands.'

The Jarsap turned his head.

'What did you say?'

On some level, it occurred to her, the anomaly. The Jarsap standing, herself seated, a simple village girl answering back her master.

'Hajur, there is another way. You don't need to sell the lands.'

The Jarsap pivoted around, his eyes rounded in surprise, his shirt splayed at the edges and taut about his belly.

'Oh? What are you saying?'

'There is someone who can take care of the lands. The trees. Dhire dai himself would have chosen this person. I know it!'

'Who is it? Do you know this person?'

'Yes. There is nobody else who knows those forests and trees as well. Nobody better suited for the job. Jarsap hajur, it is the best solution. *Binti*, please.' Another word Dhire dai had taught her. Binti, a plea.

That evening, as Rita entered the Ranisab's bedroom with her dinner tray, the old woman was seated by the electric heater, its twin rods burning. The Ranisab looked up, her face expectant.

'So, you have heard.'

'Hajur, I have heard.'

Rita rested the tray on a side table. She had to move the parrot who was in the way and lifted him up, warm in her hands. Then she gently laid the stick against the Ranisab's chair, the bird's carved face softening in strokes of orange.

'Will you go back to your village?'

'Hajur, I would like to remain here, at the Seto Bangala. Until the fighting is over. That is what Dhire dai would have wanted.'

'Of course, you can remain here for as long as you like. At least, until the fighting is over. The question is, what will you do after? What do you want to do?'

Rita thought of Aama. They would have to manage everything now by themselves. Aama, Kaaki and Neelam didi. The fields, the houses, the cattle, the vegetable patches. And until the Jarsap decided on her proposal, the mango forests.

The Ranisab was watching her carefully, 'Remember, you have potential, Rita. It may be difficult, but don't let life stand in the way of what you truly want.'

Rita hesitated. She felt a flutter where her heart was, but knew that there would be no better moment than now.

'Hajur, there is something I have to tell you. I have been meaning to, but I could never find the words. The ring . . . the one that disappeared. I took it.'

Rita expected to fall. For the weight of what she had done to come tumbling down and bury her. But instead, the moment the words left her lips she felt a lightness that washed over her and cleansed her whole.

The Ranisab looked at her.

'I know.'

'Hajur?' Rita blinked.

'I have known all along. When you get to be my age, certain things you know without being told . . .' she chuckled, 'But what I think is . . . you did not mean to do it. You see, *something* made you do it. Or *someone*. I don't know what or who and I won't torture you with questions right now. But of that, I am sure. What you did, it did not come from you.'

'Hajur, I never should have done it,' Rita looked down at the carpet, the warmth of the electric heater penetrating her skin, 'If I knew what I know now, I would never have done it.'

'Ha!' the Ranisab laughed, a gentle wheeze, and her hand spilled out of her khasto wrap, 'That ring would have left this house one way or another. Most likely it would have been sold off to fund yet another of my son's dinner parties. I am glad that at least it served a more useful purpose.'

'Hajur?'

'I suspect that ring had something to do with you finding yourself. The sudden hunger to study, this whole nursing business. It seems that ring was lucky for you,' the Ranisab's eyes stared at Rita, crinkled at the edges.

* * *

The next week, Sumnima was sitting up in the hospital bed, propped against pillows. She still did not speak, but colour had returned to her cheeks and she accepted the warm bowl of jaulo that Rita had brought in a tiffin box. Her fingers wrapped around the bowl were raw and meaty but she paid them no attention and made no effort to hide them.

'Has anyone come . . . anyone come asking for me?'

Rita was planning to tell her about Dhire dai, but now she stopped short.

'No,' she snapped instead, 'who would come?'

'I've had no visitors?'

'I'm your visitor, am I not, and I'm standing right here in front of you.'

Sumnima lowered the bowl to her lap, a shadow passing across her sunken face, her brows pinched.

'But has no one else come?'

'Didn't I just tell you? No!' Rita felt herself heat up. Then, abruptly, she changed the topic, 'Do you remember Dhire dai's mango trees? Do you remember how we used to sit by their edge, the plans we made?'

'Those plans,' Sumnima replied, her voice rasping at the back of her throat, 'were nothing but childish dreams.'

'I still remember them. All the details.'

Sumnima handed back the bowl, half eaten. Still, it was progress.

'So what, you are a nurse now?' she laid back on the pillows.

'Not yet. But I plan to be,' Rita searched Sumnima's face but it betrayed nothing, 'The Jarsap may not be paying me but he is paying for a tutor. I have finished all the content of Class 7 and 8 already. My tuition teacher said I passed all her mock exams with first division.'

'Hmph. Given the free slavery you are providing, that's the least they can do.'

'I was thinking . . . soon, you should return. Back to the village.'

'That is not an option.'

'Why not?'

'Because I have been posted here. My people need me here now, in the city.'

'Your *people* are back home in the village. And they are not getting any younger. Don't they need you too? And firstly, you need to recover. The doctor said it will take you many months to get your full strength back.'

Sumnima looked away, across the room.

Rita steeled herself.

'Up on the Dhire you didn't go with the rebels. You stayed with us instead. You stayed with me. Even now, you haven't forgotten your family, where you come from. I know it.'

'I have nothing to go back to.'

'The things and people we care about, *you* care about, are still there.'

Sumnima looked at her, a smirk teasing the corners of her mouth.

'You do realize that I cannot return to the village for my own safety and the safety of our mothers, don't you?'

Rita held her breath for a second then slowly exhaled, trying to slow her own breathing down.

'I must tell you something. The last time we met, you said something that I have been thinking about ever since. You said that up on the Dhire, someone betrayed you. Someone betrayed the rebels.'

Sumnima's lashes flickered.

'It was me,' the words came out sharper than Rita had meant, 'I betrayed you.'

Sumnima turned to her, her eyes wide and confused, 'What do you mean?'

Rita averted her gaze, stared down at her own hands. Square and dark skinned, stubby fingers. She had never looked anything like Sumnima and neither had her hands.

'One afternoon, when I was alone at the house, a pair of men came by. They said they were health workers. They asked a lot of questions. I told them about you. About the others. About what you were doing, up in the forests. I . . . I didn't understand who they really were.'

Sumnima looked at her, her face suddenly washed out, drained of its colour. Then after a while, she spoke.

'I left you behind,' her voice chafing, 'and that made you angry.' She turned away, towards the empty bed opposite, its thin bare mattress and cold steel bedposts.

Rita's throat closed up. She ran her eyes from her own fingers up to her wrist. She was still wearing the metal bracelet that Aama had given her. It used to be silver coloured once. Now it was almost completely black, its surface rough to the touch.

'But the things that you told them,' Sumnima continued, her voice fragmented, her eyes diverted, 'they would already have known. Or they would have been able to find out elsewhere. There were . . . other informers in the village.'

'Was Principal sir also an informer? Is that why he was killed?'

'What?' Sumnima's eyes were back on her.

'You once said that Principal sir was harmless,' Rita felt herself recover, felt now the familiar prodding tips of anger, her words rushing out, 'That nobody with a hole in his sweater as big as his could ever have Kathmandu's ear!'

'What . . . what did you say?'

'Why did he have to be killed? Because he caned you that one time? Or because someone above you ordered it and you just did whatever you were told?'

'I didn't . . . he wasn't meant to be killed. I didn't realize . . .' Sumnima swallowed hard, 'I didn't know that he died.'

'He was killed! He was beaten, beaten so badly, that later, he died of his wounds.'

'I did not . . . I had nothing to do with it.'

'You were there. At the same time. A commander! Surely, you had *everything* to do with it.'

In the middle of her short shallow breaths, her heart pounding within her, Rita could tell that the usual drone of the patient ward had quietened down. The patients in other beds were starting to look over at them now. Someone coughed. They could not, Rita knew, afford to continue this exchange in such a public space. She stood up abruptly, snatched the tin tray with the used medication sleeves and marched out of the hall.

The next day, Rita cornered Rai Miss outside the patient ward. Rai Miss had an impatient look about her and Rita went straight to the point.

'Have they come looking for her?'

'No. Both you and her keep asking the same question. How many times to say no?'

'So, they've not returned?'

'No!' Rai Miss huffed, 'Don't worry those people . . . whoever they are . . . won't be back any time soon.' She seemed to the verge of asking for more detail, but instead she said, 'But you will have to get Sumnima out of here. Within a few days, Dr Parajuli will have no choice but to discharge her. To be honest, he should have done so already. He has only been keeping her this long because of you.'

* * *

'Jarsap hajur!' That evening, Rita stood by the Jarsap's door, digging her toes into the carpet.

At his desk, the Jarsap peaked up above his spectacles, his face drawn into a surprised frown.

'May I have a word with you, hajur?'

The Jarsap's eyes grew bigger, as if he could hear her voice but not pinpoint its source. He would never have expected to be addressed directly in this manner by a servant girl.

'Jarsap hajur?' Rita insisted.

Cautiously, the Jarsap took off his spectacles and placed them on the desk.

'Yes?' A testing response.

'May I have a quick word with you, hajur?'

She could see the Jarsap's mind make a quick calculation, run through the various eventualities. For a moment, Rita wondered if he had forgotten all about her proposal. And finally, he said, 'Is this about your proposal?'

'It is, hajur.'

That seemed to make the Jarsap relax a little. He recrossed his legs under the desk. 'Come in.'

Rita stood by the Jarsap's desk.

'Hajur, have you come to a decision?'

'Well, I have given it some thought, yes. The choice is, as you say, one that Dhire would have made himself. But, the way I see it, there is one problem.'

'What is it, hajur?'

'This person you swear by. This person is a woman.'

'Hajur, yes, but she is more capable than most people I know. She will stay up on the Dhire. She will look after the trees, just like Dhire dai did.'

'But how can I trust a woman to be able to handle such a vast piece of land, all those trees?'

'Hajur, I don't think . . . I don't think you have much choice, hajur.'

'What do you mean?'

'All the young men are gone, hajur. Either they went away to find work, or they joined the rebels, or they fled from the rebels. There are only the too young, the too old and a handful of women left now, hajur. The woman . . . she is the best person for the job. Of that I am sure.'

The Jarsap seemed to contemplate this, his brows knitted in concentration.

'And also, hajur,' Rita continued, 'I am not sure . . . if I may say so, I am not sure now would be the best time to sell the land, hajur. What with everything that is happening . . . that has happened. I'm not sure you would get a worthy bidder or a good enough price, hajur.'

The Jarsap's eyebrows rose high into his receding hairline.

'One more thing, hajur . . .' Rita continued, 'if this woman were to take on the task . . . would she get compensated for her work? Same as Dhire dai did?'

The Jarsap blinked. Thick folds of skin hung under his eyes but in them, she saw a glint of something, a fleeting surprise that turned into something familiar, a recognition.

'I intend to keep my old arrangements with Dhire intact and pass them on to his successor. But . . .' and now the Jarsap looked away, 'but the days are no longer as . . . bountiful as they once used to be.'

The moment suddenly opened up raw, stretching out with the silence of all the things left unsaid.

Rita quickly spoke, 'I understand, hajur. But there is also an alternative.'

'An alternative?'

'Perhaps hajur, the compensation for looking after the trees can come in the form of land instead? There is a small strip, between the trees and where the farmland starts, that is sitting idle. The compensation could be in the form of a *bakas*, a gift, for a job well done, only after the woman has proven herself. Jarsap hajur, binti, she will not let you down.'

'Hmm ok,' Rita could tell the Jarsap had never considered this alternative. He reached for his spectacles, 'I will think about it some more.'

As Rita backed away, her feet grazed the knotted carpet and as she turned towards the door, she glanced up at the tiger pelt, sprawled fierce against the wall. She paused momentarily, considering it, and for the first time she noticed that two of its front canines had halves missing, the sharp tips broken clean off. As she pushed her weight against the heavy wooden door, she remembered what Krishne had said. The white house was subsisting on borrowed time. This life too, was going to come to an end.

16

The Parrot

At the hospital, Sumnima was asleep. For the past two days, she had been ignoring Rita—turning the other way—and each time Rita had laid the bowl of broth on the side table and left without saying a word. Now she opened the plastic bag she had brought from the white house, taking out the thermos, the Mahendra Malla book, and the hot water bottle refilled and warm in her hands. She was smoothening out Sumnima's dolai blanket when at the end of the ward, she heard a sudden commotion. Rita turned around to see Dr Parajuli hurrying in, tall and gaunt. Behind him, two nurses were struggling, a new patient stretched out heavily between them.

'There,' Dr Parajuli pointed, his voice a brisk hoarse order, 'bed number fifteen.'

Rita walked out on to the aisle, then made way for them to pass, and suddenly, stepped back in shock. The woman, her hair long and matted, could barely walk and was being dragged. Her face was a flaming pulp, red and purple, one eye swollen shut, another eye that looked unblinkingly out at the far wall as if it held no remaining life.

Dr Parajuli held back, sidling up to Rita agitatedly as the nurses heaved the woman to the bed.

'Damn it!' he swore, 'this is the worst kind of patient. The worst kind!'

Rita had never heard Dr Parajuli refer to a patient with any sort of emotion before and she stared at him in shock.

'You know why she is here? Who did this to her? Her own family,' he twisted his face, a bitter scowl, 'Her own people. Can you believe it? Goddamn animals! God damn those animals!'

And Rita thought, pasu. She stood there, pulsing, for a long minute after Dr Parajuli left her and hurried over to attend to the new patient. When she turned back around, Sumnima was sitting bolt upright in her bed. And now Sumnima was making to move, she was pulling back her covers, she was reaching out for the steel rod with the saline bag still attached to her veins. She was trying to stand up and Rita hurried over to her, slipped her shoulder beneath one arm, propping her up.

'Let's go,' Rita said softly, 'let's get out of here, let's go for a little walk.'

Between the wards and just before the intersection of corridors, Rita had noticed a small discreet door and she slowly led Sumnima to it now. The door screeched open and outside, wintry sunlight seeped into a narrow closed-in gali surrounded by high walls that held nothing more than cemented stairs spilling out of the hospital building, a small patch of weathered grass and multiple large water tanks arranged in a metallic row.

She sat Sumnima now upon the cemented stairs, detaching the saline bag from the rod and shading

Sumnima's head with her nurse's apron. The sun gave off a meek warmth but still, Sumnima was shivering.

'What happened to that woman?'

'She was . . . beaten.'

'By whom, what did the doctor say?'

'By . . . her own family.'

Sumnima curled her raw fingers into a fist, 'Whoever did this needs to be punished!'

And now it came back to Rita, the vines of gourd running and stretching before them, the smell of Aama's unwashed cholo pressed close against her, the stillness of fear that held them. The time after which things turned inside out. She thought of Sumnima, down in the hole below the prison walls, stretching, reaching towards the light. All this time, Rita realized, Sumnima had been seeking a way to make up for all that had happened, all that she had been powerless to stop from happening.

They sat silent, side by side, their knees touching.

Rita said, 'I have something to tell you.'

Sumnima looked at her, her eyes large and tired, deep pooled shadows carved beneath them.

'Old age finally caught up with Dhire dai. He has . . . passed away.'

Sumnima blinked. They sat silently for a while.

Then she said, 'He saw me. That day. He was there.'

'What do you mean?'

'The day Principal sir was . . . punished . . . Dhire dai was there, in the gathered crowd of villagers. Watching.'

'But you said that you had nothing to do with it?'

'I . . . I didn't.' Sumnima picked up her own fingers now, turning them this way and that, observing their meaty definitions. Then she inhaled deeply, as if she had come to a conclusion.

'There were two units placed in our district at the time. Mine and another commander's. That day, we both ended up in Rato Mato. We were only meant to make collections, muster up as much money as we could, you know, for the cause. Maybe threaten people here and there . . . frighten them a bit. But Principal sir, he did not make things easy for himself.'

'What happened?'

'Things got out of hand. The other commander, he is known for his brutality. I tried to stop it . . .'

'You tried to stop it?' Rita repeated.

'I thought they would just rough him up a bit but then they brought out the bamboo sticks . . .'

'What happened?'

'They started beating him. At first, I let it happen. But then, I could see they were going too far. I told the other commander so, but then . . . he turned on me. He started questioning me, questioning my loyalty to the cause, in front of my own unit. I . . . I didn't know what to do . . .'

Sumnima looked back down at her hands. She folded her fingers into her palms, squeezing tight until her nail-less fingertips bulged white.

'Did that have something to do with why you were caught?'

'Later, after what had been done, I came back. A few of my fighters came with me. Principal sir was still under the tree. He was alive. But the police . . . we had not expected the armed police to get there so quickly.'

'And that was the mistake you made.'

Sumnima released her hands and her fingers flooded back with colour. She rested them gently upon her knees. Somewhere, a generator sounded and now all the water tanks in front of them came alive in unison, a beat clanking and running rusty through the network of metal.

'The whole time it happened,' Sumnima continued, 'Dhire dai just stood there. In the crowd. Watching me. His eyes never left me once . . .' her voice faded away.

Then suddenly, she looked up, her fists clenched again.

'I should have done something, I should have . . .'

Sumnima was suddenly looking at her, her eyes large and moist.

'I . . . I never meant for this to happen.'

Rita remained quiet, searching for an answer. Beside her, she could feel Sumnima, the blind scraping against walls, the soundless screams swallowed by mud.

'Someone once told me,' Rita said, 'thoughts can be heavy enough to bury you, but they are only thoughts. Some thoughts, some memories, one must simply let go.'

Sumnima started shivering hard. Her collarbones protruded beneath her emaciated neck and it occurred to Rita that she had never imagined her like this. Sumnima—tougher, stronger than everyone else. Rita untied her apron, then unbuttoned her own sweater and spread it around Sumnima's shoulders.

'I think . . .' Rita found herself reaching for the right words, 'I think there may be a way to move forward. To make up for what happened. To make it up to Dhire dai.'

'What do you mean?'

'The mango forests are empty now. Dhire dai's role has to pass on to someone new. Why not . . . why not it be you?'

'But there is nothing for me there, up on that hill.'

'That strip of land is still there. Maybe in exchange for you taking care of the trees, you can get that strip of land. So that one day, we can build our guest house. Like you always said we would.'

'But how can I desert the cause?'

'I think you've given enough to the cause. And the cause . . . it has taken from us more than we have bargained for. Maybe it's time now to recover ourselves, our own dreams, our own lives.'

'There is nothing more important than the fight for equality and freedom.'

'There are more ways than one to achieve those aims.'

'How can I . . .' But the fight, Rita could tell, was weakening in Sumnima's voice.

'In a few days' time, you will need to leave the hospital. They need the bed. You cannot do much in your present condition. You need months of recovery. Nobody will come looking for you up on the Dhire.'

'I will be betraying my people.'

'*Which* people?' Rita's voice came out harsher than she had meant, 'The ones who left and deserted you here, a sick invalid?'

Rita thought again of Manju. Her high chirpy voice and eyes that danced, keeping their secrets close. And then, a stirring. Something that came close to her, then whipped away, then flitted again close enough again so she could examine it, take in its meaning.

'The people that I trained with, the people I fought alongside, the people who . . .' Sumnima was starting to say.

And suddenly, Rita understood. She remembered the sound of her slippers slapping the earth as she ran down into the village after what had happened up on the Dhire. She remembered passing the village tap, the row of Madhesi houses, her heart in her throat, her mind screaming out *Sumnima! Sumnima!* The echoing silence that came in return. Then she remembered Manju's empty house. The bent old woman from the house next door, who said, *They took everything with them*. Rita asked herself now, how could they have known to run? How could they have known to take everything with them?

'I know who betrayed you,' she abruptly blurted out, 'Up on the Dhire.'

Sumnima's eyes turned to her, a vacant white, 'What?'

'It was Manju, and her stone-seller father.'

'What do you mean?'

'Where was Manju when the attack was happening? Where was she after?'

'She . . . she escaped.'

'But after the Dhire, when I went searching for you, her family had already packed up and left. Their goats, their fowl, even their dried corn. The courtyard was swept clean. The yard was empty. How could they have known so early? To pack everything?'

Sumnima blinked, her face a pale sunken sheet in the sunlight.

'*They knew*. The attack was supposed to be a surrounding and a surrender. No real fight at all. And yet, they were prepared to run and warned no one else. *The counter-attack happened before the attack had even begun*. They let the others fight on while they fled. Why? Because it was them. They divulged the rebels' plans.'

'But why would they do such a thing?' Sumnima's head was starting to shake from side to side.

'For *money*. A man who can sell his own hill can sell anything. And his daughter is no less. They are just politicians, like all the rest of the politicians in this country. They must have been bribed by the armed police. They saw an opportunity and took it.'

'But Manju . . . not only is she still involved in the cause, she's also climbed high up the ranks now. And her father . . . he's very much involved, right here, in Kathmandu.'

'Why wouldn't they be involved? All the money you are collecting . . . where is it going? Do you even know? I think . . .' Rita stared at Sumnima hard, 'I think the small people, people like Niraj Rai . . . were simply pawns of the cause. They were used.'

Sumnima looked up sharply, 'Niraj was a fighter. He was a *hero*.'

'He was used.'

'He was a fighter, fighting for *freedom*.'

'He was fighting for someone else's profit.'

Sumnima's lips drew back now into a vicious sneer, 'You speak of others but what about yourself? What have you ever done except betray your own family? What have you achieved so far, other than being a nokkar in the big house? What—' But Rita didn't let Sumnima finish the sentence.

'Sometimes,' Rita caught her breath, 'the truth is hard to accept. But that *is* the truth. I see it all now, exactly how it happened.'

Sumnima was staring at her wordless. Then Rita tempered her voice, 'I would be continuing my classes in the village if this insurgency had not started. We both would have.'

'What do you know? You know *nothing*!' Sumnima spat out, her whole body convulsing with the effort of the words.

'You said it yourself. You said it had to be someone on the inside. Someone who knew all the details. Someone who knew the minutes and seconds. Who else could it have been and why?'

Sumnima turned away, spent, then brought her face down to her knees, burying into her hands. She stayed like that for a while, quiet. When she lifted her face back up, it was contorted, streaked with tears.

'They betrayed him,' she said, her voice cold and flat, 'they betrayed him.'

A low keening emerged, bounding off the high walls all around, mingling into the discordant cacophony of the water tanks and generator.

And Rita kept saying, 'Chup, chup, shh, shh,' just like Aama would, up in Rato Mato.

* * *

A week later, the Red Cross van was parked outside the hospital. Its door slid open and inside, stacked on the seats, were boxes of supplies and tied up plastic bags. Rai Miss stood outside the driver's window, giving instructions, and Rita shuffled back inside the building. She brought Sumnima out now and waited as Sumnima climbed into the back seat. Sumnima was wearing the green tunic and paired leggings Rita had given her, the one with the gold border but they were too short, the leggings rising up her ankles, the sleeves pulling close to her elbows.

'Here,' Rita handed over the old jute bag Aama had given her. Rita had put in a khasto wrap, a bottle of mineral water, packets of wai wai noodles and glucose biscuits. She held Sumnima's eyes for a second, then nodded as she stepped back, sliding the van door shut.

Rai Miss had helped her arrange everything. On the roads and highways, checkpoints were being put up everywhere. Only medical and aid vehicles were allowed to pass with minimal questions asked. The newspapers mentioned, once more, a possible ceasefire between the government and the rebels. But in the bhanchaghar, Krishne sniffed and said even if there was a truce, it wouldn't last. More and more people were disappearing. Plucked clean off the earth. This, Rita knew, was her only chance.

Dr Parajuli signed off Sumnima's hospital release and Rai Miss negotiated the extra seat for a patient transfer.

The driver of the van had already started the engine when she suddenly remembered.

'Wait!' Rita called out, 'two minutes, I forgot something. I will be right back!'

Rita ran back into the hospital, past the reception and down the bustling corridors until she was back in the ward. The sheets on Sumnima's bed were yet to be stripped and on the small steel bedside table sat the thermos from the white house and the Mahendra Malla. Rita grabbed the book and just before turning, her eyes fell on the small steel table. A dull square, it was nothing to look at, yet she reached down and momentarily let her hand lay upon its surface. A faint moist handprint lingered, then faded.

The driver started the engine while Rita slipped in the book through the half-opened window and as the van moved through the gates, she could see Sumnima's face in the backseat, turning back to look at her. Between them, things unsaid that never needed to be said, that were simply, always known.

Three weeks later, she received the letter.

You can tell the old man in the big house that his trees are fine. I have counted every single one of them. 1004, including the saplings. And before you worry, I don't leave the house and the forests. And nobody ever comes up to the Dhire. They are too afraid of the ghosts. Most of the farms are completely deserted. Our mothers are the same as before. You should have seen Neelam didi's face when she saw me, standing outside her house!

I keep thinking about that poem you read me, the one about the bird and sometimes, I think the poem is about finding oneself. You know, who you truly are inside and why you're here to begin with. In any case, I went to see that strip of land yesterday. It is still there, waiting. I hope you are studying hard, I'm sure that you are. I will write again soon.

'How is the new patient doing, any improvement?' the Ranisab stretched and reached for her cup of tea.

'She eats, she sleeps. And that's about all, hajur.'

'Does she say anything?'

'No, nothing as yet. Only stares, doesn't say a word, hajur. She's in the recovery ward now, but soon they will have to discharge her.'

'Have you found out where she's from?'

'No, but she's from a rich family, hajur. I can tell from the clothes she came in. Rai Miss says her bed was secured from very high up in the political ranks. It's also why she is still there, otherwise they would have had to discharge her already.'

'They probably sent her to the public hospital because the private ones would have carried the risk of recognition. Chee-chee, what a shame,' the Ranisab clucked her tongue, then was quiet, 'What will the rest of her life be?'

'They say, that it's the wounds that one can't see that are always the hardest to heal, hajur.'

'Yes. It is always the mind that has to be set free, first. I suppose it's a small blessing that at least she has someone like you helping to take care of her.'

'I do what I can. I read to her every day, hajur.'

'What do you read her?'

'The book of poems, hajur. The one I borrowed from you.'

The Ranisab smiled.

'Ok, it's getting late. Clear all these plates. Go do some more studying now, before dinner time. And shut the windows, we've had enough fresh air for now and it's getting cold.'

'Yes, hajur.'

Rita stood up. In front of her, the Ranisab's windows stretched and outside, the winter gardens, bare and bright, swept up to the far walls. Rita reached for the glass panes and just as she was about to shut them, a sudden burst of green shot past her, so close she could hear the beat of its wings right by the window frame. It swooped down into the garden, then corrected course, shooting back up again, climbing forth higher and higher against the backdrop of the distant hills. A shrieking cry pierced the air, its call lingering, filling the entire room.

Acknowledgements

A Note from the Author

This story is loosely based on the historical events that transpired in Nepal during 2001-2002, namely the earlier days of the Nepalese Civil War and the Royal Massacre. The characters are entirely fictitious, as are the portrayals of specific events they experience. The lines from Lekhnath Paudyal's poem, 'The Himal', on page 188 have been excerpted from an English translation by Michael James Hutt which was first published in *Himalayan Voices: An Introduction to Modern Nepali Literature* (University of California Press, 1991).

I would like to take this opportunity to thank the many teachers who have guided me over the years. To the very first, a Catholic 'sister' (whose name I no longer recall) in primary school who showed me kindness in a cold place and enabled me to believe. To the teachers of Rato Bangala School who set my creativity free (including allowing me to use descriptive 'adjectives' that, technically, did not exist in the English dictionary). To the teachers of Lincoln School, and especially Miss Bell, my first 'outside' reader, who always said I had a book in me. And finally, to Samantha Chang, Patricia Powell and Jamaica Kincaid at Harvard College, all of whom encouraged me to delve deeper into this craft.

A special thanks to my indomitable agent, Bonnie Nadell, who has stuck it out with me over the years. To my lovely editors, Archana Nathan and Areeb Ahmad, for elevating the manuscript. To Miray Topay for her early and invaluable advice. And most of all, to my family, who made space in their lives so that I might make space in mine . . . ultimately, it is their unflagging support that has enabled me to fulfil this passion project.